Valley

of

Decision

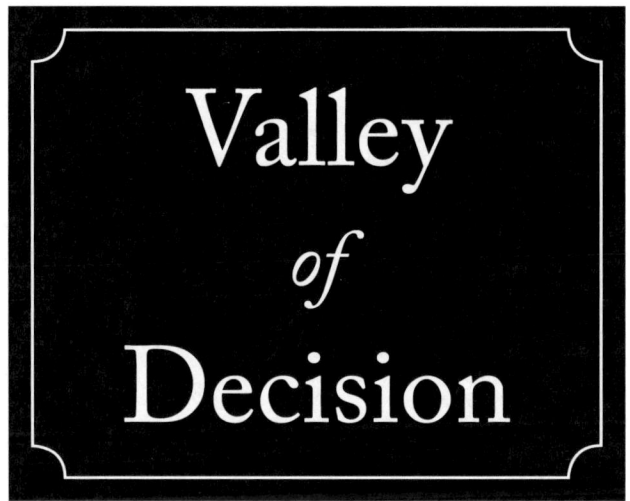

Valley
of
Decision

DAVID MATTHEW SUMMERS

TATE PUBLISHING
AND ENTERPRISES, LLC

Published by Tate Publishing & Enterprises, LLC
127 E. Trade Center Terrace | Mustang, Oklahoma 73064 USA
1.888.361.9473 | www.tatepublishing.com

Tate Publishing is committed to excellence in the publishing industry. The company reflects the philosophy established by the founders, based on Psalm 68:11,
"The Lord gave the word and great was the company of those who published it."

Book design copyright © 2013 by Tate Publishing, LLC. All rights reserved.
Cover design by Rodrigo Adolfo
Interior design by Caypeeline Casas

Published in the United States of America

ISBN: 978-1-62510-768-8
1. Fiction / Christian / General
2. Religion / Christian Life / Spiritual Warfare
13.05.03

DEDICATION

To family and friends who have made
my journey a little easier.

PROLOGUE

"God has prepared his table for his bride. When his church is ready, we will all sit and eat at his table."

"Is his church the bride?"

"Yes, and the groom has made all the preparations to receive her when she is ready."

Sam had seen so much, so many wonderful blessings, treats, and delicacies. It was almost too much for his spiritual eyes to absorb. He could not begin to contemplate all that was left to see and experience, knowing full well the majesty of heaven he had witnessed thus far was merely like a gem reflecting the sun. But there was one thing he wanted more than anything, and he wanted it now. That was to look upon the face of Jesus Christ and God his Father.

"I think I would like to see Jesus now."

CHAPTER

1

Oh, the deceit; oh, the sting of betrayal; oh, the depths that some will sink to destroy an innocent man's life. Does this bring pleasure? Of course it does. Why else follow through with such calculated vindication, bringing forth a kind of sick gratification for only the most disturbed of mind to delight in? Was it a thrill to see me sweat, a feeling of retribution in watching me squirm?

Samuel Reed fumed in bitter wrath as he cushioned his freshly cut fist in an old cloth. The cloth had been white, decorated with blue and yellow flowers scattered about; dark blood red does not become it. It had been left by an ex-girlfriend whose name currently escapes him, nor is it relevant to today's debacle. Just another girl who felt Sam's place could use some touching up—a lady's touch. So much for that; she should see her blood-soaked decoration now.

His bachelor pad would not serve as a suitable retreat. Sam had to get away. Being confined, surrounded by four terribly close walls would only serve to aggravate the situation at hand, not to mention his state of mind. He had to get out and find a place to defuse his racing, illicit thoughts.

He cut his hand pretty badly having slammed his fist into his car stereo on his way home from work. Not because his stereo was not operating properly (it was functioning as designed), nor was a less than suitable song being played by his favorite station; this was an unforeseen method of venting, and his hand would suffer the brunt of it. He had to hit something; by God, there was absolutely no way around it. He did not realize his hand was cut that badly. The cloth soaked up the blood well, stopped the bleeding, and was useless and soon discarded.

"I'm sure the pain will come later," Sam said in a daze while grunting. "I gotta get out of here." Staying put, dwelling on the day's events was not a healthy option. He felt it would only help him to lose the crux of rationality further, which experience had taught was never productive.

Yes, he had been pushed before. This was not the first time (and was certainly not to be the last) where a situation such as happened that day had occurred, pushing Sam to such a point where all he knew to do was lash out with pure fury. Reflecting on this, he knew it was not rational. He knew it would solve nothing, but whenever had "knowing" and "doing" ever been compatible in his reasoning?

Nonetheless one could only be pushed so far. But don't misunderstand; Sam was not one that was easily angered. It took time. The same way when rubbing two sticks together that you get a spark, and much longer before a flame is born. Sam would tend to skip the preliminary flicker of fire and rather plunge headfirst, being succumbed by a blazing inferno, engulfing all within range. Far be it for him to be one to snap at the drop of a hat though. No, no, no, not Sam. After all, he was rational, as rational as any intelligent thirty-five-year-old man would be expected to be by the mass populace.

The rational would always display a certain level of self-control even in the face of certain disaster. Striking out in anger (as sweet as an act of vengeance may appeal) was just not the answer, and although it bothered him to no end, he had to put thoughts of perpetrated violence to rest. Besides, he vowed never to let his temper get the best of him again. *We are to learn from our mistakes so that we will not repeat them.* That was the kind of thinking Sam needed to focus on, and he did his best. As someone once said (must have been a wise man), "He who does not learn from history is condemned to repeat it." It did not take long before he found conflict with such sayings. *But is what I'm doing any better? I'm about to run from my problems. Didn't somebody at one time say something about it being better to face your problems than to run from them? Or maybe it was fears that one's supposed to face. Whatever it is does not really matter.* "I just have to get the heck out of here!" Sam's thoughts turned audible as he found himself shouting.

"Shouting is a nonviolent means of release, so what is wrong with that, Dr. Tripoed?" Sam said on the verge of hysteria, addressing a non-present relic of his distant past. Even Dr. Tripoed would have to admit, considering the circumstances, Sam was performing famously well managing his scrambled thoughts of ill repute. Well, it was an improvement anyway.

"Calm down. Calm down, Sam," he said while rubbing the thumb of his right hand across the palm of his left in a nurturing manner. "Just get your things together and go." But where? He did not have the slightest idea. It was funny how at times the conscious mind inadvertently revealed its submission to the subconscious as was revealed when hurriedly grabbing items that confirmed he could only be going to one place: Mt. Kinley.

It's perfect. Why didn't I think about this earlier? I can't think of a better place to wind down and put things in perspective. There could not be a more logical yet comforting means of escape. He continued rummaging through his home for the essentials one would need for camping. It turned out the bare essentials were all he had. *No matter, I'll make do... Who needs a tent? I have all I need.* Although having a destination in mind and the semi-relief that came with it, adrenaline was still the driving force there, and hurry he must. He threw his things into the back of his pickup truck. He pushed the gas pedal to the floor, quickly switching gears, and gloated in satisfaction with the ear-piercing screech that followed. All those within hearing distance and some dogs beyond were victim to his adolescent rant.

Chill out, Sam. The last thing you need is a speeding ticket.

"Hmm, chill out." Sam went over that term. That was something James would say. "My dear old friend James. Not anymore and not ever again… The truth came out today, and James is a no good, backstabbing snake." But Sam had always known that; that was the quality of his character he admired most. He just never expected to be a victim of its cruelty. But he should have. Thinking back on it, he definitely should have seen that coming. As the saying went, "If you lie down with dogs, you get fleas." But in this case, maybe Sam was the dog with a multitude of fleas to go around. James was the last one he wanted to think of right then, but he could not stop. *How could he sell me out like that?* Sam thought, failing miserably in prying his mind from the day's events.

CHAPTER

2

"Dear Lord, what am I going to do when I get up there?" This was not exactly something that was thought out extensively. No, this act was very typical of Sam's method of stress management: act and trust the details could be worked out another time.

Although the mountains were not a far drive by any stretch of the imagination, they had fallen to an occasional observance, a scene whose only purpose was to serve as background for the life of one Samuel Reed. There was once a time, not all that long ago, when noticed them every day. Funny, that as his life evolved, he had not spent any time at all at his onetime refuge. He used to not be able to help himself, especially on days when painted a beautiful white in the blessed winter by the gentle caressing snow. Just the thought of it was rebirthing a longing in his spirit to get on up there, find that perfect location, cast his line, lean back, and enjoy the gentle creaking sounds and soft splash of moving water and subject to the push of gravity's lure downward, only to repeat the cycle all over again, a slave to the laws of precipitation. Whether he caught a fish or not didn't really matter. Whether with friend or by his lonesome, again, that didn't really matter. The fresh air, the pleasant aromas of Mother Nature in a cascade of scents, each one equally as diversified as the other—Mount

Kinley was once his sanctuary, and that day he would make it so again.

"I was set up, first by that private investigator and then James. How dare he. I never would have done that to him. Was he in on it from the beginning?" Sam closed his eyes and shook his head violently, trying to shake away the anger that simmered beneath the fog of confusion. *This is not the time to vent. That will come when appropriate*, Sam thought begrudgingly.

Now was the time to escape. You're going to the campgrounds where you're going to relax and free your mind of all things stressful, and then as usual the answers to the uncertain days ahead are sure to come. Like when one was trying to remember something that he knew all too well only a short while ago but then couldn't remember, such as somebody's name. He could see his or her face in his mind, he could even recall recent conversations in great detail, but for some reason, his or her name escaped him. Then suddenly when least expected, when thinking about something else completely unrelated, that name would magically appear, clear as day. In the same way the answers to Sam's immediate future were sure to come.

"My tent, my tent, what did I do with my tent?" The idea of sleeping outdoors (a man and his sleeping bag) was beginning to sink in.

"Parker Emerson!" That name with the face behind it body-slammed his train of thought. *Of course it is Parker who has my tent. The last time I saw him I let him borrow it, and I never did get it back. Man, I sure could use it now.* This sudden turn in thinking brought an unexpected joy to his heart, along with a painful emptiness Parker once filled. *Man, I miss him. Must be around ten years since I've seen him last. I wonder how he's doing. I wonder where he is today?*

Although Sam was only one year Parker's senior, he felt like he had about ten years on him in maturity. Sam always felt like a mentor to poor ole, naive Parker. But it wasn't a drag; it was more

like a challenge. A challenge to bring up Parker by the book of
Samuel Reed. A delightful challenge indeed. Parker had a timid
innocence about him, and it didn't seem to matter how severely
life kicked him around; that innocence would always remain.
Sam sometimes wondered if this was a result of blindness to the
cruelty of the world or if he was just plain dumb. How could he
not see that there was not always gold at the end of the rainbow?
And most of the time there was not a rainbow to begin with. Was
he a simpleton? When one's hand was being burned by fire, the
common person was quick to move it, being very careful to not
repeat the offense that resulted in such agony. Not Parker. He
was one not only to repeat the process but add his arm for good
measure and then be genuinely surprised when the pain began.

"What a fool," Sam said with a giggle. But coming to this
conclusion felt a bit preconcluded. Parker wasn't a fool, and Sam
knew it. Naive? Yes. A fool? No. He recalled one incident in particular. Out of the blue Parker invited him to a pub, a rather notorious one at that. It was known for being packed beyond capacity
with the most elite of twenty-something-year-olds in town, getting drunk and wild beyond control, often leaving bouncers with
their hands full. That was completely out of the ordinary and did
not reflect the peaceful, albeit geeky, personality of Parker. Sam
surmised that this had to be an attempt on his part to befriend
him beyond the traditional pleasantries that people became so
accustomed to exchanging when they could think of nothing better to say in the uncomfortable presence of others.

Sam knew very little of Parker at that time, only that he was
a very nice religious guy who worked in the same building he
worked in but on a different floor, doing completely different
things. Ten years ago Sam was at the lowest of the low job-wise,
trying to scrape together a living as a dreaded telemarketer. Sam
was never very clear on what exactly it was that Parker did, but
he knew it had something to do with distribution for some major
grocery store chains, and he made pretty good money as a result.

One of the first meaningful conversations Sam had with Parker came one day when he saw him holding hands with another man, heads bowed, eyes closed, deep in what turned out to be prayer. At first glance, that did not look like something for two hetero-sexual men to be doing, but on further examination, it became clear that that was not a display of gay affection at the work place but rather two men worshiping God. Yuck. He almost wished they were gay because religion left a bitter taste in his mouth. Not only that, but for reasons hidden, anger always followed.

"Don't you know you look like a fool, Parker?" Sam waited for Parker to dispense with the worship and confronted him alone in the elevator.

"What do you mean, Sam?" That took Parker by surprise con-sidering before that day, he and Sam had never said more than a few words to each other. Parker's I-don't-have-a-clue demeanor to Sam's rebuttal added to his growing aggravation.

"You really ought to take other peoples' beliefs into consid-eration, and not everybody believes what you believe. So if you decide you're going to make a spectacle of yourself by praying in public, realize you're going to offend a lot of people." As far as Parker could see, Sam was the only one "offended."

"Sounds like I'm in good company. Jesus offended everybody during his time. Why should I be any different?"

"Parker, I'm only going to tell you this once. You seem like a good guy, and as a person, I have nothing against you, but don't you ever at any time start preaching to me about your Jesus. I don't need him, and I don't want him, if he ever did exist."

"But, Sam—"

"Parker, did you hear what I said? Not a word," Sam insisted, his body reeking defiance.

"If you say so." Parker relented and told Sam what he felt he wanted to hear, but this outburst said more to him than Sam could possibly know.

Plain and simple, Sam needs Jesus. If he only knew the love of Christ, he wouldn't react this way, Parker concluded with genuine concern. From then on, Parker made it his mission to be a witness to him of his need for the Savior. He did his best, given the short amount of time before work to study his character. It didn't take very long for him to pick out his qualities, like how personable and infectious his countenance in the presence of others was. This would be a challenge of monumental proportions, considering Parker's social handicap to all things worldly. But he was determined, and if he had to step outside of himself by inviting Sam to a bar to get his attention, then by God, that was exactly what he would do, and did.

A man walking his dog wearing a thin red coat along the sidewalk running parallel to the busy street briefly caught Sam's attention. The man's coat was sufficient for *that day*, but he might wish he were wearing something a tad warmer come nightfall. *Man, I hope it doesn't get too cold up there*, Sam thought with a grimace. *It might get cold tonight. I should have at least brought warmer clothes. That's just like me, only thinking of the immediate present and not regarding a possible future.*

CHAPTER

3

Why would a goody-good Christian type like Parker want any-thing to do with me? If he's really looking for someone to break him out of his God-inflicted shell, he's come to the right man. I'll show him what it is to live, to really live, Sam deeply pondered.

That might definitely end up being one of the strangest Saturday nights Sam would ever experience. He was used to par-tying with love-'em-and-leave-'em lowlifes like himself, seeking the sexiest yet easiest girl to bed down with for the night. It was typical on any given weekend for Sam to be surrounded by an entourage of women seeking a night of passion with the pack leader. Sam would usually be with a small group of party bud-dies of which he stood out, with his chiseled, confident looks and engaging personality. But not tonight. Tonight was Parker's night, and he was determined to make sure nothing would get in the way of that.

As was his custom, Sam made himself right at home and tore into four MGDs before Parker could get halfway through his Seagrams strawberry kiwi wine cooler. "Really, Parker...a wine cooler?"

"Oh yeah, I drink wine coolers all the time." Truth was Parker hadn't had any alcohol since his sister's wedding two years previ-ous, but he didn't want Sam to know that.

"Wine coolers are for frigid girls, not men. Do me and yourself a favor and try to live a little tonight."

Parker got his point. He was way out of sorts with his new company and rowdy surroundings, with rock and roll music blaring at optimum volume. It was time to graduate to a new level, at least for one night. But would this interfere with the message he wanted so badly to share with Sam? *It is only a wine cooler. Sam's not going to hear a word I say anyway. But maybe he'll listen if I do something completely out of character…if I could only earn his respect, he'll be sure to listen.* Parker decided on exploring secular avenues in being a witness of Christ.

Parker had been slowly nursing his beverage the whole time Sam was downing his beer. Suddenly without warning, he engulfed the half that was left. Sam's eyes grew to miniature saucers, his lower jaw dropped, and a sound of surprised praise escaped his lips. "Woooh, all right, Parker! It's a start anyway!"

Nothing could have made him happier than to see this reaction from Sam. He felt like he finally broke through an impenetrable force field weekend only by the mutual consumption of alcohol.

"I think you need another, my friend." Just then the waitress happened to be passing by, and Sam motioned, but Parker gestured to him.

"I got this. Miss, I'll have another." He then dropped his voice an octave, doing a fair impersonation of a TV commentator. "And this time make it an MGD."

Sam just about spit out his beer laughing. Parker followed Sam's reaction with deep-down, belly hurting hilarity. She must have thought they had more than enough already.

"Hey, Kim!" Sam shouted across the growing intoxicated crowd, cutting off their little giggle fest. A rather attractive young girl responded and quickly scampered her way to Sam with his odd companion.

"Hey, Sam, what've you been up to?"

"I'm good, sweetie. I want you to meet my good friend Parker," Sam said while removing her arms from a pending embrace.

"Hi, Parker. I'm Kim."

"Hi, Kim. I'm Parker." He knew the second those four words left his mouth that introducing himself was now redundant.

Kim busted out laughing, and Sam, trying to keep himself from responding in kind, quickly reminded him, "Parker, she got that." His face immediately turned a crimson red. At that point, the waitress returned with one beer for Parker and four for Sam. Parker seized this opportunity to hide embarrassment by taking a very deep swig of his MGD.

"What's up with the geek, huh, Sam?" Kim whispered. "Shh, he's a good guy. Give him a chance," Sam pleaded quietly under his breath. Judging by a childish roll of her eyes, Sam saw that was not going to turn out as he had hoped.

"Hi, Kim, can I buy you a drink?" Parker said, trying to regain his composure but unaware of the spittle hanging from the corner of his mouth.

"That's okay. I'll just take one of Sam's if he don't mind." Not waiting for a reply, she grabbed one of Sam's beers carefully lined up on the table and pranced off without so much as a glance back."Son of a…" Sam grunted.

"Is she coming back, Sam?" Parker inquired, oblivious to body language.

"No, Parker, she's not." Sam, anticipating his next question, said, "No, you didn't do anything wrong. She's just weird. Don't worry about it. There's a lot more where she came from."

Parker was not prepared for that. Courting the opposite sex was not something that even crossed his mind. Who would expect such a thing on a Saturday night at a notorious pub full of intoxicated hotties? Most single men in the world, that was who.

If he had mentioned he wanted to talk to girls with me, I would have rehearsed, in private, a list of my attributes to share with the appropriate lady. Oh, who am I kidding? I always come off as a hope-

less dimwit that no lady in her right mind would ever take an interest in. Kim was a perfect example of that. He read Kim's face as she was leaving, and he didn't like the way it made him feel. He hoped to God Sam would not put him in that position again.

~

"Oh no!" Sam said, gazing at two men who had just arrived.

"What's wrong, Sam? Is Kim coming back?"

"No. You see those two guys that just walked in?" Sam said, pointing with his brow.

"Yeah," Parker answered, not trying to hide a probing stare.

"Don't stare at 'em!" Sam almost yelled. "I work with them, and they're a couple of jerks. If you don't stare at 'em, they might pass us by."

Too late. Sam was noticed right off. Attempting to appear engaged in conversation with company did not help. The two gentlemen zeroed in on Sam as if directed by radar.

"Hey, Sammy, how you doin', brother?" the taller one said, feeling free to take a seat, uninvited. The shorter one proved to be a little more hospitable by standing his ground waiting for some sort of gesture from Sam that it was okay to sit at their table.

"Hi, guys, I'm just kicking it with my friend Parker here," Sam said, trying to drop every hint in the book that they didn't care for more company.

Maybe they got the hint or maybe not, but Parker managed to burn all bridges of escape by exclaiming, "Hey, guys, friends of Sam are friends of mine. Have a seat."

Sam cringed. What part of "they're a couple of jerks" did Parker not understand? Further male company would only intrude with Sam's plans for the night: to be a mentor in the ways of women to an unfortunate, religious simpleton. Sam was able to sneak in a look to Parker that he felt anyone could read. It clearly said, "What the hell are you doing?" Parker returned this muted question with a look of dumb bewilderment.

"Right on, guys! Hey, drinks are on us," the taller one exclaimed.

"Gin n' tonic all around!" Sam had not indulged hard liquor in years. He gave it up and decided to stick with beer after one too many nights waking up next to women either double his age or beaten one too many times with (what some might call) the ugly stick. Besides, losing complete control was something that scared him and best be avoided. But the drinks were free, and who was he to be particular when it came to alcohol? Especially considering the tight budget he lived on those days. *They're here. Why fight it? Party time.* "Gin n' tonic it is. Bring it on!"

Sam's memory was rather hazy of the goings-on from that point on, only that as time evolved and shots became more and more frequent, their new company was no longer a nuisance but a lot of fun. Without realization from Sam, Parker was managing to be squeezed out of conversation, almost to the point where his presence went forgotten. He did his best to interject his two cents here and there, but the nightlife did not mix with the calm harbored deep in his spirit, nor could the others relate to anything he attempted to share. It didn't take long for the gin to take control of speech as Sam blurted out in classic drunken fashion.

"Hey, you guys are all right." The response was loud and energetic. "Whooh! Sam you're pretty cool yourself."

Shortly after that, Sam remembered very clearly being asked, "Hey, Sam, what do you think of Earl?" the shorter one asked, his demeanor switching to sudden seriousness, getting right up in Sam's face, dropping his tone to almost a whisper yet making sure he wouldn't miss one syllable of what was about to be said.

"I think he's a total jerk. Why?"

This was not an exaggeration. Sam couldn't stand him, nor could anyone else who worked for the man. Earl had a serious attitude problem, or maybe it was just customary to hate the boss. Either way, he could not hide his disdain for the man.

"Sam, I hired you to do a job, not to sit there and talk to your friends while pretending to work." Earl caught Sam in mid goof-off, and Sam didn't like it. Such a puny man wearing huge magnifying glasses he called "spectacles," trying to talk big and exert authority as a man to be reckoned with. Sam imagined at Earl's home it was his wife who had control, with poor little Earl responding to her every command as if she were his drill sergeant in the United States military.

Earl was right though. That was exactly what he was doing. He would tire of calling random strangers (in the middle of what always seemed to be dinner) and sometimes seemed to develop a prospect, create some rapport, think he was making a sale, and suddenly witness that person turn mean, fire some disgusting adjectives, and terminate the call in a very rude manner.

"No job is worth this," Sam repeated every time a similar incident occurred. To help the time go by faster, he would divert from the call list and instead call old girlfriends and shoot the breeze for a while and plan hot dates that sometimes actually manifested. He hated the fact that Earl called him on it, especially considering the fact that Earl had no way of knowing such an accusation to be true. Such a thing grated on his nerves.

When his new drinking pals brought up defacing and disabling the man's car, the only thing Sam could think of was retribution. How sweet the taste.

"All right, let's do it!" Sam shouted as the table rose with a newfound mission in mind.

"Are you coming, Parker?"

"No, Sam." Parker grabbed hold of Sam's arm, looking him in the eye said, "And I don't think you should either."

"Oh please, Parker, if you knew this guy, you'd understand." It was then Parker said something completely unexpected and somewhat way out of left field.

"They will eat the fruit of their ways and be filled with the fruit of their schemes"(Proverbs 1:31). A thick silence followed. All three stood there, mouths agape, unsure of what they'd just heard and without a clue how to respond. Because a response was not forthcoming, Sam could only laugh, which got everyone else laughing, except Parker.

"Yeah, whatever, Aesop," someone said, prolonging the unintended humor. And then off the three wannabe vandals went with a curious vengeance in their hearts. But this journey for Sam ended much quicker than expected. Soon after stepping foot outdoors into the frigid night air, he began to puke most severely. *Must have been that mixture of beer and hard liquor that did not agree with me.*

～

That Monday Sam's party buddies did not show up at work. After that near fateful night, Sam could not remember ever seeing them again. He also noticed Earl showed up at work without so much as a scratch on his Volvo. Maybe they got caught; that would explain their absence from work. Maybe they thought better of it and just went home. Or maybe their whole purpose that night was to get Sam good and loaded so he would not resist that endeavor and take the fall if anything went wrong and the law got involved. Now in retrospect it was the latter that seemed most likely, and if that were the case, he was glad their patsy puked his guts out when he did. *Thank God for small favors*, Sam thought.

What stood out to Sam about that night was the wisdom of Parker. He knew when to put on the brakes. Even when he was in the middle of having a good time, out having fun drinking with the guys, he knew when to stop. Sam could only suppose that, that saying that temporarily silenced the guys that Parker quoted at an inopportune time had something to do with his faith, of which he was deeply devoted. He kind of wished he had something dear to his heart like that, something precious that would keep him in line and spare him trouble and give him peace. But this was not his nature, and he enjoyed his freedom too much to want to give it up to any God or force or whatever it was. He could not deny that incidences like that developed a deep respect for Parker and his deep-seeded faith.

CHAPTER

4

As Sam pulled into the parking lot of the campgrounds, he did not like what he saw. *Oh man, why does it have to be so crowded?* Yet he knew the answer before the thought could be fully formed in his head: it was a beautiful day. The sun shone bright and emanated the kind of soothing warmth that only mid-October could produce. Such a relief coming off the record-breaking heat from the relentless, unforgiving summer that had only just ended. Sam enjoyed summertime more than any other season, but that was ridiculous. As it was, he was going to make the most of it and enjoy the day regardless of the mounting concerns gnawing at his brain like a worm or a rancid piece of cheese. But this crowd did create a dilemma for a destitute man hell-bent on being alone, isolated with only his thoughts to keep him company. *Who says I gotta stay at the campgrounds? This is a huge mountain with an unlimited amount of space. Maybe it's a good thing I didn't bring a tent, that way it will be a lot easier to do a little hiking in search of an appropriate place to fish, eat, and crash for the night.*

Sam didn't bring all that much, only what he felt would be necessary to survive one day and night outdoors. In his backpack, he had his sleeping bag, a lighter, a couple of cans of food, a can opener, a tackle box, a canteen, and a fishing pole in two parts strapped on the side. A tent might have proven to be a bit cumbersome for a hike had he one to bring. After spotting the creek most campers were utilizing to catch their abundance of mercury, Sam decided to follow it the opposite direction of where the majority were planted. A good mile or two should suffice. Although he had never ventured off anywhere away from the public campgrounds before, leaving this mountain vastly unexplored, he felt no danger of getting lost or tangling with a wild animal.

The terrain he chose to hike was not exactly easy. At certain points, the remnants of a trail would begin to manifest only to dissipate and ultimately vanish all together, soon to pick up on the other side of an unexpected mound of earth or rebirth at the end of thick, hardly penetrable shrub. At times remaining upright, keeping one's self from submitting to treading on all fours like the beasts of the field, was more than a challenge. But as he progressed, it was a challenge he was beginning to enjoy and even welcome.

It had been some time since Sam endured such a workout, and it felt good. Joining a gym was an idea, always in the back of his head, but it was there the idea would remain and fester. But that day he was finding that he was not as out of shape as he felt he should be. Was there a better method aside from calisthenics to blow off steam? Of course there was, but not having James or Barbie here to beat up, he made do. Had Mr. Carlton, Sam's boss, not been in the room when the ordeal went down, Sam would have beat the living crap out of James. Not to mention that woman. Sam had not developed the nerve to beat a woman. *In her case, I'm more than willing to make an exception*, Sam reasoned with a macabre giggle. It might have sounded a bit heinous or even a trifle evil, but if felt very good.

Whenever space allowed, his pace turned into a sprint, for no other reason than it satisfied a longing to know (at that point in his life) his body's limits. He liked the results. He sure didn't feel like a man halfway through his thirties but a young man in his early twenties who had only begun to live.

His head in a self-indulgent cloud, legs pumping, backpack rattling, and eyes focused on the twisting path ahead, he did not notice the divot right in front of him of which his left foot was sure to catch, and did, sending him flat on his face without so much as a second to extend his hands to break his fall. After slowly lifting his head from the face-plant he unwillingly pulled off and spitting out blood-flavored dirt, sautéed by a busted lip, Sam began to laugh in spite of himself. Had he an audience to witness this incident, no laughter would have been forthwith to come, at least not by him. You can be sure to bet others would have been laughing, laughing at the dumb fool that took a hard fall. That would have given birth to embarrassment, which was almost always followed by a burning kind of rage, where he could not help but respond with violence. Good thing nobody was around to see that. He took to his feet and brushed himself off the best he could. No broken bones, no holes in clothes, just a small cut in his lower lip.

His hike was coming up on two hours, and it was time to stop with the athletics and get serious about finding a spot to set up camp. When this became a reality in his thinking, something caught his eye on the path ahead: a great chasm running parallel the mountain. It ran a great length across Mount Kinley but ended just before running into the lake. It was about five feet in width, about two stories deep, and a couple of miles in length. Sam had three options to get to the other side. He could jump the five feet across, he could go for a swim (dog paddling his way across), or he could walk two miles around.

Going for a swim was the first one he counted out. Sam reasoned, *It is not like I brought a change of clothes*. It came down to whether he wanted to take the risk of making the jump across, which if miscalculated could end in serious injury, including death, or going two unnecessary miles out of the way of which zero risk is involved but a colossal waste of time. He stood on edge, methodically studying where he would leap and where he would land. Continually he visualized himself in midair and landing comfortably next to a rather large boulder. Three times he took a running start to get the feel for what he was thinking on attempting, being sure to stop exactly where his feet would soon take flight. *This is something I definitely would have easily accomplished when I was young.* "And I'm not feeling old today!" Sam shouted. His mind was made up. He would take the leap or die trying. He removed his backpack and gently tossed it to the other side, being very careful to keep it from obstructing the area he planned on landing, and he was also very careful to make sure his fishing pole would not be crushed on impact. He took a quick but thorough glance for divots obstructing his path. Everything appeared as he had hoped. *No turning back now.* Sam smiled, trying to mask his nervousness.

Just as he had visualized, he planted his feet on solid ground about fifty feet away from the chasm to give himself ample room to reach ultimate speed. His hands were in position, gripping ground with serious intensity, and his back arched in classic racing form. He visualized his successful leap and landing one last time.

As if someone fired a gun to signal "go," Sam bolted as fast as his middle-aged body would carry him. His designated launching pad came upon him much quicker than he anticipated, so much so that in midair he realized he overestimated the width of the ditch, sending him a few feet past his ideal landing pad. This was not going according to plan, which made his landing awkward and uncoordinated. The boulder he planned on landing next to was now behind him, leaving rows of greater rocks to maneuver around. Sam tried desperately to activate emergency brakes, but inertia turned out to be the dominating force, sending a stumbling Sam headfirst into the mass of a van-size boulder. He knew the second his feet hit the ground that that was not going to end well. The millisecond where he knew impact with the rock was unavoidable and his head was going to bash it hard, all he could do was tightly shut his eyes and brace for impact with an unbridled hope that it was not going to turn out as terribly as it was sure to.

Starting at point of impact, a strong jolt of vibration preceded an electrified surge of pain that screamed out all at once in every nerve in his body. A sudden flash of brilliant white light exploded in his inner eye and then flashed out to black.

~

Sam's eyes fluttered and then with much trepidation opened. "I'm alive." He said this on his back, looking up at a clear blue sky to the sound of birds chirping and water flowing. That was the first of a montage of peculiarities yet to be discovered. After diving headfirst into that rock, his body went limp, and he collapsed on his face. How was it that he was not spitting out dirt (for the second time today) when he came to? But that was a dumb question. *I went unconscious. Maybe I was able to flip myself over before I passed out. Or maybe as a result of such head trauma, I had a violent seizure and I inadvertently flipped over.* He moved his arms and then his legs; his limbs seemed to be in proper working condition, no paralysis. At the moment, he couldn't tell if his condition was something to be worried over or not. The big question was his head.

Slowly he lifted his right hand, fingers extended to gently touch where his forehead ended and hair began. Surely, unspeakable pain would cause a horrid scream that couldn't be hindered but rather shatter the boundaries of vocal control. That was not the case. He touched, fingered, and probed his head as a blind man would a foreign object. Nothing. At first touch, he moaned in anticipation of an immense agony that was sure to come but did not. After a thorough examination, he could not find the slightest indication that he suffered what could have been a life-threatening injury.

"What happened?" Sam whispered.

He rose to his feet. Steady. Not only able but also strong. Free. Such a wonderful feeling of freedom absorbed his mind, soul, and body, which he could not explain—as if all human restraints of man had fled all at once. Whatever inclination of desire was his at the very thought, or so he felt. He wanted so badly to embrace the new man, to indulge all of his spiritual attributes whatever they might be, but something buried down deep in his heart knew to do so would mean the end of all things "Sam." It scared him.

"What's happened to me?"

It could not be put into words how he knew it, but a reckoning lay ahead. His spirit knew it like he knew his own name, and he didn't like it. So he buried it deep in his subconscious where "out of thought, out of accountability" was the rule.

A spiraling circle to somewhere began to take form and develop out of nothing. Sam could only laugh in delirium. *At last, proof I hit my head really hard... I'm delusional.* The circle suddenly bent inward like a morphed vinyl record, stretching deep beyond vision's end, forming a perfect tunnel or passage to the infinite, where forever began.

"You're not real!"

Maybe he wasn't forceful enough in his tone to snap his mind back into reality because the tunnel remained, as if to keep an appointment with one Samuel Reed.

"No! I command you to leave me now!" Sam shouted with all the force he could muster. Aside from his free will, almost as if he were pushed, he drew back and fell onto his back into a deep, dreamless sleep.

CHAPTER

5

He awoke looking up at a clear blue sky to the sound of birds chirping and water flowing, the sun shining brighter and more full of life than seemed typical. The tunnel was no more; it somehow vanished along with, what felt like, most of his sanity. *Just like I thought, I must have knocked a few screws loose in order to be hallucinating so vividly.* It scared him a little, to the point where he considered going back to town and getting his head checked out by a doctor. He was not a dummy, and if severe pain or dizziness were involved, he was sure to have sought medical attention. But since that was not the case and aside from a brief hallucination, there was really no serious cranial damage, as far as he could tell.

His first thought was to continue with his hike as planned in search of that all allusive place to camp. As he arose, he took notice of his surroundings of which previously went without much observation. "This is perfect," Sam said regarding his proximity to the creek, the towering trees providing an ample amount of shade and privacy if needed. The creek glistened as the sunlight danced upon the reflective glass of its imagery. Trees standing tall in perfect posture, multiple arms stretched forth for birds to perch and autumn leaves to fall, unfolding a blanket of red, orange, and some yellows to gently clothe the naked terrain. From somewhere deep inside unfurled a welcomed feeling of comfort, and belonging at his new *accidental* abode.

On a more down-to-earth, practical sense, an intensified surreal contentment filled his soul at the thought of assembling his pole, baiting his hook, and thoroughly indulging the serenity and conquest of fishing.

"I need not look any further... This could not be any more perfect." Sam was taken by surprise at the soothing calmness of his own voice.

~

Sam smirked. *What a sport clear-water fishing is, where patience truly is a virtue, giving a man a legitimate reason to be lazy.* He watched as trout wantonly repeated the process of nibbling at the bait, only as a tease with preordained plans of seeking game elsewhere. Sam sat about fifty yards away from where this taunting occurred. What amazed him was how clear the water was. Never before on any previous expedition had he been able to see so clearly the detailed idiosyncrasies of the floor on which the creek sat. He was thoroughly amazed at how clearly he could see shiny white stones settled at the creek's bottom that could actually be gems of value. They looked like pure shining jewels. He had fished in these waters many times, and never had he seen it in this way. The water itself looked more serene, more vivid. Like a stream of clear-cut, wet crystal, yet somehow soft and exhilarating.

A vast multitude of fish like a swarm of bees mining honey scurried about, bumping into one another seeking the kind of fulfillment necessary to live. *Why then don't they take the bait? Why is it these creatures cannot see the life hanging right in front of them?*

"Lunch time, boys. Eat up."

Just my luck, I find the only school of blind fish in the entire creek. He began to space out, contemplating the thought process of a species so miniscule, when a suppressed truth awakened an unknown desire. *They might not be hungry, but I sure as hell am.*

Immediately he retrieved his can opener and two cans of food, both of which were chicken soup. It will not be warm to taste, but it will do. Clutching firmly his grip-on handle, pushing down with his free hand, steel began to puncture steel, and although the tork applied was minimal, the can opener imploded, leaving one end in his left hand and the other on the ground. As a result, he helplessly watched two screws roll into the creek.

"What the hell just happened?" In frustration, he chucked the remains of the can opener a great distance, landing in a scattered splash, and repeated this action with both cans of soup. "Looks like I'm not eating today!"

Once again he scanned his surroundings in search of a hidden answer. "Lo and behold, could that be fruit hanging from that branch? How did I not notice?" The more he investigated, the stranger the results. It was a cherry tree. If it wasn't odd enough that a tree loaded with cherries escaped his attention, what really perplexed him was that although the tree was shedding its leaves like an aging man his hair, not one shriveled cherry lay upon the ground. He picked one and analyzed it further, and then another.

"These cherries are ripe." *How weird, a ripe cherry tree in the middle of October.* He nibbled in evaluation. Tasty, succulent, fresh, dare he say delicious. He didn't mind grocery-store-bought cherries and on occasion would indulge a cherry or two especially when he could mix them in a stiff drink. But never before had he tasted a cherry with flavor so intense and so alive. So quick was his hunger satisfied, but he picked one more for good measure, allowing flavor to make love to his palate one last time.

6

The last time I was up here was with Parker. It had become commonplace for them to fish up Mount Kinley together. Although Sam didn't see it at the time, they were developing quite a tight friendship. He told himself that he enjoyed company, and it didn't matter with whom he shared his bait. But in retrospect, he could now confess that it was Parker's company he valued most. Even though he was relentless when it came to sharing his faith, Sam was clever in changing the subject. If his persistence became annoying enough, Sam would tell him straight out to shut up. Parker handled it well and would not fuss.

One particular afternoon Sam had his usual cans of beer stocked next to Parker's diet sodas in a cooler. Sam had fun jesting Parker over his choice of drink. He had a complex about his weight and felt very strongly that it was this that held him back in sweeping a young damsel off her feet. Yes, Parker was overweight; there was no denying the obvious, but it wasn't as bad as he made it out. Sam would do his best to encourage him.

"Parker, unlike men, women are not as concerned with looks. They are more about making a connection. They want a guy who will fulfill their emotional needs. And if you can do that, you're home free."

"I think I can do that," Parker said in deep thought.

"Of course you can, Parker, anyone can. But here's the catch: you only need to appear to be that guy. When it comes time to deliver, you don't even have to be around. Hell, you don't even have to be in the same zip code. You get my drift?"

As Sam was bestowing such profound wisdom, excitement was growing as he spoke of things he knew best. But confusion was an all too common look upon Parker's face.

"What I'm trying to say is when you get what you want out of the girl, split. Get out of Dodge, don't answer the phone, time to move on to the next conquest, ya see? That way you avoid all the estrogen, inspired drama no man wants to put up with."

"But what if I want to be that guy?"

"Huh?"

"You said I only need to appear to be that guy. What if I want to be that guy?"

Sam slapped his open hand on his forehead. "Why would you want that? You know what, Parker, if that's really what you want, then that is exactly what you'll get, and you will suffer the consequences."

"Don't worry about it, Sam. I don't know where to begin. I don't even know how to talk to them. The first thing you need is confidence. I tell you what, I'll set you up with Tanya's friend, Marcy."

"Marcy?"

"Yeah, man, she's pretty hot. You guys can double date with me and Tanya." Tanya was Sam's flavor of the month.

"Um…I don't know."

"Don't give me that. What did I tell you about confidence? Women are drawn to a man with confidence like a twister to a trailer park."

Parker liked the double date scenario; that way he wouldn't have to be alone with her—comfort in numbers. "Okay, let's do it," he said with a strong tone of ambition.

"Now you're talking," Sam said while crushing the empty can of his sixth beer and plopping himself on the ground the way a judge would a gavel. "Case closed."

～

Before Sam could truly absorb the scenario created on the fly, he found himself on the phone with Tanya inquiring what she thought Marcy would think of Parker.

"You've got to be kidding me, Sam."

"Listen, I kind of gave him the impression she would like him."

"Sam!"

"I had a few beers, I was a little buzzed, and I wasn't thinking straight."

"Sam!"

"I know it's a long shot, but all I'm asking is one date and that Parker could make it through the night without having his heart torn to shreds."

"And then what?"

"And then...we could say Marcy had a good time but she's not interested in pursuing anything romantic, or say an old boyfriend came back into her life or something. I don't know. Help me out here."

Tanya sighed. "I cannot see Marcy going along with this, and even if she does, you know how outspoken and painfully honest she can be. Parker's bound to get hurt."

"Just ask her to be nice to him. That's all I ask."

～

It was a damp night when the date went down. During the downpour of that day, Sam's stomach knotted and twisted in unspeakably uncomfortable fashion. *What have I gotten myself into? What have I gotten Parker into? Is it too late to call the whole thing off?* Sam's thoughts pestered the entirety of the afternoon. Unfortunately, he knew the answer to that last question was yes.

Tanya already sparked Marcy's interest in a highly exaggerated (borderline fictitious) version of Parker, and Parker—thanks to Sam—had picked the most vulnerable time to emerge from isolation. The unexpected rain of that day could only be a foreshadowing of the night to come.

The meeting place was at Tanya's, and although Sam was a half-hour early, Marcy showed up five minutes after. This was crucial in Marcy land. The ladies needed an efficient amount of time to gossip before the night officially began. Parker didn't show up early, nor was he more than a minute late; his punctuality was rather impressive.

The three of them stood at watch through Tanya's front window as Parker exited his brand new Ford Explorer, unaware of the leering spectators analyzing his taste in style. He usually wore pants pulled up a bit too high, his shirt two sizes too small, and his protruding belly hiding his belt. Not tonight. Parker was looking good. There was no denying that he put a lot of preparation and spent a whole lot of money on a virtual makeover, showcasing a tailor-fit pair of slacks with matching jacket and a slick, freshly shined pair of shoes.

"Kind of on the chunky side, don't you think?" Marcy blurted out.

"Oh, but he's such a good person, Marcy…"

"Relax, Tanya, I can see he's got a fat wallet, and that is a plus."

As Parker drew closer, Sam was able to make out what it was that he was carrying, and Marcy made it obnoxiously evident that she could also.

"A corsage! Oh my God, he's bringing me a corsage! It's my freakin' prom night. You guys didn't tell me we were going to the prom." Marcy followed her sarcasm with ear-piercing laughter, the kind that always got Sam cringing, wishing to God for the pleasant screech of someone scratching a chalk board.

Before Tanya could answer her door, Marcy jumped in front of her.

"Allow me," she said as she threw it open. "Hi," she said, displaying an almost comically huge smile.

Sam didn't know her well enough to tell if she was going to laugh in his face in mocker's delight or if the smile were genuine. Parker took a step backward in surprise at her candor but quickly adjusted.

"Hi, I'm Parker."

"Um, yeah, I think I've figured that out, and I guess that would make me Marcy."

Before he could even think of his next step in exchanging pleasantries, she stripped the corsage from his hand and, throwing it over her shoulder, said, "I won't be wearing that."

The stunned, awkward look of one completely lost almost got Sam and Tanya in hysterics.

Just then Marcy pinched his cheek and said, "Oh, you're so cute." She grabbed Tanya's hand and they trotted out to the car. Sam rested a hand on his shoulder.

"Good job, Casanova."

"She said I'm cute."

"She did say that, didn't she?" Sam said, taking notice of the visions of grandeur dancing in his eyes. Suddenly Parker bolted out the door, after the girls. He surpassed Marcy, and just before she could open the car door, he took hold and said, "My lady, allow me," and gently opened it for her.

Again Sam cringed at the screeching cackle that was Marcy's laugh. And again she pinched his cheek and said, "You are so cute," and she took her seat. The smile on Parker's face was priceless.

"So far, so good," Tanya whispered to Sam. But Sam would not allow himself comfort. How long was it going to be before Parker said or did something completely dumb and Marcy made him feel every bit the moron he was? If it hurt badly enough, Parker might cry. Sam stayed on edge the whole night, uncomfortably aware of how suddenly this tightrope the night rested on could snap.

Sam seized an opportunity to put Parker straight when the ladies attended the all-important bathroom ritual.

"How am I doing?" Sam's apprentice inquired, grinning ear to ear.

"You're doing fine, Parker. Just try to relax a little and try not to be so…high-strung."

"High-strung? What do you mean?" He knew the meaning of the word but not how it applied to him.

"You don't need to stand up every time the ladies get up to use the bathroom. You didn't need to order for Marcy, You—"

"Isn't that what a gentleman is supposed to do?"

"Yeah, maybe back in the 1940s it was, and maybe they still do that today in other countries, I don't know, but your approach here is all wrong. You're acting like a little puppy dog, and you're going to run and fetch her slippers." Sam continued to put him straight as he took Parker to dating class 101.

"Contrary to what you might have been taught, women don't respect that. The only way you're going to make her want you is by creating the illusion that she can't have you. Now, how you do that is very simple…"

Parker's silence snagged Sam's attention. The smile, along with all his confidence that shined so brightly in his eyes, was replaced with the kind of uncertainty and fear of a young man who forgot to study for his SATs.

This was hopeless. "Parker, forget everything I just told you. You are doing great."

"Are you sure? You just said—"

"Forget what I said. Your way is working, so go with it."

"Thank you, Sam. I owe it all to you."

"Don't go thanking me just yet. The night is young, my friend. Let's wait and see how it turns out, okay?"

"Okay, Sam," Parker said, mistaking Sam's ambivalence for modesty.

Sam often found himself in a pickle when making spontaneous plans and spur-of-the-moment decisions. Alcohol loosened his tongue and had left him in a situation he had never thought possible. *I mean c'mon, on a double date with Parker and Marcy? The pope might as well be dating Sinead O'Conner. What are the odds of that ever coming to fruition?* But there they were. Sam found himself nervously checking his watch. *Tick, tick, tick.* Time was toying with him. How long before this ended in Parker's heartbreak? He wished this inevitable disaster would hurry and get on with it so Sam could start with his apologies to Parker and then to Tanya and then allow time to heal all wounds.

They saw a movie after dinner, and Sam and Tanya were able to arrange through body manipulation, privacy. Predictably, being alone with Marcy terrified Parker, but it was time to be a man. *Sink or swim, either way this will be a monumental landmark in his life he might remember forever*, Sam reasoned.

As tradition demanded, Sam got busy getting hot and heavy with Tanya. This was not only a way to fill the unquenchable lust that ruled his life; this time it served a dual purpose as it did calm his nerves. Howbeit, every now and then Marcy's trademark laugh would reach and dissect Sam's eardrums, and he could only wonder what stupid thing Parker was saying that time.

~

Parker was a mystery to Marcy. Every time she wanted to write him off as a dud, he would keep his peace and not fall head over heels with a barrage of compliments most men so easily succumbed to when she flipped her gorgeous hair over her shoulder or snuck in a perfected seductive look in her eyes. Nothing. Not a word of praise—or of anything else for that matter—escaped his lips. She found his silence sexy. This guy was making her work for attention, and it was driving her crazy. Finally she gave in and shattered the strained quiet.

"Why don't you talk?"

"I'm sorry. Was I supposed to say something?"

"Give it up. Just to let you know I'm not buying it. You might be able to woo all the girls with your fancy clothes and your super manners, but I'm not buying it."

"I don't understand. Have I done something wrong?"

"No, you're a perfect gentleman, and that's how I know you're up to something. In the end, you want what all men want, and it's not my phone number."

"I just wanted to be nice to you," he said, realizing he failed but not sure how.

Marcy was surprised by his somber tone and studied him closer.

"You're the real deal, aren't you?"

Parker didn't know how to respond.

"You'll have to forgive me, Parker. I'm used to men having ulterior motives."

"There's nothing to forgive."

"Thank God, a lot of men would have cussed me out at this point."

"I'm not that kind of guy."

Marcy reached into her purse to put on a fresh coat of lipstick while asking, "Parker, what are you looking for in a woman?

For the first time that night, Parker looked Marcy dead in the eye and gently cupped her hand in both of his and said, "Beauty doesn't come from this."

"Huh?" Marcy's heart began to pound.

"Instead, it should be that of your inner self, the unfading beauty of a gentle and quiet spirit, which is of great worth in God's sight."

Marcy melted. "Oh my God, that was so beautiful. Is that from Shakespeare?"

"No… Actually…it's from the Bible."

"See, I don't get too many guys quoting the Bible to me."

"The Bible is a beautiful book, full of great tragedy and even greater grace. I look at it as God's sonnet to us."

"Well, I suppose even Shakespeare had his superiors," Marcy said. Parker laughed, and Marcy responded in kind.

The night ended as wholesome as it had begun, except Parker's confidence was elevated to a plane he never dared to imagine. The night left Marcy somewhat humbled and very intrigued. Parker planted a kiss on her cheek goodnight. Although she would have preferred a little more passion, she respected his method. *The passion will come soon enough. After all, he is a guy. Religious or not, he cannot hide his desire for me forever.*

CHAPTER

7

"I'm so proud of you, Parker!" Sam arrived at work early to greet him.

"Gee, thanks, Sam," Parker said while gazing at the ground in an attempt to avoid the eye contact that was sure to reveal restrained exuberance. Hiding his eyes only delayed the revelation his cheeks gave away.

"Well, look at you, blushing."

"Sam, please, no I'm not."

"Oh, yes you are, and you should be. You know why?"

"Why?"

"Because you da man, that's why. You are so da man!" Sam proclaimed, elevating his voice so everyone within vicinity can hear this declaration.

"I'm not either."

"Sure you are. Did you get her phone number?"

"Yes."

"Holy crap! I am now a believer, Parker. Your God is supreme! Is he taking new believers? Where do I sign up?" Sam bowed his head and waved his arms in a mockery of worship.

"Stop teasing."

"Husbands, hide your wives, mothers lock up your daughters. Parker's on the prowl, and he's horny!"

"Sam, stop!"

"I'm sorry, folks. I crossed a line. I was not politically correct. He's not horny. He's sexually challenged."

A few bystanders laughed.

"Knock it off!"

"I'm sorry, Parker. I just want to celebrate you being one step closer to manhood."

"It's okay. Just tone it down a little."

"You got it, buddy. Did you kiss her?"

"That's none of your business."

"Oh, I get it, a gentleman doesn't kiss and tell. I never was any good at being a gentleman. But you don't need to say anything. I know you kissed her."

"How would you know that?"

"Oh, it might have something to do with the fact that although you just yelled at me, that silly grin has not at any time left your face."

"We have another date planned for Friday."

"Whoa, that was quick. Slow down, little doggie."

"I couldn't help it. She was glad I called."

Sam's demeanor made an abrupt change. "You couldn't help it? Parker, be careful."

"Of what?"

Sam wanted to tell him that Marcy was not only known for being wild but was also known for getting around. He wanted to tell him of how highly he respected his purity and devotion to an unseen God, and he would hate to see that die at the hands of a vixen.

But the only thing that came out was, "Just don't rush things, man."

"Don't rush things," Parker repeated with lackadaisical sincerity.

Sam recognized the effects of one deeply smitten had blind-sided Parker with powerfully absent-minded force. He remembered very clearly the first time love clamped its razor-sharp talons into the baby flesh of his unguarded heart. *There is nothing I can do to protect him. He will learn the hard way, same way I did.* Sam immediately rebuked such thoughts. *I never thought he'd survive the first date, and he did great. Maybe they're met for each other.* He couldn't help but chuckle at the idea. But Sam's original opinion was correct, only delayed.

Cloud nine would fall short in describing Parker's aura. He was walking on air—more like floating on air, with little Cupids gently carrying him softly through his workday, only stopping at intervals to smother him with kisses. Unaware of the big, dopey smile that permeated his face, he was one completely smitten, with an overflow of endorphins massaging his brain.

When the workday ended, Parker blurted out to Sam, "I'm going to talk to her about Jesus."

"Don't do it, Parker!"

"I think she'll like to hear it."

"Do you like Marcy?"

"You know I do."

"Do you ever want to see her again?"

"Of course."

"If you start telling her she needs to be saved, I promise you, you'll never see her again."

Parker said nothing as he walked off with his head hanging slightly low.

The sharp contrast from one Monday to the next was almost beyond measure. His countenance, demeanor, the very essence of who Parker was, was tragically distorted.

"What happened?" Sam bluntly asked as Parker paid him no mind, shaking his head side to side, passing him by like a rich man would a peasant.

Sam followed close by. "What happened? Did she dump you?"

Parker mumbled nonsensical ramblings. "I didn't mean to hurt her. Girls like flowers. She was almost naked. I didn't know what to do. I'm a fat slob."

Sam forcefully grabbed him by the arm and led him to an unoccupied, unkempt recreational room. "Slow down. Now tell me what happened."

Parker pulled himself together and explained as best he could the previous weekend. It was Parker's intention to take her to dinner, followed by a romantic drive up Mount Kinley, and then a Bible study under the stars. Apparently, Marcy had other plans. Parker was greeted by a beautiful woman in stunning red lingerie as he entered her darkened, candle-lit cove of passion. Marcy paid no attention to the flowers he presented but was aggressive and intrusive with her hands. She kissed at lips that were not kissing back.

"Don't fight it… Let me please you."

"Marcy, what's…please what are you doing?" He wrestled her hands off of his belt, but she would not give up, slipping her hands under his shirt.

"You know you want me. You can have me. Tonight I'm all yours," she whispered in her best attempt at seduction.

Parker successfully kept her from removing his shirt and did his best to back away from her advances. Her hands returned to his belt, and her kisses advanced to his neck.

"Marcy, this isn't right." He backed into the front door he had entered, and it nudged open. That was his only option of escape. He turned himself around with half his might, jerking loose her wandering hands, sending Marcy stumbling back and falling hard on her rear. Parker ran to the sanctuary of his vehicle, hearing all the way a collage of profanities, adding more clutter to a disoriented lack of clarity.

All that night Marcy avoided Parker's insistent attempts at contact. She scoffed at his pleas of retribution left on her voice-mail. She took great delight in answering the constant ringing of her phone, in order to deliver an earful of spiteful insults. Finally the ringing stopped after she exclaimed with fearful venom, "Listen, you fat slob, you call here again, and I will call the cops and will have you arrested."

~

Marcy's anger remained at peak level for days to come. No one rejected Marcy, not when it came to sex. The bitter sting of humiliation was new to her, and she hated it, along with its executor. That was the way she has made multitudes of men feel after having worked them up to a crescendo of endorphins and then coldly mocked their attempts at enticement. Never had she expected to be on the receiving end of such a rejection. Marcy hated the way it made her feel, and never again would she open her heart to someone so pure of heart.

~

Not long after that, Sam found a better job as a used-car sales-man. He and Parker promised to keep in touch, and they did for a while, but the paths of life led them in two very different directions. The last time Sam saw him, Parker was a changed man. He was the same moral, peace-seeking, God-loving person he always was, but something was different. A spark had flickered out. That was how Sam knew that Parker loved Marcy. They only had one real date, spoke on the phone only a few times, but Parker undeniably and unfortunately had loved her.

CHAPTER

8

Dusk had arrived like an expected and unwanted guest. It would be dark soon, and it was time to prepare for the black of night, along with the prescient elements to follow. As the sun began to drop below the horizon, so did Sam's sense of security. Already there was a chill in the air, reminding him of his lack of clothing that might prove to cost him greatly had he not brought a lighter. The thought of seeking wood for a fire had only just birthed in his thinking when his eye spied beside the cherry tree a nicely stacked, freshly cut mound of wood.

"What the…"

I know I'm not too sharp today, but how is it possible that I didn't notice this wood? The organic, aromatic aroma that scented forth, begotten of earth, awakened his senses. Pleasant memories of December 1 flooded his mind of a happier time when his father would single-handedly, on that special day, cut down a fresh Christmas tree to be enjoyed by family for a month to come.

"Who cut this wood?" Whoever it was couldn't be far. The strong scent gave away its freshness, and it could only be within an hour the wood was cut. *But that's silly. I've been sitting here fishing well over an hour.* Again Sam checked his head for bruising or some kind of swelling, and again there was nothing for touch to reveal. *I'm truly losing my mind.* Yet the so-called miraculous appearing of the wood was only a prelude to, perhaps, a greater mystery.

Why put it here? This he dwelt on rather than the how. How it escaped his attention, he'd rather not even think about. No point in exploring the origin of its manifestation. It would only lead to questions Sam could not answer, and being the rational guy he was, if an answer was given that dwelled beyond what was rational, it was his lifelong habit to block it out, and that he mastered.

He created an adequate fire pit, stacked a few blocks of wood, and within twenty minutes had a nice fire raging. Not a moment too soon because the temperature seemed to drop at a rate he was not accustomed to. *Oh my Lord, without this fire I would have been in for a long night.*

As the night grew darker, the fire shone brighter and its heat intense. The cold proved to equal in severity, he found, when briefly stepping aside from the angry dancing flames to relieve himself. He could not have been fast enough, feeling that a man in a T-shirt on a night as cold as it was, without a fire, might have a real chance of freezing to death or at the least catching the pneumonia that would kill him later. Maybe this was an exaggeration, but it felt accurate.

⌒

Lying flat on his back, he felt a bit overwhelmed at the star-lit beauty of the night sky. Billions, possibly trillions, of stars spread across the universe as if flung.

As a child, he once threw a handful of pebbles at a handmade castle of Play-Doh. Some stuck; some didn't. It seemed our creator always hit his mark. Sam didn't need Parker to tell him God existed. If he was anything, he was a realist. And as far as his reason carried him, something had and never would come from nothing. There had to be a hand behind it all, a transcendent causal agent. Scientists had a real problem with anything they couldn't tangibly touch and scientifically explain. As a result, as with Darwin, they pulled any theory out of thin air and called it fact and manipulated biology to prove it. The very existence of man, the earth, and the universe was proof enough of a power far greater than man. Sometimes to see things as they were made it real and sometimes not. Sam fell under the latter. In this case, for Sam, seeing the evidence of matter, the existence of existence, beholding all that his eyes were designed to perceive was enough.

As far as the origin of that hand went, who knew? Every religion claimed to know, and all beliefs were varied; no one could agree. He had a certain amount of respect for all religions because at least they were trying to figure it all out. No way, though, would he choose any one religion to rule his life. To do that would be to say he knew better than all other religions, and he was in no way about to make so bold a statement. To do that would be calling every other form of belief wrong, and who was he to say groups of millions, some of whom had given their lives, were wrong?

If he were forced to wear a label, he would settle with "theist." He was once referred to in like matter, and out of curiosity he looked it up.

> Theism (noun): Belief that one God created and rules humans and the world, not necessarily accompanied by belief in divine revelation such as in the Bible.

Yep, that pretty much sums me up. He was glad to have a term to identify with. As highly as he respected Parker, Parker was guilty of circular reasoning. He always tried to use the Bible to prove the Bible. His fallacy was he perceived the Bible as fixed proof and quoted from it without first providing evidence of its authenticity.

Arguably, the Bible's central figure was the man Jesus. History might prove such a man at one point did exist. But not history, nor any human being, could prove that his outrageous claims of divinity were truth.

As far as the nature of God went, as powerful and creative as nature dictates he was, it seemed evident he was a being that did not have nor desire an interactive relationship with man. Man desired this, and as a result, biblical fairy tales were invented to fill that void, and among them dwelled the audacity of a place called heaven.

The majority of religions had this common precept of this make-believe place where peace and tranquility reigned forever. How easy the majority fell for such a mass delusion. When the body died, we died along with our consciousness.

Almost as if to prove this point, a falling star streaked across the frigid night sky, as if on cue, and burned itself out. That meteor was constructed by the hand of a God out of nothing, and to nothing it returned, and we were no different. There was no purpose behind any of it. To Sam, all existence might as well be an extravagant experiment, and maybe in another million years God would check in on us to see how we were making out. It was the depravity of man that was proof enough that God did not intervene in his affairs.

Why did such horrible things happen to good people while the evil prospered, living off the fat of their abundance? Where was the justice in that? Where was the justice when Sam's cousin Freddy Nosfer died at the hands of a drunk driver bringing gifts home to his wife and five kids for the holiday season? Freddy's atheism didn't bother him at all. Why should it? He was a good man who loved his family. Who would have the heart to fault him for that?

The drunk driver only served twelve years in prison of a twenty-year sentence, getting out early for good behavior. Meanwhile, Freddy's children had to grow through their formative years without a daddy. Where was the justice?

Where was the love in innocent children being raped and murdered? What kind of God would allow such atrocity? Certainly not a loving God. All religions, all of mankind for that matter, needed to have an awakening to the fact that he had left us alone in the world, and precautions needed to be taken in fending for oneself.

So make the most of it. Have as much fun, make as much money, score with as many babes as possible, because life was short, and we had no way of knowing when our something would return to nothing. And *no one* was keeping score.

~

Sam's eyes were beginning to grow heavy, and thoughts were coming much slower, and as the onset of nodding out was developing, he heard a definite rustling among the trees, beyond where fire exposed the dark. Suddenly he was alert. More rustling. It must be a wild animal, but what animal would come so close to a fire? Sam didn't know enough about wildlife to answer that question. It didn't seem likely that any animal would be brave enough to come so near, so raging a flame, and yet it was moving closer. In hopes of scaring it away, he threw a rock in that general direction. That was when Sam heard a sound he knew no animal could make, leaving every hair on the back of his neck standing at frightful attention. A giggle from the black bounced off the trees.

Sam clenched his fists.

"Who's there?" he shouted, trying to sound masculine but unable to hide a twinge of shakiness in his voice.

"Who's there?" a voice mocked.

For sure this had to be one of the most wicked-sounding voices he had ever heard. Sam stood frozen, straining to see through the darkness that hid this visitor so well.

A silly thought crossed his mind: *Is this your wood? I'm sorry. I didn't know who it belonged to.*

More giggling of an inhuman nature followed, but this time Sam could make out that it was two deviants striking untold terror into his heart. Again they mocked Sam, "I'm sorry, I'm sorry, I'm sorry, *I'm sorry!*"

One voice was deep and guttural while the other was more like a screeching hiss. The sound traveled as if mic'ed but without reverb. The last shouted in a terrible growl as they ran off into the black that birthed them. Sam exhaled.

"What the hell was that all about?" He sat back down, trying desperately to slow the terrible rhythmic pounding of his jostled pulse.

CHAPTER

9

It wasn't until about an hour later that Sam was finally able to laugh. He laughed hard.

"Man, those guys scared me good." He could only wonder what kind of drugs they were doing to get the idea of scaring the bejeezus out of a lonesome camper.

"Where do I get me some of those drugs?" He laughed again, but it was cut somewhat short when he remembered the demonic-sounding cackle that was almost successful in loosening his bowels.

Just like in a horror movie. Yeah, I felt just like I was in a horror movie, and I'm the star. That's not good. Don't the stars of those kind of movies always end up mutilated in some way or another? No, it's the star that always seems to make it out alive. It's the poor fool in the opening sequence that doesn't stand a chance. So how do I know this is not an opening sequence?

Oddly enough, it was this kind of thinking that calmed his nerves as he curled up in his sleeping bag in search of his dear, old companion sleep. He began to drift. He felt a presence. His eyes flew open in less than a heartbeat, and standing before him was a child. Sam scooted backward, rubbed his eyes in hopes of a vanishing illusion, but the child remained. He had to be between eight and ten. He had a freshly cut lip, tangled hair, and a troubled look about his face, his glazed blue eyes showing great long-ing and despair. He communicated with Sam without use of spo-ken word.

"Please, don't wake up, mister."

"Who are you?" Sam replied.

And just like that the boy was gone. "Josh!" Sam shouted with arms outreached as if trying to pull the boy back from the dimension he was pulled into. For the briefest of seconds, Sam knew who the boy was; everything made sense. As fast as clarity ascended, so did the cloud of confusion return.

"What's happening to me?" Sam bellowed. "Who's Josh? I know no Josh. I've never known a man or a child by that name." He thought long and hard on the image.

"I've never seen that boy before in my life." *Can all of this be blamed on my phantom head injury?* He sourly came to a bit-ter conclusion.

"I'm having a mental breakdown. This must have all started with the turmoil at work. I can only assume losing my job that I loved so much had a greater psychological impact on me than I've realized, literally causing me to flip out. And I have been graphi-cally hallucinating ever sense." This he felt compelled to come to terms with.

"My God, I hope it's not that bad," he said, fearing he might end up like his great-aunt Jeanine. She was never quite the same after witnessing Uncle Louie, her husband of forty-six years, go headfirst through the windshield of their 1942 Ford Sudan Tutor. His neck was broken instantly.

The vehicle in front made a sudden, unforeseen application to the brakes. She was wearing her seat belt while he was not. If it wasn't bad enough that he bounced on the asphalt twice, the unsuspecting RV that struck from behind succeeded in violently pushing the Sudan forward another twelve feet, further crushing Uncle Louie and forever altering Aunt Jeannine's state of mind.

Losing my job is a far cry from what she went through; it doesn't even merit the comparison. He put an abrupt stop to this line of thinking. *Sleep is the answer. Everything will become clear; the fog will lift.* For the third time that night, Sam drifted.

~

An intoxicating, succulent aroma of hamburger meat frying over an open flame tantalized desire. An undeniable and thoroughly provoked yearning guided his steps. As delicious the cherries were, they could not hold his hunger any longer. He followed a trail that had only just come into being. He had never been this way before, yet it was somehow familiar. He had no idea where he was going, but he knew the way.

The shrubs grew more grassy and full, and as he progressed, the trees grew thick and taller, all in a row. One had fallen down and lunged across his path. He stopped and analyzed the massive tree with full sincerity.

Sam was drawn into the simple yet complex way nature had in development and formation.

Its interwoven dimensions, in such minute fashions, intrigued his inner soul. He found himself attempting to comprehend the brilliance of one simple section of bark. He began to lose himself as he transcended into its fabrications. Its beauty engulfed him, and they became as one.

Lying not far from the tree—half on the trail, half in shrub— was a handcrafted staff. Sam picked it up; right away he enjoyed the feel. As he contemplated its origin and he who so carelessly left it behind, a lamb stumbled onto the trail from the hedges.

She looked Sam up and down and vocalized a predictable, *"Baahh." She thinks I'm the shepherd.* "I'm not your shepherd, lit- tle lamb."

Sam walked more hurriedly in hopes the lamb would not try to follow but rather find the true owner of the staff. She followed at a rapid pace.

"No, don't follow." He threw down the staff and ran, but still she kept up. "Fine, little lamb, I give up. I'll be your shepherd... Soon we're going to have ourselves a nice meal together."

Baahh, said the lamb as if in agreement.

A familiar tune played out in Sam's head: *Sammy had a little lamb, little lamb, little lamb. Sammy had a little lamb, and to the beast she will go.*

"Wait a minute. That's not how the tune goes."

He could not shake it. Over and over again it played itself out: to the beast she will go, to the beast she will go, to the beast she will go.

"No, I love this lamb!" That was news to him but true. He cupped his hand under her snout and, looking the animal in the eye, declared "No one can snatch you out of my hand. I will give you shelter."

They walked another two hundred yards when a mysterious thick fog engulfed them for a spell. He need not worry about his little lamb, as she kept contact with Sam's leg step by step. As the fog cleared, a long line of sheep stretching a great distance stood before them. Sammy's little lamb immediately took her place last in line. As far as his eyes could gaze, the line twisted and turned and seemed to drop off at its end, but to where he could not make out. This must be where the shepherd feeds his sheep. As if to confirm this, a billow of smoke mushroomed skyward. So many sheep to feed.

Leaving Sammy's little lamb behind, unaware of the vegetarian diet of sheep, he sprinted toward the line's end in hopes of bringing back a rib for his precious little lamb and thanking the shepherd for this great feast. If only he had not thrown down and left behind the shepherd's staff, he was sure to be thankful in getting it back.

Upon arrival, Sam fell to his knees and vomited, having discovered the delightful aroma was not hamburger but lamb all along. One by one the sheep leapt into the unforgiving flame as if drawn by an unseen source of pure evil. But the sheep would not die but thrashed about, wailing in agony, burning but not consuming.

"No!" Sam cried. As fast as his feet would carry him, he sprinted the full length to where Sammy's little lamb was left behind.

More sheep had arrived, and Sammy's little lamb no longer brought up the rear. They all looked the same. Which one was his? There was no way to tell. Frantically he tried using force to break up the line, pushing one lamb after another this way and that. They only regrouped and fell back to their position in line. He picked up what he thought might be his little lamb and began to retreat when his little lamb bit him, but still he held her even as blood dripped from his wrist.

"No! You're going the wrong way. You've been lied to. This way is damnation!"

CHAPTER

10

A vocalized yelp sprung Sam from the deep of a twisted sleep. The sun shining bright beat a soothing warmth upon his face. He felt as though flung back into the here and now. Water was flowing ever so gently, and birds chirped. The fire had died but was still simmering and crackling a little down at the bottom. He wanted with great fervor to leave.

A squirrel scampered about gathering and storing in preparation for the winter soon to come. A cluster of varied birds perched and whistled songs in celebration of the new day; schools and schools of morning trout swam on, being viewed as clearly as yesterday. It was all so beautiful.

"I don't care. I'm getting the heck out of here. Maybe yesterday was all a temporary psychotic departure from reality, but I'm not going to stick around to find out."

Shame—the festering, prevalent emotion when he thought of last night. The thought of two jackanapes getting away with creating such a sick dread in the depths of his soul challenged his masculinity, and he failed most assuredly. *If only they'd make their presence known now, in the light of day, I'd beat the living crap out of 'em. Then we'd see what's so funny,* Sam considered while skipping a stone across the tranquil waters.

The most important thing was now that he had a sufficient amount of rest he felt he was thinking with a clear head and believed firmly that he might be able to salvage his job. *Maybe it's not as bad as I thought. I know I screwed up big time, but I'm sure I could get Mr. Carlton to give me another chance.* Sam walked over to the cherry tree for a quick breakfast when a new freshly cut mound of wood forced a frightening shock, drawing his attention to the supernatural.

He thought of James. This was his area of expertise. *What would he say? Could he know something of things that appeared from nowhere? I've mocked, demeaned, and belittled everything he tried to tell me of the supernatural, and now I find myself in a dilemma I don't have an answer for except that there are forces at work here, I know nothing about.* Thinking of James brought back feelings of anger and betrayal.

"James might know of hidden things, but he's not the better for it. He sold me out like a bastard stepchild."

~

Sam worked with James on a car lot selling the best in used automobiles. Sunshine Discount Used Cars hired Sam without experience in the field because when being interviewed, he exhibited his mastery in powers of persuasion. He harbored such a gift beginning at an early age when he could just about talk his mom into anything, no matter how steadfast she stood in her convictions. Often she'd remark, "You should be a politician." Other times by various individuals he was told he should be a lawyer. But none of those ridiculed occupations sparked his interest. However, sales did.

His skills were sharpened very young. He learned quickly how to coerce and manipulate his young friends to do his bidding. Often it would entitle tasks that would suffer Sam great discipline by the powers that be if caught. For a season, this worked, until the inevitable occurred. When his patsies suffering the consequences of their actions, it was Sam's name that came up time and time again. And time and time again Sam suffered a greater punishment than his predecessors, being labeled as "the bad influence." He learned to live with it throughout his adolescence. It got to a point where this "bad influence" suffered more than deserved.

Astute children soon learned when caught misbehaving, a sure ticket out of discipline was the very mention of Sam, whether he had anything to do with it or not. "Sammy told me to do it" was the cry heard around town, and Dad didn't like it, threatening to send him to a boarding school if it persisted.

All these things were lessons learned and lessons applied. Learning to persuade and avoid trouble in the process was sometimes a fine line, and Samuel Reed perfected not crossing it by becoming more clever and crafty in his schemes. He got through high school with a spotless record. Spotless as far as the world knew, but Sam knew better.

CHAPTER

11

It was warm but not terribly hot when Barbie arrived at Sunshine Discount Used Cars. She wore extended high heels of which she had yet to master, her gait somewhat awkward, leading way to an occasional stumble, but this was not effective in slowing her pace. She panned from one little car to the next almost frantically. She was tall, at least she appeared to be, with very long, gorgeous wavy blonde hair.

She was packing quite a rack, Sam guessed 32Ds, and across her tight pink shirt was written in purple "Party girl." Of course she fit Sam's area of expertise like a glove. A tall hot blonde that was sure to fit every blonde joke ever uttered. Who could ask for anything more? He gave himself a quick look in the reflection of a Buick car door window, straightened his tie, and strutted his way to meet the acquaintance of his next conquest/sale.

Sam had an eye for the naive. They could make his job oh-so-easy, but if he wasn't careful, they could also prove to be a colossal waste of time. And it was all about knowing the difference, as any good salesman would. So often human subtleties and little quirks could say so much without having uttered a single word. Something told him that not only would he be able to swindle her into a bucket of mechanical junk, but he'd have no problem retrieving the obligatory phone number, which would lead to a definite night cap.

"Hello, miss, can I help you?" Sam said, his smile oozing confidence.

"Um, yeah, I'm—" The blonde lady missed a step, losing her balance, and conveniently Sam was on task to keep her from falling on her pretty little fanny.

"Careful now."

"Oh, thank you. It's these heels. I don't know why I wear them."

"Don't you worry about it. No harm done."

She stood her ground for a stitch in time and said nothing, a lost faraway look in her eye, as if she forgot why she was here.

"My name is Sam."

"Hi, Sam." She blushed, smiling while using her hand to cover her eyes like a little school girl in the presence of her first crush.

"My name is Barbie."

Barbie. Why am I not surprised? "Nice to meet you, Barbie. Is there anything I can help you with? Anything in particular you're looking for?"

"Yes, I would like something small and cute, preferably red."

Spoken like a true babe without a clue. Did a make, year, or gas mileage even cross her mind? No, she wants a small red car. Oh yeah, and it's got to be cute.

Perfect timing that James should happen to arrive to start his day of work. When Sam saw him pull into the lot, he figured now was a good time to challenge his skills of conviction by unloading a lemon on a sexy dimwit. *I'm going to sell her the white Caddy.* Sam was looking forward to shining fresh in a method of trickery and reaping praise in the salutations of his predecessor.

Sam and James enjoyed taking new arrivals on test runs. It was rare that a flaw was found, but the 2008 white Cadillac was an exception. Instead of reporting this find to their beloved boss, Mr. Carlton, they decided to have a little competition in who first could get away with selling it. The challenge lay in the fact that the Cadillac had a tendency, on occasion, to jump from fourth to fifth gear on its own. Something told him that Barbie would give him the victory in this contest.

"A small red car for you? I think not."

"What's wrong with that? I like 'em small!" Barbie exclaimed, chewing her gum while twirling her hair like a true multitasker.

"Please tell me you don't say that to all the guys."

This sly stretch at a sexual innuendo might have gone completely unnoticed had Sam not smiled really big, cock his head, and wink. Barbie giggled.

"Stop. That's not funny."

"I do apologize. It's just you have got to be the prettiest thing I've seen all day, and, sweetheart, it's been a long day."

In the cutest, little girl tone, Barbie submitted, "Thank you."

"We have an assortment of those tweaked little pieces of Asian roughage on the south side of the lot if that's what suits ya, but honestly, I have to believe you're better than that."

Barbie's brow lay heavy, and her jaw dropped in suspense.

"Better than that?"

"Oh, for sure. I'm sure you know what people think of an attractive blonde in a cute red car, don't ya?"

Barbie followed closely in anticipation of a new revelation. "What do they think?"

"Well, I thought it was common knowledge, but I guess I'll have to fill you in." Sam, raising his eyebrows and stroking the stubble on his chin, continued. "Please forgive me, but when they see a cheap car, they think cheap woman."

"Huh!" Barbie hit a high octave in her screech. Sam had to use restraint to keep from covering his ears.

"I'm not saying that's the way I feel, but, honey, when you've been in this business as long as I have, you pick up on certain things."

"I don't see why anyone would think that."

"That makes two of us, but people are shallow. For instance, when I see a lady riding in a Bentley, the very last thing that crosses my mind is a cheap woman. No, on the contrary, I'm thinking respectful, distinguished lady."

Barbie reached across her shirt, grasping her left shoulder at a casual attempt at hiding her Party Girl logo.

"I don't have that kind of money."

"Of course you don't. Very few people do. Even if you wanted a Bentley, I don't have one to sell you." Sam effectively convinced himself that although a Bentley was out of the question, being a model, she was sure to afford a Cadillac.

She could only be a model. What else could she possibly do with half a brain? "Well, since you're the expert, what do you recommend?" Sam stroked his stubble again, scanning the lot, and pretended to brain storm.

"Well, since I know you don't want to feed that typical blonde stereotype, how about a car a little bigger?"

"Bigger?"

"Exactly, my dear, a bigger car is saying you've really made something out of your life."

"You really think so?" Barbie was beginning to show signs of interest. Appealing to her sense of the superficial was the bait, and she was nibbling. He had to be sure to not reel her in too fast or he might lose her.

He escorted her toward the habitat of the Cadillac and said nothing, with an unrealistic hope she'd pick it on her own. But since things were never that easy, she asked about every vehicle but the main target. Sam was clever in his denouncements of her every inquiry. Leading, without her knowing, to ask a second time, "Seriously, since you seem to know me so well, what do you recommend?"

"Okay, if you're going to force an opinion out of me, I'd go with the white Cadillac."

"A Cadillac, huh?" Barbie rubbed her hand across the hood almost seductively and tapped on the windshield with her long, red, well-manicured press-on nails.

"It is nice."

A test drive was the next step in this hustle, and as luck would have it, he ran into James while retrieving the key.

"Don't tell me you're selling her the gear jumper," James said in envious awe.

"Yes, my friend, that is exactly what I'm doing," Sam gloated, slowing his jaunty step to bask.

"You've got to be kidding me. Okay, so what's she going to say when the Caddy jumps gear?"

"To be honest, I don't think she's going to notice."

"Is she that dumb?"

"Yes, my friend, she is that dumb."

James responded with tempered hostility, "The only reason you always seem to win our little competitions is because you get so lucky like this."

"Maybe so, maybe not. See you on the flip side, James," Sam deferred, strutting his way back to the Cadillac. James grunted something inaudible.

James has a lot to learn. Where luck runs out, skill takes over. It's the same way with poker. Sure, some luck is involved, but it's skill that's going to win you the pot. The same way skill is going to win me this delicious pot, Sam thought while checking out Barbie with lustful intent as she leaned back over the Caddy. *Leave it to a model to strike a pose unaware. It must be second nature; they just do it without thinking.*

Sam encouraged her to stick to the streets during the test run, figuring that would keep her from shifting to fourth gear and thus avoiding a possible impromptu revealing of mechanical failure. He did not count on his intent being challenged as Barbie became persistent in her desire to maneuver this drive to the interstate. That was out of the question, so when put in such a bind, lie.

"Oh, I'm sorry, but it is Sunshine policy to stay within fifteen miles of the proximity of the lot."

"Why is that?"

"You know, I'm not exactly sure as to why, but I'm sure you know how corporate can be, with all their red tape. I bend a rule just a little, and next thing I know, I'm in the unemployment line."

"Well, I wouldn't want you to lose your job."

"Thank you so much, Barbie. And on top of it, when you're dealing with an anal-retentive boss, it kind of ties your hands to the liberties you want to share with your clients."

All went according to plan, the gears stripped of an opportunity to jump. As they finished the drive, Sam asked, "So what do you think? Do you want to take this baby home?"

"It is a very nice car, and it is smooth, and maybe I need a change like this in my life, but—"

"I get it, you're not sure. I'm moving you too fast. I tell you what I'm going to do," Sam said as he grabbed a notebook and pen from his breast pocket. "I'm going to give you my cell phone number, and you can give me yours. That way if you have any problems or have any questions, you can give me a call at any time."

"Okay, I'm following, but why should I give you my number?"

Sam handed her his number and clasped her hand, displaying his winning smile while looking her deep in the eye. "Because you want to go dancing with me tonight."

Barbie paused while processing this information. "Huh?"

"Look, I'm not going to play any juvenile games. If you have something better to do tonight, tell me now so I can call someone who knows how to have a good time."

She chewed on her bottom lip and then slowly licked her top, making Sam weak in the knees. She then closed in, getting right up in his face.

"Oh, I know how to have a good time, sweetie," she said in a low, sexy whisper. Barbie took his pen and scribbled her number. While stuffing the paper into his front pant pocket, they embraced. Sam was thinking, *Right on. She's even easier than I thought.* Just as their lips touched, which was sure to be a prelude to a passionate make-out session at the workplace, Barbie pushed him back, turned, and ran away. Stunning. How quickly she adapted to her heels as she ran in them like a pro.

"Hey…what…what about the Caddy?" Sam yelled. She didn't so much as glance back but hop into her Lexus and screech down the road, waving at Sam in a curious gesture of mockery.

James, who must have been lurking in the shadows as these odd turn of events transpired, made his presence known.

"Well, well, well. Sammy, it looks to me that our little contest is still afoot."

"I don't get it. I just don't get it," Sam repeated, contemplating where he lost her.

"I don't get it either. When you guys came back from the test drive, I thought she was a definite slam-dunk. What happened? How could you let a dish like that get away?"

"I think she was playing me."

"Playing you?"

"Yeah, I don't understand it, but I think she was playing me from the start."

"Why would she do that?"

"That's what I'm trying to figure, and it's driving me crazy."

He tried to quickly scan the registry of his mind of disgruntled ladies, but the list was just too great. Could this have been a strange act of revenge?

"I know you don't want to hear this right now, but according to your horoscope, it is not supposed to be your week."

"Oh, please. You know what, James? You are right. I don't want to hear that crap right now. As a matter of fact, I don't want to hear that ever, you got it!"

"I'm just saying."

"Say all you want, I'm going home." Sam clocked off a half-hour early. Mr. Carlton didn't mind. On further speculation on the ride home, he remembered she gave him her phone number. At a red light, he fished it out of his pocket, expecting to find a false number, but to add further confusion to the scrambled circuits of his ability to reason, what was written was "Gotcha."

CHAPTER

12

A strange eeriness filled the atmosphere at work. Sam had yet to clock in, but upon arrival, he felt it thick. Maybe it had something to do with fellow employees avoiding eye contact or going out of their way to stifle communicating with Sam as if he had contracted a communicable disease. *What the hell? Did I forget to put on deodorant this morning?* Sam gave his pits a quick whiff. *No, that's not the problem.*

Jill Esterhouse was one of whom he despised, for she was Sam's strongest competition as far as volume in moving product went. He could have sworn that for the briefest seconds she wore a sad face.

She's not sad about me; she's sad for me. What on earth is going on? "Perplexed" would fall way short in describing Sam's demeanor.

As soon as he spied James's Skylark on a day he was not scheduled to work, James came running.

"James, what is going on?"

"Sam! Mr. Carlton wants to see you, and I promise you I had nothing to do with it." James then gave Sam a quick hug. He did not hug back.

"Nothing to do with what? What is going on?"

James repeated, "Mr. Carlton wants to see you," and sped off.

Sam gingerly stepped inside Mr. Carlton's office. The joyful, portly black man that usually occupied his desk was replaced by a downcast, portly black man. Mr. Carlton was not alone. A thin, tall woman in a corduroyed skirt that reached down to her ankles, sporting a thick pair of eyeglasses with short brown hair, and a full brown paper bag resting against her feet sat beside him, staring Sam up and down.

"Mr. Carlton, you wanted to see me, sir?"

"Yes, Sam, have a seat."

Mr. Carlton was a good man whom Sam enjoyed working for. He delighted in meeting with his employees every morning to dish out a healthy dose of encouragement and to spark the flame of confidence and trust to start the day.

He invested much faith in Sam, recognizing his natural-born, God-given skills in sales. Often he entrusted him with the responsibility of training new recruits, James being one of them. He was patient with his staff, and when one would lose a sale, it was common to hear him say, "It's all right, you'll get 'em next time," or, "Don't worry about it. You're still learning." Sometimes he'd go as far as to bring religion into the mix, and not only for job-related purposes. If he found that someone was dealing with difficulties with life in general, he might remark, "I'm going to pray about it," or, "Don't worry. I'm praying for you. God's got it covered."

The simple-minded found comfort in such words. One day Sam was able to sell a brand new Mustang with all the trimmings. Mr. Carlton saw the joy in Sam's eyes and said, "Congratulations, Sam. Praise Jesus!" Sam wasn't sure what a dead carpenter from two thousand years ago had to do with it, but he appreciated the sentiment. It brought him great recompense to bring a smile to the face of his humbled boss, but what was this?

"Sam, I know you've had the pleasure of meeting Mrs. Suswan."

Sam rose to his feet like a gentleman and reached out to shake her hand.

"No, I don't believe I have—"

Mrs. Suswan rose to her feet and clasped his hand into hers, in the same manner Sam did to Barbie the previous day. She then looked head-on into his eyes and smiled something awfully.

"You don't remember me, Samuel? I thought we had something special."

A flicker of recognition smacked him upside his head. "Barbie?"

"No, actually the name's Kate Suswan, a.k.a. Barbie."

"What? I don't understand."

Kate then with much venom began to empty her bag. She threw down onto Mr. Carlton's desk a blonde wig, a pair of high heels, and an apparatus obviously meant to imitate the appearance of large breasts and her Party Girl novelty shirt.

"I don't understand…"

"She's a private investigator, Sam," Mr. Carlton interjected.

"What…who?"

"Sam, she has shocking allegations aimed at you."

The last thing Kate retrieved from her bag of tricks was a miniature tape recorder. "And I have all the proof I need right here."

"Proof of what? I didn't do you wrong." Sam was completely flustered, losing the gift of speech.

"You wanted the car, the white one, Caddy…Cadillac! We drive test…um, test drove… You liked, said was smooth… I did nothing wrong!"

"Oh, really?" Kate said sprightly.

"Apparently someone has filed a grievance against you, and they hired Mrs. Suswan to investigate your work ethic," Mr. Carlton summed up in as few words as possible.

"Oh really? Well, I did nothing wrong. Go ahead and play the tape," Sam said with such confidence, Mr. Carlton almost believed him. Lord knows he wanted to.

Sam was hoping beyond hope, in the deepest recesses of his heart, for a bluff. There was nothing on that tape except what she was trying to get him to admit to—a haphazard, howbeit, bold attempt to get Sam to incriminate himself. Not going to happen. Just as he feared, Kate was not shaken in this undertaking but gladly lifted the recorder above her head and pressed play.

She played the device from beginning to end. Every word said, clear as day. Sam's insides twisted and turned upon Mr. Carlton hearing the depths of him perpetrating melancholy deceit. It hurt. There was immense shame involved in being exposed in an attempt at ill-gotten gain, but more so when someone so good, so pure of heart, was struck so deeply by the arrow of disappointment by someone in whom such trust was invested.

What could Sam do but protest? Upon hearing the sexual innuendo, Kate declared, "Not only do I plan on filing fraudulent charges on him, but I might be able to get him on sexual harassment."

"That's ridiculous! I meant nothing sexual by that!"

Mr. Carlton went to bat for Sam. "Mrs. Suswan, I hardly think you have enough to charge him with sexual harassment."

"Maybe not. Too bad audio could not pick up his facial expressions. I assure you a jury would have seen it no other way." Upon hearing Sam refer to Barbie/Kate as a cheap woman, Mr. Carlton dropped his sullen head and rubbed his eyes.

"This is all hogwash!" Sam shouted, trying desperately not to swear.

"Sam!" He never heard Mr. Carlton use such a tone, and it served its purpose in shutting him up for a bit.

Kate continued taking control, very much like an attorney before a judge. She stood with pride in front of Mr. Carlton and questioned, "Sir, is it Sunshine policy not to drive beyond fifteen miles during a test drive?"

"No, ma'am, there is no such policy."

Sam sat quietly but fidgeted as she played his lie of so-called Sunshine policy when it came to straying from the proximity.

Did Mr. Carlton say anything in response? Sam couldn't tell you, as his head had slipped into a shocked state, mumbling incoherently of tricks or whatnot.

"Sir, is it Sunshine policy to sell vehicles known to have mechanical failures such as stick-shifts that jump out of gear?"

"No, ma'am, it is not," Carlton responded firmly. Sam just about jumped out of his seat.

"If there is anything wrong with that car, I know or knew nothing about it! How could I know?"

"Oh really, Samuel, then how about we ask James?"

"James? What does he have to do with anything?"

Carlton summoned for James, who for some reason was still lingering around the lot. He shuffled his way into Mr. Carlton's office like a schoolboy caught throwing rocks at girls.

"James, did you know the white Caddy had a malfunction in its shifting mechanism?"

"Yes, sir, I did."

"James, did Sam know?"

"Yes, sir, he did."

"He's lying!"

Turning to Mr. Carlton, Sam said, "Sir, he's lying!"

With authority and power, Mr. Carlton thundered, "Sam, shut up!"

Kate Suswan, seemingly oblivious to the commotion, continued, "Sir, is it Sunshine policy for your employees to hit on your customers..."

Sam had heard enough. He knew his remark in referring to Mr. Carlton as anal-retentive was coming up and could handle no more. He could hold back his choice of words no longer, letting the expletives fly, and he stormed off the lot in a drama-driven hissy fit.

CHAPTER

13

Sam gathered his things in step with the ominous desire to vacate the mountain. He was sure to find a message of termination on his answering machine upon arrival from none other than Mr. Carlton. He could hear it now: "Samuel, I'm disappointed in you, and I'm sure you understand, regarding the circumstances, I have to let you go."

If Mr. Carlton would leave it at that, it would be cool. It could be handled well enough. But no, he was sure to add, "I'll be praying for you, Sam."

That's exactly the kind of thing he did not want to hear. It was like pouring salt on open wounds or teasing the broken-hearted. He might as well be told Santa was not going to bring him presents that year. His skin crawled at the thought of being spoken to in such a condescending fashion.

Oddly enough, he knew he was going to miss this abode. The days anyway. The unexplainable welcomed feeling of comfort and serenity along with all its strange perks was a camper's delight. Yet the night was the exact opposite, Sam feeling on the verge of insanity. What a horrific experience. Sam took one last look at the freshly stacked wood. It served as a reminder that this trip's oddities could not be explained through mere head trauma or psychological banter. The wood was still there. This was real. *Time to get the hell out of Oz.*

Sam stood once again on the edge of the great chasm. Methodically he tapped on the boulder that was sure to cause dangerous head trauma but did not. No way would he repeat such a crash. Once again he visualized his leap and landing.

There lay no boulders to obstruct his landing on the other side. If his feet failed him on impact, the worst that could happen might be a skinned knee. He swung his backpack back and forth, readying to toss, when the sound of laughter caught his ear.

It was coming from about fifty yards from where he had camped. He steadied himself and carefully listened. Two men for sure. Naturally, the first thing that crossed his mind was the more than likely possibility that these two were the comedians that delighted in striking the fear of the unknown into a lonely camper.

Rather than head on home as planned, a simplistic curiosity—what was it that curiosity did to the cat?—could not be subdued. He had to at the least see them in the light of day and, if all went well, communicate.

Sam was able to quietly sneak up from behind. They stood in the creek—the tall one with water to his knees, the other to his waist. They wore matching suspenders and chewed tobacco as if in a race, often spitting in sync, as if choreographed. The short one spat on land, the other in the water. The short one reached up and gave the tall one a backhanded slap.

"Don'e you be spittin' in that d'ere wad'a, Leo, yo scad dem fish fo sho. I shooda bot a bucket."

The taller one, Leo, agreed.

Judging by this exchange, Sam surmised this was not the first that the shorter struck Leo. It almost seemed to be something he had grown accustomed to, as if ritualistic in frequency.

Enough had been seen. Sam decided it wasn't worth wasting his breath on a couple of rednecks and began to tiptoe his way back the way he came.

"Sam! Sam! Sam!" the taller one shouted out.

Sam stopped in his tracks, frozen at the mention of his name. The men didn't even turn to look at him but remained focused on reeling and casting, casting and reeling.

How could they possibly know my name?

"Yeah, it's me," Sam replied, somewhat baffled.

The two men turned around with awkward, dumbfounded expressions of their own as Sam approached.

"Whoda hell are you?" Leo asked.

"I'm inclined to ask you guys the same thing. I don't know you. How is it you know me?"

"Ged a load ud d'at, Leo. Dis fella come up on'd us outta of God knows where, and he'd think we know him."

"Come on, I just heard you yell my name three times."

"Mister, duh only ting I yelled tree times was damn. Ed yo name Damn, mister? Looky here, Leo, dis man name is Damn." They broke out in screeching laughter.

"Is yo laz name It?"

"I tink yo right, Carl (the taller one). Dis feller name is Damn It."

Another seemingly unending fit of laughter followed.

Sam could not possibly have felt more embarrassed. "No, what I thought you said was Sam, which happens to be my name. Sorry I bothered you guys."

Leo wanted to continue with the teasing.

"Sam? You mean like Samsonite?"

Carl reached up and slapped Leo. "Shut it, Leo, ed not funny no mo'."

"What you be doing round d'ese here parts, Samsonite?" Carl asked. Leo smirked but held back laughing.

"That is not my name," Sam responded authoritatively.

"I says it is," Carl retorted, challenging Sam's resolve. In like manner, Leo took a step forward with chest bulging and a sickly grin deforming the already malformed contours of his face and tobacco stained teeth.

Sam read them clearly: I dare you to disagree. See what happens.

Sam had no fear. If it came right down to it and a tussle broke out, he was sure Leo would come at him first, and being the big baboon that he was, there was no doubt he would want to utilize his upper body strength in punishing Sam, and he was sure to be slow. When he made his move at Sam's face, neck, head, whatever the case might be, Sam only needed to duck down, attack his legs, and come up with a rock to the chin, and timber, the giant would go down.

When Carl sees what was done to Leo, he would be sure to run off like the little coward he was; easy as that. Although everything inside him wanted to take them up on their little challenge, six months of anger-management classes kicked in. *This is so not worth it.*

"Samsonite it is. You guys can call me Mr. Sonite."

Leo looked at Carl for insight into the odd situation at hand. Carl looked back at Leo for a long four seconds of trite silence. Carl could hold back no longer, his stomach restricting in a torrid release of laughter. Of course this was the okay for Leo to follow in high-pitched melodious harmony. Sam chuckled along with them but was unable to reach their level of treble.

"Sam, you all right," Carl declared.

"So, you can hook us up wit some luggage, Mr. Sonite?" Leo rhetorically asked.

Sam lifted his hand as if to slap him and mimicked their backwoods southern slur. "Shut it, Leo, ed not funny no mo." They then shook hands in confirmation of harmony.

The relief taken in defusing what could have turned out to be an inauspicious situation was more than satisfactory. They made idle chitchat of the mundane, while all along Sam wrestled with the idea of bringing up last night's scare but decided on letting it rest.

Suddenly, without warning, things got uncomfortable once again as Carl took a sudden interest in Sam's fishing pole. He stared at it longer than what was comfortable, like it was something never seen before. Finally he commented, "Where'd you go and get that d'ere pole from?"

"Gosh, I don't know…at a sporting goods store some years back, I think."

Carl dropped to his knees to analyze it further.

"Well, dat sho is a nice one." This sudden interest in Sam's very ordinary fishing pole made Sam a tad uneasy to say the least.

"Just an ordinary fishing pole, Carl. I think it only set me back about fifty bucks."

"Let me aks ya." Carl's eyes gazing up at Sam somehow took on a shade of yellow. "Yo fishing fo fish, am I right?"

What kind of question is that? Sam answered as reasonable as one would expect. "Of course, fish." Not sure what else to say, Sam tried to make light of such an odd question. "You wouldn't expect me to be fishing for men, would you?"

There was something different to the laughs that followed. Although it was the same boisterous reaction Sam had come to expect from Carl and Leo, that time there was absolutely no mistaking the unsettling twinge of fear they failed in concealing. The yellowish tint to the white of Carl's eyes somehow reverted back to its natural color.

Sam had heard somewhere at sometime that such symptoms could be a sign of jaundice, but never had he heard of eyes that could switch color in a matter of seconds. Just because he had not heard of it did not mean it was not possible, and as far as he was concerned, what he didn't know filled an infinite number of warehouses. Nonetheless, seeing it in Carl's eyes, on top of his strange fascination with his pole, made him terribly uneasy.

"It was nice meeting you guys, but it's time for me to head on home."

"Okay, Sam. Doan you be fishin' fo men now." Again with the laughing.

Sam began to make his way back the way he came when Leo said, "Hey, look at dat, Carl. Samsonite goin' da wrong way."

"Hey, Sam, you know dat duh wrong way, doan ya?"

"Actually, guys, this is the way I came."

"You crazy. You mighta killed yoself jumpin' dat… Shoot, you gotta gash on yo head already."

"What!" Sam fingered his head anew and ran up to Carl. "You see a wound on my head? Because I don't feel anything."

"All I see is yo fohead, dummy. What you trippin on?"

"Come on, you just said I have a gash on my head."

"I did not either. You gotta clean out yo ears, dummy. What I said was if you gonna jump dat hole in da mountain, you'd gonna bash on yo head already. I didn't say nuttin' 'bout no gash."

"That is so not what you said. You said I have a gash on my head. Didn't he, Leo?"

"Dat's not what I hear. I hear bash."

Sam, finding no good in arguing, relented.

"Is there a better way to get to my truck? I need to go through the campgrounds to get to it."

"Sho is. You only needs to continue in da opposite way in da way you wanna go, den you gonna come up on a fork. Now listen, Sam, dis ed very impotant. You must take da left-han path. It'll take ya wheres you wanna go."

"Okay, left-hand path, got it."

"Might I ask, where does the right-hand path lead?"

Leo got right up in Sam's space. *What's this? Are Leo's eyes yellow now?* Sam stared with fascination.

"Dat's where you don't wanna go."

Sam got an unwanted close view of his teeth and crinkled his nose in defense to Leo's putrid breath.

"I got it, guys. The left path is where I want to go, and the right is where I don't want to go. Simple enough. I take it that going this way is going to be a longer hike?"

"A little bit longer, but safer. It gonna circle you back to the grounds…les'you wanna fall down dat deep ditch in da mountain."

~

Just as Sam had been coming up on what he guessed to be a three-hour hike into the great unknown and just as he began to curse himself for exercising such idiocy in hearkening to the direction of two fools, a fork in the road lay ahead. He sprinted the rest of the way to its genesis and contemplated his direction. The left was wide and well traveled, twisting and turning a great distance. The right was thin and narrow, leaving only enough room for one man in single file. No twists and turns on that path; it went perfectly straight. It too ran a great distance, farther than his eyes could see on a clear day.

It certainly seemed to Sam that the left path would be the clear choice. Using the rationale of his heart of hearts, he felt strongly that both paths, eventually, led to the same destination. Evidently, the left-hand path was the easier and thus quicker route. The right was so scarcely traveled that it could hardly be discerned, as moss and grass stretched across, almost covering it completely. *Who am I to argue with such a great majority?* Sam reasoned.

Still, being the curious creature he was, he felt compelled to go right, for a quick look-see at the path he was leaving behind. He only took about five steps when a thumping sound mildly shook the mountain ground, echoing through the trees and distant canyon caves.

What on earth…?

Thump, thump, thump, thump. Sam scanned all around in search of its source. The echo had him twitching his head side to side seeking he who bounces sound. *Thump, thump, thump.* With each thump, the sound grew louder, drawing closer.

A figure of a man was rapidly walking his way on the wide path from the direction Sam was apt to take. *Who on earth is this guy? What is his deal?* Sam thought. He could not figure how it was possible that one man could by his mere gait shake earth so prominently.

He studied his coming with bewildered wonder. Upon his eyes adjusting to the man who walked with thunder, he could make out that he wore a uniform.

Surely this was a park ranger. *Am I not supposed to be here?* Sam wondered. *Maybe there's some rule I don't know about.* He considered that maybe he was treading upon private property, in which he'd be glad to pay a fine or whatever, as long as that guy could confirm his way to be true, and if not, the park ranger could at least direct him. *Thump, thump, thump, thump.*

The rumbling made a little more sense when Sam saw that with each bone-crushing vibration, the ranger planted each step with fury, as if he were trying to crush a large rat with one fatal crush. This made his gait awkward and unnatural; it was almost funny to watch, but not quite. Although such a manner of fluidity would slow most people down, taking the time to exert so much strength and power into each step, somehow for him it did not. Sam would swear that he moved quicker as a result. A mysterious rage summoned his presence, and Sam was a possible obstacle upon his path.

Loose rocks were shuttered free from the space occupied, for only God would know how long, rolling and tumbling to gravity's end.

This only added to the commotion, stirring birds to take flight and rodents to relocate nests.

Sam stood his ground as the ranger approached and successively hid the quivering in his legs. The ranger almost looked like he wasn't going to stop but was going to blow right past Sam like he wasn't even there, like a man on a motorcycle in regard to a traffic jam. Sam went to move to his right, and the ranger moved to his left in response. Thinking he was going to be run over and stomped upon mercilessly, Sam raised his arms in defense. "Whoa!" At the last possible moment, the ranger came to a complete standstill.

The ranger stood at attention like a private before a general and said nothing. He was massive in height and ample in girth, like a seven-foot body builder doped up on steroids. Sweat oozed from his pores, and he had a fetid stink, like one dipped in toxic sulfur. His nostrils flared in sync with the rapid pounding of his heart.

"Thought you were going to run me over," Sam said with a giggle. The ranger did not smile, the ranger did not laugh, and the ranger stood stoic, his expression void of all emotion. He gazed upon Sam as if waiting for something.

～

Sam was ten years old again, and his father had just received his progress report.

"Samuel Reed, come here."

Sam stood before his father knowing that he knew all the bad he had conducted during the light of day in the confines of broken school rules. His father would say nothing but only stare into the guilty eyes of his misbehaving son, much the way the ranger was now. Sam could not, he would not, endure it long, but confess all the vanity committed under the sun to his father who already knew. Just as if he were ten all over again, he rambled on to the ranger all the wrong committed on his turf, his mountain.

"I'm sorry. I didn't know I wasn't supposed to stray from the campgrounds."

Still the ranger stared.

"Was I not supposed to light a campfire in that area? I'm sorry. I should have known it was a hazard."

Still he stared, and Sam grew more flustered.

"The tree? Was it the cherry tree?"

At this, the ranger's eyes widened.

"That's it then. I ate from a protected tree and lit a fire on private property. Whatever the penalty is, I'll pay it. Go ahead and write me up a ticket or fine or whatever."

"That tree is wrong. It is death." The ranger grunted in rage.

That's funny…I feel fine. "I promise I won't touch it again. I'm actually on my way home."

"Don't go that way. You should never…you do right…always go our way, always have." His words were simple and precise.

"Huh?" How strange that the ranger would refer to the cherry tree as a "way."

"Stay on wide path, where many go. You do right to do so. You always go with us, you do good. Enter through gate." The ranger's pupils danced while he spoke, drawing Sam in and holding him tight. It seemed the ranger had control of the tantalizing jig his eyes performed. The pupil of one eye would shrink while the other expanded; one eye would slowly move up and down while the other would swiftly zigzag side to side. Sometimes they moved together while most of the time not. Suddenly the simplistic way in which the ranger spoke was vital to Sam, every word of great significance.

The ranger then crossed his arms and nodded at the left-hand path in a gesture that said move it.

Sam spoke without meaning, "Yes, the left-hand path, I go… I follow." It would have been a fair mockery of the ranger if done on purpose.

CHAPTER

14

He emerged from a deep state of hypnosis, what might have been thirty minutes to two hours later. Who could say? He had stayed true to the left-hand path just as the ranger's suggestion evoked. He thought about the park ranger and his inept attempt at speech. Really, they must be scraping the bottom of the barrel for park rangers these days.

He didn't seem to have the wits about him to acquire and maintain a job as demanding and thoroughly involved as what one would expect from a park ranger. He began to consider that the park ranger might have been indulging in illegal drugs before he came upon him. It certainly would explain a lot, especially that tripped-out look in his eye.

The bizarre gymnastics his eyes performed were successfully kept from Sam's memory; he only knew that there was something very strange about them.

LSD—I bet he drops acid on the job and trips hardcore. What's the world coming to? The guy is probably having psychotic, paranoid delusions that I'm going to tell his superiors... Maybe he is mentally retarded. Not severally but mildly. Don't they have programs or something for the mildly retarded to help them get jobs they can handle?

But a park ranger was hardly the sort of job Sam could picture a retarded guy being able to handle. The guy must have been high.

~

Already, the evening had arrived, which came with it a foreboding chill in the air. As was yesterday, today brought with it a pleasant touch of warmth. But if last night was any indication of the night to come, Sam was in big trouble. This served in quickening his pace to a jog in hopes with every turn of this zigzagging, never-ending journey, he would triumphantly cross the campground boundaries and thus his truck, along with his living reality.

As evening gave way to night, so did chill to cold. His fears confirmed, he sprinted, not just to get home but to stay warm. He brought himself to an unscheduled end pass and analyzed how far he had come and how much farther he had to go. *I know how far I've hiked, but I don't have a clue how much farther.* Sam stressed as he contemplated the distance yet to travel. He groaned from somewhere deep within. He could not help but think how if he had jumped the chasm a second time as he had originally planned, he would have made it home before nightfall to enjoy the warm subtleties of a roof and heater.

The anxiety, frustration, and boiling anger he had successfully kept in check all this time was beginning to simmer over.

"Thank you so much, Carl and Leo, for thinking of my well-being and leading me out to the middle of freakin' nowhere. Thank you so much for that. You're a couple of funny guys—really, really, really funny guys," Sam said, his voice rising in frustration.

"And let us not forget our friend, the psycho park ranger, with his heavy feet. Quite a cast of characters all hell-bent on me taking the wide path… Why? So I can freeze to death!" Sam shouted while kicking loose dirt. On what might have been on the verge of losing it completely, he walked that line steadfast in not crossing. This occurred when he removed his backpack from his tired, slouching shoulders in search of his flashlight. Although it was much too dark to see, for some unfathomable reason he also could not feel it.

"What the…"

He flipped his backpack upside down, allowing all his possessions to fall freely onto solid ground. He distinctly remembered resting his flashlight beside his canteen and tackle box, but they were the only two items that fell. His canteen split a trail of water in two, encompassing his left foot. While his tackle box shattered on impact, sending his lures, hooks, weights, bait, and needle nose pliers scattering. He madly searched other compartments, knowing full well it would not be there, and sometimes it hurts to be right.

A fragile man on the precipice of crossing a very thin line that was sworn upon to never cross again was cruelly pushed over by phenomenal circumstance.

~

He was fifteen the last time he was that angry. He only wished Carl and Leo were there right now. They would be recipients of wrath unleashed. "We'll see who laughs last!" Brutally, he would teach them a thing or two. He wouldn't mind facing that park ranger again either.

"Bring it on, big guy!" In this state of mind, he felt capable of intimidating the devil himself. He walked over to his tackle box and kicked it hard, but the impact did not send it flying as far as he thought it would. He watched it break into pieces as he slammed it against the mountain. Much in the same way he slammed Chrystal, his seven-year-old cousin, against his bedroom wall some nineteen years ago.

CHAPTER

15

The genesis of his unpredictable wrath was hard to pinpoint, but he could very well remember losing it in 2nd grade when Alison Duarty beat him at a not-so friendly game of Hungry Hungry Hippos. He picked up the board and slammed it down on her head. She ran home crying. How dare her hippo swallow more marbles than his? Such incidents continued throughout adolescence. These things remained at a juvenile level, but quickly graduated to a more mature, dare he admit, criminal extreme not long after. Sam acquired two tight friends in his high school years, Marcus Stiney and Jim Glazier. They shared in their hatred of authority, despised their social peers, and reveled in the creative when it came to breaking rules. Quietly, they were an intrinsic force, representing the darker side of school spirit, and nobody knew it, exactly the way they wanted it. Marcus Stiney already obtained a bad boy reputation having spent time in Juvenile Hall for selling illegal Fireworks on school grounds. Jim Glazier had no such reputation, but not for lack of trying. One only need to regard their lackluster upbringings for an explanation.

～

The upbringing of Samuel Reed was not so dreary or unfortunate. His parents, Marvin and Maggie Reed, loved him immensely and showed their love through nurturing and supporting Sam in his gifts and passions. They did not forcefully lead him one way or another in life but allowed him to make his own decisions and carve out his own method of success and happiness. They were there to catch him when he fell, which was often in his preteen years, and as maturity grew, they watched and applauded his every triumph. When Sam got out of line and rules were broken—as they so often are throughout adolescence—they disciplined as was appropriate.

The absolute best they could do for him was to protect him from the self-seeking vipers in life out to gain prosperity through outright foolhardy deception. Their goal to steal the spoil of him who worked so hard for every cent and indulge in that they did not work for.

On the top of this list would be organized religion. They advertised salvation through the giving freely of one's treasure. And if you gave enough, you'd be sure to own the most luxurious of suites located in the center of heaven—with a window and everything—and just maybe you would get to eat the scraps that fell from God's table.

"Stay clear, my boy, stay clear," his father repeated on many an occasion.

Of all the wisdom bestowed upon Sam over the years from his well-meaning father, that was one that stuck. No way would he be swindled by any hustler, religious or not.

They did such a good job telling people what they wanted to hear. "The creator of all the universe loves and wants to have a personal relationship with you"—that's how they set you up. Who didn't love to be loved? Sam had to hand it to them being so clever in their rhetoric, but wasn't it funny how they could never end a sermon without pleading for money? Apparently the God of all the universe and his boy Jesus got low on funds pretty often. Not to mention God's mouthpiece, the blessed pastor of God's flock, needed a couple thousand to make his monthly payment on his new Mercedes Benz. The piper played his flute, and how easy did the children follow. Not Sam, not ever, thanks be to Dad.

CHAPTER

16

Their rebellion was performed quietly in secret and methodically carried out. They spoke to no one of the spiteful reproach festering in their hearts of all things social. Dumb jocks were target number one, and condescending teachers who thought they knew better than all and flaunted a prissy attitude with it were number two. Depending on the mood and opportunity, really anybody could be on the list. The main focus there was not so much anarchy but fun. It just so happened that anarchy could be a whole lot of fun.

That was back in the day before security cameras inundated school grounds. There was a small measure of school security that walked the premises, but nothing they could not avoid. One only needed to learn their schedules and then hit the gaps hard. Never did they commit the same crime twice, and if they did, it would have been carried out in alternative ways. Their acts of vandalism were cleverly spaced out. Never at the same time of day or a schedule followed. Sometimes they hit months apart while other times they hit two days in succession. No one could catch on to any one pattern, but staff did keep their eyes open, keeping them on their toes, allowing the creative juices to flow.

Great delight came as a result of the administration of small, petty crimes. The swiping of a baseball bat that had been left behind in a dugout and using it to randomly smash up lockers was a perfect example of how they conducted their brand of lawlessness. Of whom? They did not know, nor did they care. That was the fun part. When it was time to retrieve or place books and various items into or out of one's locker, Sam, Jim, and Marcus were innocuously within the vicinity to see which lucky student received the coarse surprise to heighten the school day.

As can be imagined, a variety of emotions were always prevalent, although sometimes (usually with the females) a degree of sorrow was involved depending on the items that were destroyed. For the most part, it was the rage of their victims that sent the expletives flying, as well as some fists, destroying further the already damaged lockers serving as malignant amusement for the boys.

The three of them were clever; they were smart and shared their actions with no one. Praise in pulling off such dastardly activities without getting caught would not leave their faction.

It was Jim who decided to give their little group a name—a simple name, nothing evolved or profound, but it did sum them up quite accurately. The Perpetrators. Sam imagined it as a name a punk rock band would use, and didn't punk bands primarily preach anarchy in their music? Well, at least the old-school punk bands did and were loud about it. It was perfect; it was them.

During first period English, one boring Monday morning, Sam's mind began to drift as it usually would, and rather than work on the assignment given, he mentally stroked his ego. The Perpetrators had been causing havoc for almost the whole school year, and no one, not one person at any time, was remotely close to fingering them. He squinted haughty eyes and smirked a display of pride, exhaling any lingering guilt. He scribbled down The Perpetrators into a notebook piece of paper along with the crimes committed and ones yet to come as if in a trance and scrambled to second period woodshop upon the ringing of the bell. He thought nothing more about what he wrote or where he stuffed it, thus evidence yet to be found.

Visiting the bike rack and slashing random tires did not provide the same excitement it once did. Even when they transferred the blade to the teacher's parking lot, the thrill was gone. It was unanimously decided that The Perpetrators causing the usual stir among the student body was getting old.

"Before this year ends, lets hit em' hard," Jim said with a look of crucial sincerity.

"I reckon that's not a bad idea. Whaddya got in mind?" Marcus responded in a fair impersonation of Clint Eastwood in one of his Westerns, spitting out his gum in place of tobacco.

"Yeah, let's get Billy Warnick," Sam said, liking what he was hearing.

"You must be crazy. I was thinking more along the lines of Chris Fesonmer," Jim retorted in mild surprise.

"A man gonna cross Warnick, he better get mean…real mean," Marcus said while adding twisted facial expressions, really capturing the good, the bad, and primarily the ugly.

"Let's get em' both."

"Both?"

"You just said we should hit 'em hard," Sam reminded Jim.

"I'm not sure how we're going to pull that off, but I'm on board. What about you, Josey Whales, you on board?"

"I reckon."

CHAPTER

17

B illy Warnick looked over his report card one more time. Nothing had changed; he still had that D- in English.

"Dad's not going to like this." Billy followed with curses. Notre Dame would not take him with grades like that. *Hate to do it, but I'm going to have to threaten or rough up some poor kid so I can copy from his paper. Hey, it got me through middle school.*

An easier way would have been to get the kid to do it all for him, but he was smart enough to know that that was a sure way to get caught. Any teacher with half a brain and eye could tell the difference between the choppy chicken scratch that was Warnick's handwriting as opposed to just about anybody in the whole school.

Billy shared his father's dream of playing football for the Fighting Irish. As a junior, he already fit the profile at six three, pushing three hundred pounds, and with tremendous skill to boot. He was well on his way to being a starting defensive line-man. Upon miraculously graduating from Juniper High School with a 2.0 grade point average, he was sure to have multitudes of colleges calling, most of which he would politely decline. All except the call he had dreamed of since he was nine while playing Pop Warner. But this was not the end of the dream. Upon setting

Notre Dame's all-time sack record and somehow graduating with honors, he would most certainly be drafted by the Green Bay Packers for a ten-year run and his success ultimately landing him in the Pro Football Hall of Fame. Sensible or not, you couldn't tell Warnick otherwise. His father instilled such confidence into the boy that he could look at his future in no other way.

Although, truth be told, Billy could care less what college he attended as long as he was playing the game that occupied his thoughts and frequented his sleeping and waking dreams. Only because he loved his father he set his heart on Notre Dame, this way a dual fantasy would be fulfilled.

Despite Billy's threatening psyche and unreadable silence, which only helped to fuel the fear of the unknown in his peers, he had a gentle manner about him that only surfaced when taking the time to get to know him. Billy had no friends, only team buddies. They were there to praise his play on the field, hug him when preventing the opposing team from scoring, but not one he could genuinely call his friend. At one point, the revelation hit him that maybe he only liked football to get attention, not only from his father but his peers. Such thinking made him feel like a sissy, so he wiped it away, never allowing his mind to return to such girly reasoning again.

Even when persuading smart kids to let him copy, he was not as harsh as some might think. Without having to, he offered to act as, what some might call a bodyguard, in return. This was not a method in assuring the smart kid would go through with it but a lousy attempt at befriending the terrified lad. It never worked. Billy was sensitive, and although it hurt his feelings, he never let on. However, if one were to sadistically verbalize cruel mockery, Billy would not hesitate to powerfully thump that careless individual upside his head—as was the case with freshman Troy Edmenton. He committed a cardinal blunder in referring to Billy as fat. Had he said "huge," Billy would have kept his cool; no big deal. After all, such a word could be used in many different ways. He might be huge in stature, huge in mass/strength, or he might have a huge heart. Huge he could handle. But fat? It was not easy to use such a word without a negative connotation involved. That was an insult, no way around it.

Troy had been walking the halls in between periods with a couple of friends discussing the up and coming game when he blurted, "Shoot, if we really want to win, all we need to do is have Billy Warnick lie down on the line of scrimmage and have the team roll him down field. He's so fat he'll clear a path in no time; instant touchdown." A rather lame joke with no basis in reality (especially considering Billy played on defense), but nothing moved faster the spoken word than gossip in high school.

Before the day was halfway done, Billy sought Troy out and without so much as a salutation struck the puny boy. He went down hard, unconscious before he hit the ground. He was out for a good ten seconds, completely at a loss as to what happened when he came to.

Billy was suspended for three days but was glad because he knew word got out not to call Billy fat. Probably not a good idea to insult him period.

∼

It was a typical Wednesday, filled with the usual monotonous activities he had come to expect halfway through the week. The day was overcast and sticky, and he planned on a cold shower upon arriving home, after first mowing the lawn as he promised his mother. The bell had rung to end the school day, and Billy fingered his way through the lunchtime trash he had routinely stuffed his pockets with, until he found the key to unlock his bike located at the school bike rack. He stuffed his backpack with his textbooks and readied himself for the ride home. He had no reason to believe his life was soon to change forever.

Something was different and rather odd. A crowd had gathered and seemed to be studying Billy's bike in particular. What on earth was going on? As he grew closer, all eyes were fixed on him.

"Look at your bike, Billy. Aahh Chris loves you, Billy. Check out your bike seat, Billy."

He could not make sense of all this, so he hurried to his bike for an answer. There written with a pink marker upon Billy's black bike seat was a message:

I love you, Billy. Call me: 458-5261

Chris Fesonmer

He stared at this message as if English were his second language. Those three words *I love you* melted his heart, but someone shouted, "Are you going to kick his ass, Billy?" Billy snapped out of his daze and translated the message to its simplest form. People said Chris was gay. It was not right for a boy to like a boy like that. That was wrong. The crowd awaited his response, and he knew what they were expecting.

Regardless if he wanted to or not, he acted out with fake rage. If he was anything, he was a crowd pleaser. He picked up his bike with a menacing grunt, lifting up the rack chained to his wheel, as well as all the other bikes all lined up in a row, and slammed it down onto the pavement. His front wheel bent on impact, and the chain was freed from the rack, dangling from the damaged wheel like a freshly severed umbilical cord. He would have preferred to leave it at that, but uncertain of the appropriateness or magnitude expected of one subservient to a homosexual pass, he figured one more tenacious outburst should do.

Some were cheering him on, while others were at a loss and stood idle, slacked jawed in wonderment, and yet a smaller group of three could not have found it more hilarious, gripping their stomachs in uncontrolled laughter. Billy grunted a second time, lifting his bike and thrashing it into the other bikes with a mighty crash, falling one on top of another like a row of dominoes, causing unrestorable damage to a few. That theater now performed, Billy quietly picked up the remaining frame of his Schwinn and headed home on foot.

CHAPTER

18

Completely oblivious to the goings on eastside of campus, Chris Fesonmer waited his turn in line to board the school bus. His one-time friends he used to share the bus with suspiciously found alternative methods home, once Chris's sexuality came into question. But there came Alex, seemingly out of nowhere, in horrible disarray. Chris hadn't spoken with him since he defeated him a few months previously when playing Nintendo 64's Nascar 99. Alex vanished from his life not long after, but there he was in a state of absolute panic.

"Chris, when you get off the bus, run straight home, lock your doors, and call the cops."

"Huh? Why? What's going on?"

Alex did not answer but turned to run off, but Chris grabbed him by his sleeve.

"Billy Warnick is after you!"

"What? Why?"

Alex said no more, twisting himself free, and ran off as quickly as he had arrived, leaving Chris with a gamut of questions unanswered.

"Billy Warnick is after me." Dear God, why? But he knew why, that was easy enough to guess. Didn't take an Einstein to figure that one out. Billy was officially a member of the gay-bashing clan.

"I can't handle this anymore. Why can't people just leave me alone? It is time for me to stand up and put an end to this."

A tear almost secreted out of the corner of his eye, but he held it back. He was just so very tired.

As recommended, he bolted home once the bus arrived at his stop, quicker than his feet could carry him, and promptly dead bolted the door. "The cops?" *No way, not today.* As much as fear flowed through every pore in his trembling body, he would not submit to its crippling malaise. He would, he needed to, he *must* face Warnick alone. As feminine as he might come off at times, he was born male, inhabiting the same measure of testosterone as any other male on the planet. Win or lose, he would take a stand. The thing was he had no plans on losing. Billy had the advantage, no doubt there. Not a problem, Chris would merely have to even things out. While storming the immaculate cleanliness of his parents' bedroom, he found what he was looking for in their closet behind nicely folded towels: his father's golf clubs. He pulled out his 9-iron, griped it tightly, and swung at air.

"This will do just fine. Bring it on, Billy!" He then set himself up a comfy spot by his living room window, crinkling the blinds so he could gaze out, gripping the 9-iron, awaiting his executioner.

Chris had a certain way about him that was very feminine, whether it was the way he spoke with others, a little gesture he would make unknowingly with his hand, or just the way he wore his clothes in a kind of flamboyant fashion. There was something about him that screamed "queer." Somebody at sometime, somewhere at school said Chris was gay, and his life had been hell ever since. On a number of occasions he found himself running for his life to reach the shelter of home. Gay bashers were after him, and one day they might get him, but not today.

"Don't flatter yourself, Billy. You're not the first, but you will be the last." Chris was somewhat shocked at the confidence of his own voice. He never thought of Billy Warnic as one who would be part of the gay-bashing clan, but now he knew better, didn't he? People would soon know that he could be as masculine as anyone else.

He gazed intently and listened oh so carefully for the sound of footsteps coming up the drive. He would not be caught unaware. When soldiers knew an attack was imminent, it made it so much easier to set up the ambush. The most important weapon aside from foreknowledge was patience, of which Chris stored in abundance.

At the top of the hour, a strange, squeaky rattling tightened his moist grip on the club. That could be him. When the source of the rattle slowly came into view, it was only the little neighbor girl peddling an old, rusted, beat-up tricycle. It looked vintage, like it came straight from the seventies.

He used his shirt to wipe the club free of the nervous humid perspiration that also stuck his shirt to his back. A shadow moved behind the dumpster across the street. *That would be a perfect place to hide if Billy were trying to sneak up on me.* Using his fingers, he opened the gap in the blinds just a little more. That did not help to see behind a dumpster. He did not see the shadow again. Trying to maintain a measure of clarity, he concluded the shadow was no more than his tired, strained eyes playing tricks.

He had great hope that his parents would not come home from their respective jobs until the confrontation had ended. He would rant and rave of how he stood up to the big bully. That would be uncharacteristic enough, which would sure make his father proud, win or lose. But again, Chris didn't plan on losing. If all went as planned, this would put an end to those who were so intent on harassing and beating him up. It would be a victory that would demand instant respect from his school, putting an end to all the vicious rumors.

"I'm not a homo!" Chris shouted at the uncaring walls.

As the sun began to set, school having ended a few hours before, Billy was a no show. As Chris was beginning to believe that this was all a cruel joke played on him by his old queer-hating friend, Billy showed up.

My God, he's huge. Chris swallowed hard. He was ready. Billy didn't look as expected. He wore a nice cashmere button-up shirt and had his hair parted nicely to the side, and his pants were corduroyed. He looked like a young man on his way to church on a Sunday morning. Odd, to say the least. Chris would not allow that to derail his plans. Billy was probably on his way to a hot date and decided to throw in beating up on the little queer boy as an afterthought.

He approached the porch, timid. He stopped, turned around as if he was going to walk off, took two steps, and then turned back around and slowly continued his way to the porch.

"What's he doing?"

The original plan was to wait for him to knock, unlock the door, and then throw it open and start swinging away like a mad-man. Billy would never expect it. He began digging into his front right pocket searching for something. *A knife? He's looking for his knife. He's come to kill me.* He bent down, for some reason taking interest in Chris's welcome mat. This was it. He mustn't delay. Chris recognized his opportunity and must take it now. Slowly, ever so gently he unlocked the deadbolt, all the while keeping a tight eye on Billy. He threw the door open as visualized and swung down with all his might onto the kneeling giant's head.

Billy stood up in crazed shock, wobbling. Chris swung back the club, ready for blow number two, when he saw Billy's eyes. They were wild, twitching, and moving in ways God did not intend. He was stumbling backward, trying to focus, trying to retain balance when his eyes rolled in the back of his head, and he went down.

"Yes! What you think now, Billy! Huh! What you think now!" Knowing perfectly well Billy was not going to get up, thus the threat to his physical well-being averted, it was time to put the second part of his plan into action. He stormed back inside, grabbing the phone, and called for a paramedic. He had no intention in taking anyone's life only to defend himself and hoped Billy would not perish as a result.

He returned to the scene of the confrontation, pulled up a piece of patio furniture next to Billy, had a seat, and awaited the sound of an ambulance in the distance.

He surveyed the damage he had inflicted. As far as Chris was concerned, a paramedic couldn't get there quickly enough. Billy's unconscious body went into what Chris surmised were convulsions. His body shook, a gurgling sound followed a sticky white liquid leaking down the corners of his mouth. *Please hurry. I can't stand to watch a kid die right in front of me, here on my porch.* Watching Billy, this titanic hulk, in such a sorry state, incapable of hurting a fly, almost got Chris feeling sympathy. Almost. He couldn't allow his emotions to go there. *After all, he came to kill me.* He looked over at his welcome mat for the knife he would have undoubtedly dropped nearby on impact. Have a nice day, two frogs exclaimed from two Lily pads.

Where's the knife? He scanned the area but did not see the knife. Panic took root as an ambulance was drawing closer.

"What did you do with the knife, Billy?" Chris shouted at his critical victim. It was then that he noticed the corner of a note sticking out from under the two smiling frogs. It was placed so that his name was clearly displayed. Chris's heart skipped a couple of beats and then sped up. His hands shaking, he grabbed the note, hardly able to open it, and read a fourth-grade level of writing.

> Chris, I got your message on my bike seat. I am not gay. But thank you for saying nice things. I won't let people be mean to you anymore. We should hang out.
>
> Billy Warnic

"My God, my God, what have I done?"

Blood was streaking from the hole in Billy's head down his cheek, scattering around the foam from his mouth and all together settling in the middle of his chest, staining his shirt a dark red. He took off his pinkish/purple shirt with tiny blue polka-dots scattered all about and tried to create a tourniquet, but it wasn't happening, so he ran indoors, repeating, "Oh God, oh God, oh God..." and ransacked his parents closet, grabbing as many of the nicely folded towels as he could carry and again tried to plug the oozing hole in Billy's head.

A knife! Without a knife, the police will think I acted in cold blood. Again he returned indoors, this time in search of a knife to plant on Billy's person. Grabbing the first butcher knife he found in the drawer of silverware, he ran back out. A police car had arrived just in time to see Chris run frantically from his home holding a butcher knife standing over a large bleeding kid. As trained, the two police officers exited their car in no time flat, drawing their pistols. The second Chris saw that police car, he knew his life would never be the same and a dam full of tears broke.

"Drop the knife!" an officer shouted. He watched his tears fall to the ground in a spaced-out daze and still held the knife, unable to grasp the command. *This isn't really happening.* The officer's crept closer, and their second attempt broke through.

"I said drop the knife!"

Chris was then able to understand the aggressive tone, although he heard it muffled, as though he and the officer were submerged under water. He released his grip on the knife, allowing it to fall.

What Chris remembered so vividly above everything else of the worst day of his life in the following years he was incarcerated was the perceived super slow-motion fall of the knife onto the tear-stained pavement, banking off handle then onto tip and back to handle, its motion increasing in rapidity—handle, tip, handle, tip, handle, tip. Chris watched in fascination the laws of inertia, and just as the object in motion was on the crux of resting, the police took him down.

All other details faded from memory and resurfaced only during the terrible nightmares that followed, never allowing him to forget that horrible day when he almost killed Billy Warnick. Forever that day burned in his collective memory of that miserable time he crippled Billy Warnick for life.

CHAPTER

19

The following Thursday morning a thick gray cloud of sorrow swallowed the initial bolt of shock upon Juniper High School receiving the all-too-real news that their star defensive lineman, Billy Warnick, had been brutally attacked and was in a coma and might not live. A sullen, miserable feeling permeated the school atmosphere. Those who laughed so hard at Billy's expense and those who cheered Billy on when damaging his own property grew awfully quiet. Sects and small groups of kids would discuss these things in private, seemingly never growing louder than a whisper. An investigation was underway.

Rumors spread like wildfire. Some said Billy was ambushed by Juniper's arch rival, Clearwater High School's inferior football team. Five team members overpowered him and threatened to beat him, each with a baseball bat, if Billy didn't verbally state "Clearwater Rules" recorded onto a cassette tape. Billy agreed to that but at the last second said "Clearwater High sucks! Juniper Rules!" Then they proceeded to beat him mercilessly. This tall tale didn't last long.

A more believable rumor had legs and could have been true. After pretending to be angry at Chris and throwing his tantrum at the bike rack, he hunted Chris down and confessed his love. No longer telling fables in his closet, he came out and confessed his love for Chris to his father, who could not handle it, unleashing furious righteous indignation upon his gay, could-have-been-a-football-star boy. The common belief was that his father had hoped to kill him, where a straight God could straighten him out in eternity.

Even that story didn't seem very likely to Sam. His stomach hurt. All through the day he wanted to puke. He skipped lunch, too overcome to eat. On a couple of occasions he visited the bathroom and dry heaved. He had not contracted the flu, nor had he eaten anything spoiled, his was a sickness of the heart. "What have we done?"

Sam could see it in Jim's somber demeanor. He felt the same sick guilt. He wanted to talk about it, or maybe he didn't. He would open his mouth on the verge of words and say nothing. As if he thought better about whatever it was he was going to say, he barricaded faulty words behind tight lips. Marcus, being the wicked deliverer of impious humor, used his backpack as a prop for Billy's bike and crashed into Jim's and Sam's backpacks, grunting as he did so, capturing yesterday's outburst with remarkable accuracy. To Sam's surprise, Jim did laugh, although he tried not to. Sam did not laugh. On the contrary, Marcus was only adding coal to a simmering fury on the verge of boiling over. *We might have murdered an innocent human being. We took a gigantic flying leap across a line that served no purpose in being crossed, except for the futile fact that we wanted to be entertained*, Sam reflected with true disgust. When Marcus thrust his backpack into Sam's a second time, in spite of the stern look upon Sam's face that clearly said, "Cool it," Sam snapped.

He could be cruel, and he could be callous, but what Marcus was doing was beyond cynical; it was pure evil, and Sam could take it no more. Without warning, he wrestled Marcus into a headlock.

"How can you be such a jerk!"

Marcus tried to break free, but Sam would not allow it, gripping tighter, causing Marcus to gag. He used his body weight to slam Sam against a wall, but Sam only gripped tighter still.

"We might have killed him, you son of a—"

Jim tried to break them up, to no avail. All the commotion brought about a crowd who ran to see the fight.

"Break it up!" A teacher who happened to be within the proximity separated Sam's death grip on Marcus's neck. "You two cool it right now. The last thing we need is another one of you kids sending each other to the hospital and jail."

That said it all. Now he knew the rumors were bogus for sure. It wasn't his father, and it sure wasn't a rival football team. It was Chris Fesonmer, *the flamer*, who somehow managed to overcome the inherited weakness of his sexuality and deliver such a whooping that Warnick might not live through the night. And Chris, behind bars, waited to see a judge. Who knew?

"I'm sorry, Sam. I was way out of line," Marcus admitted as The Perpetrators ended the school day.

It was then that Sam announced what they all knew inside was inevitable. "We're done. The Perpetrators are over. I don't know about you guys, but I want to stay out of prison."

They survived the school year untouched, unscathed, creating tremendous havoc, and no one even knew that small group of vandals known to themselves as The Perpetrators even existed, and they never would.

～

Upon arriving home, Sam could think of nothing better to do than crash. Lights out; nobody's home; do not disturb. He had never experienced such a day so full of sorrow and tremendous guilt, creating such a sickness he had yet to shake, causing his very bones to hurt. A good nap might help him to feel a little better. He entered through his front door, dropped his backpack on the living room couch, and chucked his cap at the TV someone had left on, turning it off on impact as planned. Now that the television was off, Sam could hear his mother snoring away in her bedroom, sounding like the dying motor on a moped. *Holding the fort until Dad gets home from work, I see. She's got the right idea.* As he approached the hall where three doors away lay his bedroom, and he saw something he had never seen before: his door ajar.

Sam could be rather careless when it came to other people's belongings, or other people's lives even. When it came to his things or his life, that's where he got anal. Nobody, at any time, was ever allowed in his room without first getting his permission. His parents knew that about him and respected him enough to not only allow him to create his boundaries, but to also not cross them. He heard a rustling. *Someone is still in my room, and it's not Mom or Dad.* His guilty conscious shouted, "It's the police! They found me out. Should I run?"

That's when he heard the unmistakable laugh of a little girl. He apprehensively stepped into his room and found his seven-year-old cousin Crystal going through his things. He had completely forgotten that Crystal was supposed to stay a few days with the Reed family to get to know her cousins. His room was a mess. She had managed to crawl and set free all worthless accumulations of varied piles of stuff from under his bed and ransacked his closet, pulling out boxes and yanking down hangers. She emptied the boxes into a sloppy pile in the middle of his room. Papers, pictures, and clothes made up the bulk of the mess.

"Crystal!" Sam shouted, startling the little girl. "What are you doing in my room? What are you doing in my things?"

"Hi, Sammy," she said with a delightful smile, oblivious to privacy transgressed.

"You are not supposed to be in here," Sam said, grabbing old pictures out of her hands. She only grabbed at more things, and this time and the following times to come, when Sam went to take his possessions from her, she would throw them across the room, laughing all along and sending him after.

"Crystal, you're going to be in so much trouble!" he said, trying to create a nice, organized pile of his own.

"What's this? It smells funny."

She had found Cousin Sammy's old marijuana pipe. Sam's eyes widened in paranoia.

"Drop that!" He caught it before it hit the ground. That's not for little girls." Sam was not a pot smoker. He tried it a couple of times, and all it did was make him sleepy. He forgot he even owned the paraphernalia until the roaming hands of Chrystal reminded him. This was a game to her.

"What's this? What's this?" she would ask, never giving or expecting Sam to answer, as she would continue to throw everything she picked up. Sam was beginning to lose his cool. This was not the day for this. All he wanted to do was sleep.

"What's this? What's this?" She managed to find an old eighth-grade picture of Sam and his middle school girlfriend, Carly, holding hands at Disneyland.

"Sammy's got a girlfriend. Sammy's got a girlfriend. Sammy and Carly sitting in a tree, k-i-s-s-i—"

He snagged the picture from her hand before she could finish spelling. He tried to stuff it underneath the pile he was growing when Chrystal blurted, "What is Perpators?"

She somehow managed to find the only notebook piece of paper where Sam just happened to lackadaisically scribble down the only pieces of evidence that could potentially incriminate The Perpetrators—not only this but dates, names, and relevancy of their attacks, each guilty parties name written in clear black and white. The torment that had been molesting his thoughts—Billy, Chris, his fight with Marcus, the end of The Perpetrators, his fears, his tension, and his anger—all surfaced at once. Sam lost control, flying across his room at the mention of the word Crystal was finding so hard to pronounce, resting his hand on her little chest, and he slammed her with all of his might into his wall.

She hit hard, causing a rumble to vibrate tile, rattling the foundation the house was set on. Her back hit first, and her head whiplashed a more powerful jolt. Instantly she collapsed and grasped the floor to keep the earth from spinning and rolled onto her back, wide, terrified eyes staring up at the ceiling as she gasped for air. God-awful sounds like a seal crying for food escaped her throat. *My God, she's dying.*

"Crystal! Crystal! Breathe! Please, dear God, breathe!" He picked her up and, holding her in his left arm, patted her on her back. He had no idea what else to do.

His mind reverted back to childhood when he glanced at death's door while choking on a chicken bone. His mother picked him up and patted forcefully upon his back. It was not the Heimlich maneuver, but it worked. The chicken bone was dislodged upon the kitchen floor, and Sam lived to gorge another day, and likewise Crystal coughed and then sucked in as much air as could be handled. This was followed by a barrage of tears and a desperate cry for her mommy.

Upon the crashing shake of the house and Sam's cries of "breathe, breathe, breathe," Sam's mother was wide awake. Not finding Crystal asleep by her side as she had left her, she jumped to her feet and crossed the distance to Sam's room in record time.

"Oh my God, Crystal what happened? Sam, what did you do to her?" she asked as she picked up the frazzled child and held her in a motherly embrace.

"I...I...I..."

Unable to find the words to explain this, Crystal shouted in between sobs, "He pushed me against the wall really, really, really hard."

"Samuel!"

"Mom, it's not like that... She made a mess of my room, and I was trying to get her to stop, and she wouldn't listen and—"

"So you threw a seven-year-old girl against the wall?"

"I didn't mean to. It was an accident" What could he say? How could he explain this?

"It wasn't an accident. He did it on purpose!"

"No, I didn't. I swear it was an accident!"

"Sam, things like this do not happen by accident," his mom said, always being practical.

"Where were you? Weren't you supposed to be the one watching her?"

"Samuel Reed! It doesn't matter where I was or what she was doing in your room. It is *never* all right to abuse a child."

"Mom, I know that. I didn't mean—"

"Samuel, what is this?" Mom found the marijuana pipe laying in plain view. "You're doing drugs now? Is this what you do with the privacy we've allowed? Things are going to change in your life, young man. You just wait until I tell your father."

~

Mom was right. Things like that didn't happen by accident. The kind of destruction that befouled Chris and Billy didn't happen by accident either. They were calculated, well planned, and methodically carried through. Sure those things could lead to unforeseen circumstances, but don't try and tell Sam he was not the one responsible. On that day, he knew better.

CHAPTER

20

C hris Fesonmer faced a rather lenient but fair judge. As serious as the charges were, because his life hung in the balance, it took all the restraint he could muster to keep from bawling like a baby at the prospect of life in prison. Thanks to the powers that be, life in prison was not an option. Relief was not forthwith to come, for Chris's mind went blank at the reading of the verdict; he was lost in a daze. *This is not real... Please, God, wake me up.*

Chris spent the remaining two and a half years of his pre-adult life in Juvenile Hall and wasn't officially a free man until his eighteenth birthday. The judge was lenient. He took into consideration Chris's age, his clean record, and the fact that he had been harassed on a number of occasions over his sexuality. He deemed that Chris was not a threat to society, but he did tag on to his sentence five years of probation.

$\sim$

This guilt did not so easily subside in the days, weeks, months, or years to come. Billy did eventually—after four months—emerge from his coma, which allowed Sam tempered relief. It was not the full recovery hope had envisioned. Billy teetered like a seesaw from life to death, although life finally the victor, the dank black that filled his nights and days erased any memory experienced of the hereafter or anything in between. He awoke to an existence he could hardly call a life. Stripped from a young man with great hope and aspirations of a glorious future was his ability to grip, walk, and talk.

For a grueling ten months, he worked with a physical rehabilitation therapist regaining his ability to grip, just as if he missed that encounter with a 9-iron. He had to work harder when it came to regaining fluent speech. He regained his ability to pronounce and annunciate his words without slurring. One could not tell he had a problem in this cognitive area unless they paid close attention. It wasn't easy to make out his flaws, but they were there, and Billy knew it. Above everything, he wanted to play football again and worked his legs with furious intensity; even his father pleaded for him not to overdo it. His resolve paid off in a big way, raising him out of his wheelchair onto a walker, then to a cane, and eventually he was walking free of any support. As far as he pushed himself and the miraculous progress made, one thing he could not overcome was a noticeable limp that would accompany him the rest of his life. Billy Warnick never played football again.

Never had he a conscious recollection of the day that morphed his life and shattered his dreams. Aside from a vivid nightmare of tiny blue dots dancing a jig upon the soft tissue of his brain, scarring nerves in its wake, he remembered nothing. This dream was reoccurring, and he always woke in a hot sweat feeling disoriented, confused, and scared. Even his crazed fit with his bike went completely forgotten, seemingly that entire day deleted from memory.

∼

Samuel Reed was forced by his parents to take anger-management classes where Dr. Genarious Tripoed instructed a group of nineteen, Sam being the youngest, through seven steps to sanity through the eruption of fury and loss of control:

1. Recognize stress

2. Develop empathy

3. Respond instead of react

4. Change that conversation with yourself

5. Communicate assertively

6. Forgive but don't forget

7. Retreat and think things over

Mechanically he followed and participated in the course someone created and Dr. Tripoed insisted on teaching. Sam was surrounded by wife beaters and child abusers attending via court order. He never felt at any time that he fit in or deserved to be there. However, he was more than willing to do whatever it took to regain the trust of his folks of whom he loved dearly. Of this list of seven, only two he felt he could use and made a point to remember, one and seven. Two through six he shuffled through the internal shredder in the who-gives-a-dang file of the mind.

Upon graduation, his parents appeased, Sam played the part of a rejuvenated boy. He even went as far as to thank them for making him take the course. Life returned close to normalcy, but not quite. He always felt like he was being watched rather closely, especially upon any occurrence where something might happen that just might get Sam's blood boiling just a little, and just maybe Sam might have a reaction not in sync with his upbringing or schooling. Suffice it to say, Crystal's routine visits were closely monitored from that point on. Sam would only retreat to the solitude of his locked bedroom a recluse rather than have his every action questioned and inspected.

21

As a man without a flashlight induced to follow a trail with no end on an ice-cold night with no coat, he was thankful to the powers that be for a clear, cloudless sky, allowing moonlight to emanate the path he was disillusioned to follow.

He was still very frustrated, and it was this antagonistic frame of mind guiding his steps. He was aware that he had already erupted in fury, but his way back to sanity did not seem so clear cut in this situation. *I am going to freeze to death. I am going to die up here. This would be a good time to put step numer four into practice and change that conversation with myself, but quite frankly, I don't care anymore. I got nothing waiting for me back home. No wife, no kids, nothing at all to show for the life I've lived, and now no job. If I die, I die,* Sam concluded sardonically. *Thank you very much, Dr. Tripoed, but no thanks.*

Nagging thoughts of "should haves" continually pestered.

I should have asked the ranger more detailed questions, or better yet I should have followed him. But I am going the direction that he came from; logically I've got to run into something. Logically I should, but what about this trip up Mount Kinley has been logical? What about this trip has panned out the way it was supposed to?

Pondering these things only would succeed in aggravating him further because there were no answers. No answers in a practical sense. *Maybe I'm having an out-of-body experience. That's what James would probably tell me.*

Crickets chatted up the night, although almost completely drowned out by a cacophony of other insects, amphibians, various nocturnal birds, and four-footed beasts spicing up an otherwise dreary night with no sense of direction or purpose. No longer could he hear the steady flow of moving water the creek provided, and he wondered how long and how far he had strayed from its evanescent charisma.

He retreated his arms inside his T-shirt in hopes of creating body warmth, but to no distinguishable avail. His hands were growing stiff to cold, difficult to open and close, the ability to feel all but gone. If a dead man could speak, would he describe rigor mortis in any other way? Knowing full well the importance of keeping his blood flowing and heart racing, he quickened his pace to a steady jog in spite of the whipping, biting cold numbing his cheeks. With every jogging step, his eyes fastened upon the path that could be seen, his vision jostled along with the rhythm of his step.

The spotting of several figures blacker than black zigzagging across his path about one hundred yards distance could have been a pack of wolves or wild dogs. The fact that they stood upright in silhouette of man could be explained by sheer exhaustion, the hypnotic lure of a full moon, and the freezing temperature stunting the ability to perceive accurately. The astonishing fact was that as Sam drew closer, his perception remained the same, and what his eyes beheld not morphing into a more realistic form of the easily explained was a bit harder to figure.

Fear gripped his heart, and he slowed his pace, seeing now more clearly the figures that moved like spirits but had the faces of man and flight of wind. In spite of this ethereal gathering of the unknown, time was taken in unison in regarding the intruding man. Twelve eyes beaming a gothic red from hoods of black gazed intently upon the intruder with no reason in being. Sam stood astute, even though the trembling that was birthed in cold continued in fear for his very life. Again in unison, the figures moved counterclockwise, side to side in a circle, as if this were an act of worship or a summoning of some sort, and removed their hoods, revealing their image, blacker still. Then, without exception, each ran one behind another further down the path, disappearing before dark could swallow each image, one by one.

He dropped to his shaking, feeble knees in puzzled astonishment. "What was that, what was that, what was that, oh my God, *what was that*!" Sam erupted. Each time the question asked grew louder in succession. This was not an act. This was real. No smoke and mirrors, real as real could be. He knew what he saw, and it was not a trick of the eye when they vanished before, covered by the thick of shadow into the bosom of night. His every belief was challenged in a matter of two minutes.

One thing he knew and could not be convinced otherwise of was that these beings were not human. What then were they? Such a question could only lead to an unlimited quantity of more questions with answers he was hardly prepared to receive. But then if the first could be accepted, those that followed could only fall in line with an anything-goes frame of mind. Though these six figures took on the form of man, men they were not. A large chunk of reality had to die in his rational mind to believe this way, but die it must and with great fight it did.

What else have I believed all of my life so deeply is wrong? Sam thoughts betrayed what he knew to be rational. There were no longer any boundaries to what he was willing to accept or believe. In a matter or moments, cults, religions, creeds, all and any form of dogma ever perceived crossed his mind, leaving any and everything on the table as possible truth. Those six spirits—yes spirits, Sam could see them in no other way—held the answers to any question he could ask, and they had inexplicably vanished. Such spirits wore night as a shroud and fed off Sam's fear as some sort of wraithlike nourishment. He desired to enter into the ring they mysteriously circled to investigate their odd manner, but fear gripped his soul, freezing his knees to dirt.

"This is ridiculous. I have been scared ever since my first night up here. That's it. No more fear."

With all the courage he could muster, he took to his feet and tiptoed his steps, heart racing, and again dropped to his knees. This time to investigate more clearly the ring they followed. A musky black essence was somehow a result of the ring completed. A light floating mist hovered six inches above a thick, sticky black goo but did not touch. Strange. Strange indeed. He did not know, nor could he figure, what the strange substance might be. It was left behind in the same way a speeding vehicle left behind skid marks when slamming on breaks, tattooing a freshly paved road.

He entered and stood center in the freshly smoldering ring. Warmth gently regulated his body temperature upon entrance. This black goo (whatever it was) emanated borrowed heat, something welcomed. The cold had somewhat lost its sting upon the unearthly visitation, spiking the kind of adrenaline that forgot sensation but undoubtedly would return, again causing Sam to fear for his very life. Not now. Not inside the ring.

This inspection failed to answer questions but created more. *What if they come back and find I've trespassed their space, their ring, and they're not happy?* That thought snuck by Sam's terror radar, so grabbing it by its fleeting tail, he wrestled fear into submission.

"Screw those spirits or whatever the hell they were. I don't care if they do come back!" Sam exclaimed indignantly. "Bring it!"

Upon such a declaration of challenge, a persistent, almost nostalgic lure of familiarity seduced his attention to the mysterious encompassing mist.

"What on earth is this about?"

Again he dropped to his knees to analyze further the vapor-like remnant of those left behind. *It has substance. If I wanted to, I think I could move it merely by breath alone, and it will not disintegrate to nothing but stay completely intact.*

He had never seen or heard about anything like this on the periodic table and wondered if anyone else had. The substance seemed to float as if under the influence of a low-grade helium. It was adorned in a lithium color of gray, but somehow able to see through like a Radon gas. He wanted to put this to the test but feared that such an unknown element might be able to enter through his pores upon touch and biologically, maybe, cause nerve damage or act as a poisonous agent to his respiratory system. Who knew? He surmised coming into direct contact might create the same kind of risk as if he were to swallow mercury, along with the certain death sure to follow, and yet he was unable to keep from slowly lingering his head ever so close, until finally completely engulfed in the alluring undistinguishable mist.

Sam could feel the slow, trance-like movement of his head directly into what might end in death and yet could not stop. His heart, soul, and spirit shouted, "No!" "Danger!" "Caution!" This could not be thwarted. All sense of control vanquished, submitting to an unknown force, possibly of sadistic intent.

~

In an instant Sam found his legs lifted, his body in horizontal posture, fifteen to twenty feet high, gazing down at a God-awful scene. A man wearing a hospital garment with the top of his head, from eyebrows up, wrapped tightly with bandages as he lay in a pitiful condition upon what could have only been a hospital bed. A small group of people surrounded this man, carrying the burden of great sorrow. What caught Sam's eye from his vantage point was the attempted comb over of a few strands of hair across a severely balding man's head. On any other occasion, he would have paid no mind, but on this special day of great circumstance, he recognized the follicly challenged man as his father.

How could this be? His mother then entered the room and fell into the arms of her husband and wept profusely.

"Mom! Dad!" Sam shouted, but just as he had come to expect, he could not or would not be heard.

He spied more closely the injured man, the source of such sorrow, and although he knew it before he even thought it, the horror of recognizing himself as that man shook him to his core. *How can this be?* Raising his hand to check his head and his hand passing through the empty space his head should occupy awakened him to a new reality. *I am here and at the same time I'm not. I am there. This cannot be. I am on Mount. Kinley... This is a hallucination.*

Aside from his parents, many other people, mostly of Afro-American decent, surrounded the injured Sam. Among them stood Mr. Carlton. Lined next to him were cousins Rick and Terry Nosfer. Sam had never known or seen many of them. There was a man he could not make out. He stood behind Mr. Carlton with his hands underneath his shoulders holding him up. Mr. Carlton was an emotional wreck, and Sam felt if it wasn't for the unknown man holding him he might collapse. As far as Sam could tell, he had never seen that man before, but somehow he was familiar, generating a countenance of strength, as if capable of carrying all of Mr. Carlton's sorrows.

As hard as he tried, he could not see the stranger's face. He seemed to be able to manipulate angles, keeping himself from being identified, as if he knew Sam was outside his body and attempting to recognize. Sam reached out to touch the back of the stranger's shoulder, and instantly upon contact he found himself back on the mountain sitting just outside the circle of elicit wonderment.

He reached for his head and this time found it between his shoulders, exactly where he left it. "Oh thank God. It was all a hallucination. One seriously vivid, tripped-out hallucination."

He looked over at the strange, lingering mist; below it the black substance crackled and pulsated.

"It was all due to those fumes I inhaled. Geez, I wonder how many brain cells that stuff killed." Never had he experienced so vivid a hallucination. So vivid he could smell his father's after-shave. *As far I know, hallucinations are strictly visual; the remaining four senses don't play a part, do they? I could be wrong. There can be no counting out the power of the mind, can there?*

I'm sure just seeing Dad would spark my memory of the smell of his aftershave, Sam reasoned. *The image of me in critical condition would naturally trigger the part of the brain responsible for sound, thus the beep, beep, beep of a EKG supposedly monitoring the rhythm of my heart.*

Why did I see what I saw to begin with? There's just no telling. Maybe it was symbolic of issues I'm dealing with subconsciously. I'm not a psychologist, so I'm not going to go there.

In his youth, he had heard from those submersed in the drug culture of LSD and peyote trips explained to him in great detail. He came to the conclusion that those who explained such experiences either failed miserably in telling their tales or the hallucinogens themselves proved trite in comparison to the alluring chemical he inhaled.

It was almost like a new reality or dimension was created or he was briefly transferred to an alternative universe of variable circumstance and outcome. That sounded too much like something he'd see in a *Star Trek* episode and had to laugh in spite of himself.

Sometimes to see things as they were made it real and sometimes not. Sam finally concluded this experience as one of those rare occasions where seeing was not believing.

CHAPTER

22

Dr. Dan Patton awoke on the brink of what he had hoped would be a two-hour nap that typical night some two weeks ago when introduced to a man in very critical condition. It was never the best of circumstances when meeting the acquaintance of patients with life-threatening illness or injury. This was what one quickly became accustomed to when you've devoted your life to doctoring those who couldn't help themselves. Life in the ER was seldom subservient to any schedule.

Had the unconscious man been brought in a few hours earlier, maybe brain activity would have been animate. Nobody could say for sure when the man managed to knock himself unconscious and how long he lay before help found him. Dr. Patton would do what he could and treat him as if he were his own flesh and blood, but he was limited only to as far as modern medicine would allow.

As long as a pulse could be found, there was life, and life was always worth fighting for. There was a soul very much alive occupying that critically damaged body. As long as there was life, there was hope, and although the doctor had never seen someone emerge from so deep a coma, it would challenge his deep-rooted ethics to even consider losing so fragile and yet profound the foundation hope rested.

His mother and father holding one another in grievous despair, hardly able to handle gazing upon their beloved son in such a volatile state, hovering like a fragile weight teetering the equilibrium of life and death, would be seeking a positive word from the good doctor to spark any twinge of hope, no matter how miniscule, that their son might live. He might. He might not. That was the plight of his comatose victims. The only concrete information that could be shared with family was uncertainty, and sometimes the bearer of bad news—or no news for that matter—coud share as deeply so grievous a lament.

Dr. Patton would be on this prestigious list. His biggest fear was not that he would be looked upon as a weak man who wore his emotions on his sleeve, but that eventually his reservoir of tears might one day dry up as callousness set in. Could he work so hard in saving the lives of people if he was not continually identifying with the pain and sorrow and grasp for hope families sought every day? He thought not.

The love of the man, known from his identification as Samuel Reed, from his parents, family, and friends who alternated visits was very evident. It could be seen in their tears, in their worry, and in the gentle tone when following the encouragement of Doctor Dan to speak to Samuel of their love and faith that he would awaken and return to them once again. This was not only good therapy for them—although some of his colleagues might argue—but was good for the patient as well. After all, no one could say for sure what went on in the mind, if anything, of a comatose victim.

Some came back with amazing stories of some wondrous afterlife so great they dreaded returning. Most didn't seem to remember a thing but the black of deep sleep. Yet a very small few had reported a hell-like existence in some nether world where recompense for a selfish life lived reaped a fool's reward. Doctor Dan Patton preferred the first. He never subscribed to any faith, but he knew the power behind it, seeing for himself the results of those who stood beside their critically injured loved one and prayed, as opposed to those that didn't.

Samuel Reed (as far as Dan could see) had no one praying over him. That was, no one from his immediate family, but there was one. A large black man came in first thing every morning, dropped to his knees, held Sam's hand, and prayed through tears. Dan admired him straight off and hoped one man's prayers would be enough. One day, time permitting, he might approach the man and maybe converse on matters of faith. Dan, being the objective man that he was, would be more than willing to hear out a man so deep into the supernatural, and in return the man might like to hear stories of encouragement Dan had experienced firsthand late nights in the ER.

CHAPTER

23

Sam found himself at a crucial impasse; a decision must be made. Either continue as he had on a path that had been eating up precious time, grating on his nerves with no discernable end. The other option was to double back, find that fork on the path, and try his luck on the straight and narrow. *Who am I kidding? That's not going to happen*, Sam concluded in defiance. *Not after I've come this far. The spirits went this way; that's good enough for me.*

Something was different. It did not take long before he figured out what it was. Sam said, "It's not cold anymore." How could that be? If anything, it should be colder as the night entered, he surmised, the beginning hours of morning. It wasn't that the temperature rose a degree or two. He felt nothing, as if temperature itself ceased to exist. Like a soothing numbness suffocating his sense of touch. He wasn't about to complain over this odd change in sensation. After all, for a moment he actually felt strongly the cold might take his life after all. Turned out inhaling that stuff did serve a purpose.

"If I play my cards right, I might make it off this mountain alive," Sam said with a twinge of excitement.

He quickened his step with a ferocity not yet seen. It amazed him the difference in movement without the cold stiffening his joints. He zigzagged his way along the twisting path. Flashes of his current state in life crossed his mind, and he couldn't wait to return to life as he knew it, but with dramatic changes to be made. He would enjoy every sandwich, every ring of his alarm clock that used to annoy him to no end, every swig of orange juice he drank on every working break, and the pleasant arousing aroma of waking up to the flavor of the weekend's perfume. He would savor all the big and simple things life had to offer on a whole new scale.

He moved at such a rapid pace he felt he was crossing miles of terrain at a rate he could never have achieved in high school. Mosquitoes must have been attracted to the stink of perspiration as they followed and buzzed and bit. Sam did not care enough even to swat them away; he would do nothing to interfere with his pace. One thing did more than slow him down; one sudden realization brought him to a complete standstill. His landmark goal to reach where the path veered sharply around the mountain came and went. He thought he was certain to see familiar terrain, possibly even the pavement where his truck rested, but upon reaching revealed no such thing.

CHAPTER

24

Brilliant, spectacular light in the far but reachable distance blazed about a massive structure, like that of a mansion. "How can this be?"

This was wrong on so many levels, but Sam's awe-inspired fascination with what his eyes beheld allowed him to save his questions for another time. Never had he seen anything like this, not even in the movies. Yet here it sat on a remote area on Mount Kinley. Slowly he walked in bewildered wonderment trying to make sense of the lights that danced in free will.

At least now I have a goal to reach. I will check to see if anyone's home, and they can tell me how to get back to my truck... Shoot, maybe they'll let me crash here for the night. Wouldn't that be something? Sam wasn't exactly thinking straight.

His goal to reach the mansion became his central priority and dominated his every thought as he followed his path into a clearing that stretched out about a hundred yards and might serve as a rest stop. Sam had no intent on resting, but somebody else did. There sat a man upon a tree trunk looking cool, calm, relaxed, and pleasant enough to be around.

"Are you from that mansion up ahead?"

"You might say that."

"Really? Is that your place?"

"No. This mansion is under construction."

"You're kidding me. How much more are they going to add?"

"Depends on the owner."

"It certainly does. Must be nice having that kind of money."

"Money has nothing to do with it."

"How would you know? Do you know the owner?"

"I know him very well."

"Listen, buddy, I have no idea why it is you're out here in the cold, and I'm sure you have your reasons, but if I were you, I'd be asking this guy that you claim to know if he could set me up with a bed for the night, and while I was at it, I'd ask if he could set up my new friend, Sam, with a bed as well."

Sam reached over to shake the stranger's hand. The stranger took to his feet, all smiles, looking Sam in the eye, and shook his hand and said, "It is a pleasure, sir. I am Shamir."

I'm not going to even try to pronounce that, Sam thought.

Shamir wore a flannel shirt, faded blue jeans, brown worn high-top hiking shoes, and had a thick black beard with gray intruding at his sideburns. He was probably somewhere in his early forties and kind of reminded Sam of the character Al from that old nineties sitcom *Home Improvement.*

"I am here because God called me to be…for your sake, Samuel."

"Oh really. Well, isn't that interesting. You talk with God often, do ya?" Sam said, laying on a condescending tone pretty thickly.

"I do," said Shamir without skipping a beat.

"Well, isn't that something. Next time you guys get to chatting, you can ask him a whole lot of questions for me…" Before Sam could ramble off a series of questions, Shamir responded.

"Pray, Samuel. The more you pray, the more is revealed."

"I don't pray."

"I know."

"Listen, I'm not sure that I believe God exists. I mean not in the traditional sense of the word. Don't get me wrong. I believe a creator somehow put everything into existence, but you only need to look at how thoroughly messed up this world is to know he doesn't interfere in our lives or our affairs. And if you're one of those who is going to tell me God is in control of everything, then I'll tell you straight out I have some serious issues with the character of God."

"He knows that you do, and he understands your confusion."

"Does he? Does he understand why when I see a poor Ethiopian woman, skin and bones, on the cover of *Time Magazine* begging for food for her children, I gotta wonder what kind of sick God would allow such depravity in the lives of the innocent?"

"Samuel, God loves that woman and her children very much."

"Does he?"

"Have you not heard that it has been said, 'Do to others as you would have them do to you'?"

"Of course I have. Everyone's heard the Golden Rule," Sam said, using his fingers as quotes.

"Then why haven't you met her need, or others just like her?"

"How do you know I haven't given to charities like that?" Sam only needed to gaze at the eyes of Shamir a brief second to know that that lie didn't fly.

"Okay, so I haven't. I get your point. If we all followed the Golden Rule, there would be no starvation in the world, am I right? That's what you're saying?"

"Partly. God has provided all the provision necessary to live comfortable, content lives in relation with his Son here on earth. It is up to you to provide for those who have not, for Jesus said, 'You will always have the poor among you.' Sam, he also said, 'Whoever gives one of these little ones even a cup of cold water because he is a disciple, truly, I say to you, he will by no means lose his reward'"

"Wow, you're really into this Jesus stuff."

Shamir smiled.

"Listen, I really don't want to get into a theological argument with some dude I just met up here in the middle of"—the mansion snagged his attention—"somewhere."

Sam snapped back to reality, although for more than a few seconds his mind wandered.

"So tell me, why are you out here?"

"Why are you out here?" Shamir responded.

"Geez, do you answer every question with a question? I'm out here because I got lost trying to go home. And you?"

"Same reason."

"You mean to tell me you're lost out here too?"

"No. I'm here because you're lost out here."

"Huh? But you're not a park ranger."

"What you say is true. I am not."

"Then why should you care?"

"Because God cares very much."

Sam wanted very badly to question this man's sanity. On the surface, he could make the argument that this fellow was not playing with a full deck. After all, he was by his lonesome, on a frigid night, with no camping equipment (as far as Sam could see), sitting on a log, and claiming to speak with God. One would say he fit the criteria—and then some. But Sam found it rather difficult to jump to such a conclusion. He also found it rather difficult to put his finger on it, but something about this man called Shamir seemed very genuine.

Sam had always had a gift in knowing how to read people. It was one of the tools of the trade when it came to being a salesman. For the most part, he knew when he was going to have an easy sale, and he also knew when he was going to have to work his tail off. There was so much that could be read in body language that the windows of the soul might not reveal. Not only that, but tone could say everything.

Was there a measure of exuberance and excitement of an inevitable purchase, or was there a shaky cloud of fear of being swindled that must be dealt with? When a potential customer said they're interested and they would come back, did they mean it? Were they sincere? He had watched Shamir very carefully while he spoke of God and his purpose in being on the mountain, and not once did he pick up on a lie. Everything he said he meant. Seldom had he met someone so sincere, but his words were loony, no way around it. How could someone with such sincerity speak such fallacy? Sam had to remind himself that even the insane could pass lie detector tests. Although Shamir might full on believe every word he uttered, that didn't make it true. Sam would continue on in conversation with Shamir, but he was going to study him closely.

"What you're saying is God is intervening in my life right now. Why now? What is so special about now?"

"God is answering the petition of one John Carlton."

"John Carlton? Mr. Carlton? You mean my boss Mr. Carlton?"

"Yes."

"Whoa!" Sam jumped back. "Mister, I don't know you. How can you possibly know my boss?"

"God knows him."

"Of course. Why didn't I think of that? Well done…very good. You got me good." Sam shook his head in disbelief and rubbed his eyes with thumb and forefinger. "Impressive. Now tell me, how do you really know of my boss? What's the trick?"

Sam, on a number of occasions, had been amazed at magicians he had seen on television that appeared to be able to read minds. Of course, there was a trick to it, but he had never been able to figure it out or crack the code. Somehow, someway Shamir had been able to not only retrieve his boss's last name but also his first, of which even Sam was unfamiliar with. If he had been asked by anyone Mr. Carlton's first name, he would have answered, "Mister."

Shamir said nothing but awaited the shocking wave of realization to settle in Sam's reasoning.

That is impossible. There is no way he could have known. Sam slowly sat himself down on the log Shamir once occupied.

"Who are you really?"

"I am Shamir, servant of the Most High."

"I think I believe you. Earlier along this path I saw six black spirits, or they were dressed in black. I'm not exactly sure. Are you a spirit like them?"

"I know of whom you speak. They are the fallen of which I am not. They will have you believe that I am. Do not listen to them, Samuel. They speak only lies."

"Why do they lie? What is their purpose?"

"They seek to lead you astray, a dweller of dry places."

"Dry places?"

"You are almost there now, but this need not be."

"Of course not," Sam said, unsure what he was agreeing to.

"You will come upon two gates—one wide, the other narrow. 'Enter rough the narrow gate. For wide is the gate and broad is the road that leads to destruction, and many enter through it. But small is the gate and narrow the road that leads to life, and few find it.'"

"But I don't understand. Why? Why do only a few find life?"

"The God of this age has blinded the minds of unbelievers, so that they cannot see the light of the gospel that displays the glory of Christ, who is the image of God."

Over the years it had become more than commonplace to vehemently argue such outlandish spiritualized statements. Not today. He had seen more of his share of the supernatural to not allow his mind to fester in a vacuum of doubt. Had his mind been blind all his life? *If you say so. Sure, why not... Evidently. To what degree?* He is fearful to know.

"When you say servant of the Most High, are you referring to God? Jesus? Or—"

"Yes. And the Holy Spirit," Shamir answered quickly as if there were no other options.

"What you say is very interesting, but that might be because you're a convincing person, or spirit, or whatever you are. It is usually Jesus freaks, like yourself, that are the most closed-minded. I bet you would be one to tell me that your Jesus is the only way to heaven."

"He is."

"You're proving my point. I don't think it's possible to be more closed-minded than that. By you saying that, you're virtually declaring that anyone who does not believe as you do, most of whom are very good people with their own convictions, having to do with the way they were raised, are not going to make it to heaven when they die. It makes sense to me that each individual will move on to whatever their belief of paradise might be." Sam was on a roll and couldn't restrain his tongue. "So if their God is Jesus, Buddha, Allah, Confucius, or whoever or whatever it might be, they will move on to be with that deity."

"God is one."

"Is he?" Sam smirked.

"Samuel, if this is so, who will you pass on to be with?"

Stunned into silence, all matter of speech stripped from his throat at Shamir's question. He hadn't believed in God since he was a boy of about twelve. He was his own god. Therefore, there could be no paradise for him in the afterlife. That made him feel sad, but not without rebuke.

"You tell me, dude, what should I expect when I die? Or anyone else on this planet who doesn't believe in Jesus? You seem to know it all. Answer me that question."

"'The Lord is not slow in keeping his promise, as some understand slowness. He is patient with you, not wanting anyone to perish, but everyone to come to repentance.'"

"Perish? What does it mean to perish?"

"To perish is to die in your sins, to reap the hellish consequences your sins have sowed, eternity without him."

"I'm without him right now. I think I'm doing just fine."

"Sam, he has always been with you. He has never left your side. He is here, even now." Shamir glowed a peculiar radiance that seemed to magnify his every word.

"Funny, I don't see him."

"Yet, he *is*. 'For since the creation of the world his invisible attributes are clearly seen, being understood by the things that he made, even his eternal power and Godhead, so that men are without excuse.'"

"If what you say is true, all of mankind is without excuse for not believing in God's Son. I find that extremely hard to swallow. You seem to know the Bible well, and you quote from it to prove it. That is circular reasoning, my friend, and wouldn't stand up in a court of law."

"If the Bible were one book, your accusation would stand, but it is a compilation of sixty-six books inspired by God, written by forty authors, over hundreds of years in duration, yet every book glorifying Christ. Because of this, believers are not guilty of circular reasoning, as you put it."

"You really know your stuff. I'll give you that. But can you explain to me why a loving God would allow such suffering in the world? I mean, really, how could a loving God allow innocent children to be raped and murdered?"

"How can he not?"

"What!" Sam shouted in disbelief.

"*Loving* is the word you used to describe him. Can God be loving if he removed you of your choice to do evil?"

"I think so."

"If you were forced to love God, would it really be love?"

"No."

"If you were forced to do good, would it truly be good?"

"I would assume the results of doing good would most likely be good, but I would agree that it is never good to force anyone to do anything against his will, unless they were sequestered as a penalty for breaking the law. Now that's a different story," Sam responded quietly, unsure where the stranger was going with this but maybe having a faint idea.

"Without choice to be truly good or truly evil, God would not, he could not be a God of love. He is sovereign and can be no other way."

"But innocent children… I just can't…"

"With sin, there is consequence. If not on earth, then under it. Pray for those lost to Satan, for God has no pleasure in the demise of the wicked. God loves you enough for you to will good or evil. Alas, man has chosen evil. Yet, in spite of this, 'God so loved the world he gave his only begotten son, that whosoever believes in him will not perish but have everlasting life.'"

"I've heard that scripture before."

"Yes, you have, and now again."

Sam was given a lot to think about and, unsure how to proceed said, "I have so many more questions."

"All will be revealed, very soon. I am called now Samuel, but I will return upon your petition. Pray. The more you pray, the more is revealed. Fear not. He is with you."

Shamir took to his knees and, upon interlacing his fingers-in posture of prayer-for the equivalent of a few seconds, shot upward like a bolt of lightning streaking the border of hemisphere before time could calculate movement and then burned out or simply vanished; Sam could not tell which. Sam saw him very well. The man in flannel was no more a man the second his knees touched the ground, as his countenance transformed something beautiful, something angelic.

Sam stood, dumbfounded. What did you say to something like that? The words did not come, and in a way he was glad for it. Almost as if in a trance, his legs slowly moved one in front of another. The mansion lay ahead, and that was his goal to reach. Wasn't it?

25

S omewhere, for some reason, Mr. Carlton is praying for me. Why? What's the big deal? It's not like people don't get lost from time to time. I'm sure God's got other, more important issues on his plate to deal with—wars, starvation, global warming or climate change (whatever they're calling it these days), and child abuse. The list is endless. Shamir, that angel is a wise man…being…angel whatever he was. I went easy on him. If he truly has a direct connection with the creator of the universe, I shouldn't have wasted time asking him softball questions. Pray he said. I don't think so. Not to a God who either has limited control when it comes to eradicating evil or has control but chooses to allow evil to have its demented way.

Either way this is a God not worthy of contact, let alone praise. "Let Mr. Carlton pray all he wants. It's not going to change anything. It's not going to change who I am," Sam said defiantly, as if beckoning a challenge.

Mr. Carlton on a number of occasions had invited Sam to his church, Blessed Hope (nondenominational). Sam passed by it daily on his way to work. "Come as you are" the sign spelled out in the front yard. However, hung over on Sunday morning was not the kind of first impression he cared to make.

Especially, if he were in the more than likely scenario of challenging the pastor on his beliefs. Carlton never went out of his way to make Sam feel guilty or whatnot, at least not intention-ally, but for some reason Sam always did feel a certain measure of guilt when he said no to Mr. Carlton's proposals. John Carlton was persistent in his invitations, and Sam thought that maybe one day he would take him up on it. If not for anything else, just to see.

~

Upon contemplating on the strangest experiences he had ever witnessed those past couple of days of his life, and the idea of trying to get friends to believe these things actually happened, suddenly there was a *crack, crack, crack, crack* sound echoing off the mountain and trees.

Its source came from somewhere off the path but not too deep into the woods. *What on earth could that be?*

As badly as he wanted to arrive at the mansion, he could not kill this aching curiosity to identify the cause of the continual cracking. It sounded like someone was chopping down trees. Who would do that at that hour, being sometime past midnight? Common sense took a stab at intruding with his desire to find the source. *Maybe someone chopping down trees at this hour is not the best person I should be meeting. I mean, after all, he has an axe.*

It was at this very moment that Sam noticed something familiar. A hazy white mist hovered at ankle level, accenting a trail into the thick of wood toward the sound of the commotion.

"I've seen you before."

Whoever was chopping trees left that behind. The mist then swirled like a miniature ankle-high tornado, increasing its spin in speed. Something then began to form and to manifest into the shape of a fist. The twirl continued as the form of a finger extended, pointing directly at him. The finger then began to move in a waving motion, beckoning Sam to come hither, like a ges-ture of a ghostly phantom hand directing traffic. Just like that, the spinning ceased, and the phantom hand vanished, leaving the mist in its steady hover.

The shrubbery was thick, but as the hand beckoned, he followed the mist with varied difficulty. Someone had come that way—not only the mist but the cracking confirmed it. Why was it the shrubbery showed zero indication that anyone had passed that way? Bushes should be bent, twigs broken, and maybe a footprint or two should be distinguished in the softer dirt. But there was none of that, only the mad chorus of chirping of that of disgruntled crickets. The mist avoided going deeper into thicket, which would have made it impossible to follow and made a sharp left turn, favoring where mountain touched ground. Sam followed sideways. Room only allowed for his backpack cascading the mountain, his arms protecting his face from the whip of branches and the painful snag of thorns and thistles.

～

It wasn't one but two men swinging axes and chopping trees. A growing mound of freshly cut trees lay ten feet from their executioners, and beside the lumber was a nicely crafted massive, not yet used, fire pit.

Sam recognized the two men right off. Carl and Leo he believed their names were. Just as when he first came upon them early that morning, he again saw them from behind. How it was they somehow got ahead of Sam on that wide path was a pickle to figure, but soon it all made sense. Evidently they followed the straight path, the one they were adamant he not take. *It could be the only way they got ahead of me.*

"Hey, guys." Sam spoke loud enough to be heard, but they paid no mind and without so much as a glance over shoulder they continued to swing their axes as if the only thing in the world that mattered was the falling of the trees at hand.

"Hey, guys…it's me Sam…from earlier."

"Sam from earlier, whatya want?"

"I'd like to know why you guys gave me some bogus directions?"

"What you say?" Carl asked in midswing.

"You heard me. Bogus directions. You told me to take the wide path when you guys obviously took the narrow path."

"Wrong! Wrong! Wrong! We did not, we cadnot, and we will'd not ever follow d'at straight and narrow, ya hear!" Carl exclaimed in furious retort as both he and Leo turned with their axes and eyed Sam with psychotic gawks.

"Okay then, you mind telling me how you got ahead of me?"

"We are where'd we supo'd to be."

"Yeah, ya dummy," Leo said.

"That's not really an answer, Carl."

"Sh'o it is. You just too dumb to see." Leo almost snarled.

"Ju'd like you is where'd you supo'd to be," Carl said as though it made perfect sense.

"I'm where I'm supo'd…I mean…where I'm supposed to be?" Sam said, almost falling victim to their infectious slur. "What on earth do you mean?"

He caught on that these two rednecks were attempting to speak in riddles to avoid answering his question and redirect his anger. Had Sam not seen the glorious mansion ahead, he might have vented his anger more vehemently upon those who misdirected. Just as he had some hours ago, he concluded those two morons weren't worth such attention.

"We mean what we says. Let he who has ears to hear, let him hear," Carl said in a disgusted mockery of something he had once heard.

"Whatever." Sam left it at that and changed his demeanor to one soft spoken. "I, at least, want to thank you guys for leaving me wood at my campsite. It came in handy."

They both looked at Sam as though he were speaking in a foreign tongue. Sam didn't care for clarification on this matter, so he tried a second time for a more meaningful subject.

"I'm hoping I'll make it to my truck shortly after sun up."

At this, Carl and Leo bellowed in high treble laughter but with no reason as to why. Sam couldn't help but smile. These two laughing hyenas were kind of comical in their own way. It reminded him of his old incarcerated perpetrator friend, Marcus Stiney, who loved to laugh at the expense of the unfortunate. He was currently serving ten to twenty for beating his abusive father almost to death. Abusing him was one thing, but his mother, he would not have.

At Sam's third and final attempt at finding something worth discussing, he said, "I'm on my way to that awesome mansion up ahead. You guys know anything about it?"

Carl and Leo's eyes widened, and Sam wouldn't believe it if he didn't see it as the white of their eyes transformed into a dirty yellow, swallowing white like a cloud the sun. Leo threw down his axe in inexplicable fright. Carl tried to hide fear, leaning on his axe as if it were a cane, but there was no hiding the tremble in his knees, nor in his voice.

"You say you see a mansion?"

"Yeah, of course, how can you not? You can't see it now through all these trees, but if you go out to the path, you'll see it clear as day... Stop messing with me. There is no way you could not have seen it."

"Mister, if you're telling me yo see a mansion, d'en I'm a telling you, d'ere aint no way you gonna find yo truck."

"He out here, Carl, I is telling you, he ed out here, he ed out here, Carl. He ed out here," Leo ranted. "What au we gonna do?"

"Shut it!" Carl yelled, followed by a forceful jumping wallop. As tall as Leo was, a jumping slap was the only way Carl could deliver correction with full force.

"Dided serious now... You aint never gonna to find yo truck, so you best get over d'at, ya hear?" Carl paused, choosing his words as carefully as possible. "Da' mansion you say you see is under construction."

"So I've been told."

"Say what now?"

"It's the guardian, Carl. I tell ya, it's the guardian. I tell ya, Carl, it's his—"

Carl lifted the back of his hand in threat, shutting Leo up.

"I really don't know what or who you're talking about, but I did meet some sort of spirit out here not too long ago. He called himself Shamir."

Upon hearing this, Leo wanted to explode, voicing his fears, but the stifling back of Carl's hand kept him in check.

"Listen, Samuel, just because that there mansion you see is there doesn't mean it ever has to be lived in. It never has to be finished. Do you get what I'm saying?"

"No, I don't. To be perfectly honest, I don't have a clue what you are talking about."

"You will, Sam. You will very well."

"Why do you fear him? It has been obvious since even before the very mention of his name you guys have been scared for your very lives."

"We are not scared for our lives, Sam, but for yours."

"What could you possibly mean?"

"Listen very carefully, Samuel…" Carl said this as the yellow in his eyes began to spin counterclockwise. "What you say is true. This man called Shamir is more than a man. He is spirit, the spirit of servanthood, and it is his plan to make you subservient to the will of his master, just as he is, who wants nothing more than to poison your soul in the grind of guilt."

"I've seen many spirits tonight."

"There are many spirits and many gods. The six you saw previously worship the supreme god of freedom. He is the one we praise, and so should you."

"Not sure how much more free I can be. I mean, I have no wife, no kids, and no boundaries. I come and go as I please, I do what I want, and I have all the freedom I can ask for."

"You say true, Samuel. Your Shamir serves a God who desires only to weigh his servants down with the heavy burden of boundaries, rules, and commands with the stiffest of penalties for those who transgress his law, which is impossible for any man to keep to begin with."

"Sounds like a fixed game."

"You say true, Sam."

With such praise, Sam began to fill as though he were being buttered up. It was a tactic he had become used to imploring upon his customers at work. It was a matter of becoming the most agreeable person on the planet when pertaining to trivial matters. He'd be lying to say he didn't feel like being on the receiving end of such a tactic now.

"What's the catch?"

"Whatever do you mean?"

"What you're saying sounds great. I mean, who doesn't want the freedom to do as one wills, but the thing is nothing is ever that easy, and in life there are always consequences. Always. If everyone on earth ran around doing exactly what they felt like doing all of the time, there would be nothing but chaos, and to be frank, I don't think mankind would have survived as long as it has without rules and consequence. In other words, I get it. I get why religions around the world invented rules to follow, or commands, whatever they want to call it. They do create a measure of…control, shall we say. On the other hand, I certainly do not believe in an all-powerful God who will throw us into a pit called hell for all eternity. That completely contradicts the whole precept that he is a God of love, like the preachers like to teach."

"Although I do disagree with you on the whole concept of rules and commands, I will say this, Samuel, you are no fool, for you will bow your knee to no one. Remember, to always question and never receive is the only way to achieve immaculate ascension."

"What? Like being my own god?"

"Aren't you?"

Sam had never thought of it that way. "Sure, in a way I guess I am. I like the sound of that."

"Indeed, as you should."

Again Sam had that uneasy feeling of being buttered up. Having never believed in an afterlife to begin with, the very existence of spirits did confirm for him that there was something after death. The idea of a grand forever party in a place called heaven sounded great, but being the realist he was, he continued to feel that such a place existing was highly unlikely. Where Shamir had flown off to, he did not know, but wherever it was it was no place worthy of man. Sam would never forget how beautiful Shamir's radiance was upon transformation. *Wherever he went, he'll never catch me there. I don't belong*, Sam concluded, a bit downcast.

As Sam began his departure, he said, "Well, guys, it has been... interesting...to say the least." As he adjusted his backpack to take his leave, the stack of fallen trees caught his attention, and he could not leave without the question being asked.

"Why on earth are you guys out here, this hour of the night, chopping down trees?"

"There are many things we do you are not prepared to receive," Leo finally said something that didn't sound like a joke. *As a matter of fact, what happened to that thick southern accent of theirs?*

"Really, Leo? Well, why don't you try me?"

Leo opened his mouth, probably to answer, but Carl beat him to it. Speaking in a loud voice of seminal irritation, Carl said, "It is what we are to do until word is fulfilled. Our time is very short."

"You could not have been more right," Sam said, turning to Leo. "I haven't a clue what he means."

Leo then intrusively spoke.

"We are to chop down every tree that does not bear fruit..."

"And throw it in the fire!" Carl finished for Leo in an insane-sounding yell. Sam did a quick three-sixty.

"That's a lot of trees." This brought about a double in-sync fit of laughter. Sam jumped at his next chance to speak to say, "Next thing I know you guys are going to be telling me that it is Jesus who is making you do this."

At the very mention of that name, both men dropped to their knees, noticeably distressed.

Leo shouted, "How dare you say that!" He covered both ears the way a child would on command from a parent when adult language was being used on a late-night TV program.

"Never say that name. Do you hear me? *Never!*" Carl threatened. Leo then began to violently bash his head on solid ground.

"You best get outta here."

Sam hesitated.

"*Get steppin'!*" Leo cried.

CHAPTER

26

An extravagant fence that looked identical to one he had seen as a child in some old black-and-white movie and was particularly fond of surrounded the ten acres of land the mansion sat. The gate was open. Beautiful was the grass and so very well manicured. In spite of night, Sam could see very well. A gentle light came from somewhere/everywhere in the beautiful yard. Not too much but just the right amount for the yard to be seen and admired. He had seen small lights placed along sidewalk pathways so as for the path to be seen in the black of night at various homes, and he looked intently for such lights, which would have to number in the thousands in a yard so grand. He looked close but could see no such thing. It was like each individual blade was emanating a small fraction or degree of light of its own.

"How is this possible?"

He entered through the open gate to cross ten acres and address the home that seemed to bask in its own spectacle of radiance. His walk seemed to pass in no time as he witnessed the grass wave back and forth in unison, without the slightest breeze as cause, all about and around as if this were a welcoming. Sure enough Sam felt welcomed.

As he arrived, he stood upon the very large porch and looked upon and marveled the structure that was unusual to anything he had ever seen. This was something constructed of no earthly materials. He could see this. He knew it. No cement mixed with water, stucco mixed with lime, and zero wood hammered. It reminded Sam of a Southern-style colonial home with fence and marble columns he admired so. It was almost like the architect shared Sam's taste to a tee.

Just like the gate, the front door was left wide open. *Guess the owner doesn't care about getting robbed.*

"Hello?" Sam called, sticking his head inside. "Is there anyone home? Hello?"

The sound echoed off the walls and traveled up a spiraling staircase, but no one answered his inquiry. *Hmm, guess no one's home.* Sam slowly sashayed his way inside, feeling very much like Goldie Locks. He imagined in this scenario it would not be three bears coming home to find an intruder but maybe a man out night hunting, wearing those see-in-the-dark goggles, a shotgun in hand, who just might not take kindly to a stranger invading the home front. *Why do I torture myself with such thoughts? Obviously no one lives here yet. I was told a couple of different times that this place is under construction. Why don't I listen?*

"I have free reign of this place, whoo!" Sam hooted. "How nice. I am going to sleep well tonight."

To his left was a comfy, relaxed, come-on-in-and-kick-your-shoes-off type of welcoming room where maybe a pool table or some hi-tech Wii-styled video games would be an ideal place to play. In any other house, this would be a living room, but when you compared the dimensions of this home, room by room, you'd see this was more like a vestibule

The funny thing was that there were no electrical sockets anywhere he could see. *When the owner comes to move in his stuff, I think he's going to share a few choice words with the builder, architect, or whoever's responsible. I mean, c'mon, how do you forget electricity?* Some things, like furniture, at some point had been moved in but, not much else.

Crossing over to the right, he entered what normally would have been considered the kitchen. A ginormous table capable of comfortably sitting a hundred or more people took up the bulk of the downstairs.

There was nothing where a refrigerator should be, not even a proper hook up. There was no stove.

"This is a dining room or what some people call a banquet room. But how can you eat with nothing to cook with? And how many people have this many friends?" Sam said, tapping on the table. This was all very weird, yet exciting. He felt like a man on the crux of solving a mystery.

Making his way down a hallway to thoroughly explore all he could, he took notice of the walls themselves and saw that they radiated the same sort of gentle light the front lawn did, just enough so that he could see well enough, even into secluded corners where at least shadow should dwell. There were no shadows. He had the same peculiar feeling beholding the walls that he did the grass. *Both are alive. But how is that possible? It's not possible. Walls are inanimate objects. Houses, even mansions, are inanimate; there is nothing alive about them.* Try as he might, he could not shake it. *This mansion is alive. Or maybe it's the light in it that's alive. Kind of like a soul. I can't believe I'm thinking this way. A mansion, alive? I think it's about time they get my straight jacket ready,* Sam thought, and with an insane, tripped-out look in his eye, he said, "You hear that, Ma? They're coming to take me away...haha hehe haha," Sam sang, feeling just as loony as the song evoked.

Sam slowly made his way down the illuminated hall, curious of so many things. Before he could open any doors (twelve in all), the sound of moving water from the furthest room back raised an eyebrow.

Is that the bathroom? Could it be that there is functional plumbing? Bypassing all doors to his left and right, he stood at the door in question with hand on doorknob, somewhat frightened. The sound of flowing water was much louder the closer to the door.

The only thing he could figure was that maybe someone left the bathtub running, and he was going to open that door and a wave of water was going to rush over him and damage the entire first floor. But he knew well enough that if the water was going to get past the closed door, it would have long before he arrived. Wouldn't it?

Howbeit, the backroom was not a bathroom. It was absolutely like nothing Samuel Reed found possible to even imagine in a backroom of any house. Two large embankments facing each other thinned the flow of water that came from the mountain's river so that it could effectively follow course through two adjacent holes perfectly constructed in both facing walls. The creek started on the mountain, passed through the mansion, and continued its travels where gravity led.

Words were somehow carved out on the embankment facing anyone who opened the door: כפי שאמר הכתבים, מחוץ לבטנו נצא נחלי הנהרות הזרימה של החיים במים הוא מאמיו לי, Of course, having only spoken English the entirety of his life, such carvings might as well have been written in Vulcan. Given the magnitude of the things he has witnessed as of late, he surmised that whatever it said was probably very powerful.

Light was brighter in this room. Not because the walls said so, not even because the sun might be beginning to rise (and it probably was), but because of magnificent, radical jewels—emeralds, sapphire, pearls, and diamonds, diamonds, diamonds, along with various other jewels Sam was not educated enough to identify. All different sorts were displayed in twelve bins, each lined in an auburn-colored fabric, circled the room, transferring a brilliant light that screamed life. In front of each bin sat a stone of high value and on top of that a pearl of great price. Each stone in size was relative to the size of a football but with far greater weight in mass.

Immediately upon his mind absorbing what his eyes were seeing, he swung his backpack off his shoulders, unzipped the largest compartment, and dumped all of his now-worthless belongings. He darted from bin to bin, grabbing many handfuls of jewels to the point where his backpack morphed and deformed from its original shape.

"I'm rich, I'm rich, oh my God, I am so rich."

He could only nab the smallest of jewels because the most luxurious of the lot, the absolute and greatest of worth, he was certain had to be the stones of which were far too big and way too enormous in weight to fit in any backpack.

"I can't believe this. Can this really be happening? I'm never going to have to work another day in my life!"

With an amplified abundance of excitement in his heart and incalculable amount of wealth strapped to his back, Sam desired to explore further this house of tremendous wonder and surprise. He looked back at the bins his hands had ravaged, and it looked to him just as full as when he had arrived. *Hmm, is anyone going to know that anything was taken?*

Sam looked back at the stream that flowed steady but strong. Where once had been carved in a tongue undecipherable was now written, "He that believes in me, as the scripture has said, out of his belly shall flow rivers of living water." This had been carved in the exact same handwriting.

I had wondered what the first message said, so the spirits interpreted it for me in plain English. "How thoughtful. Thanks, guys," Sam said to thin air. "Really doesn't make any sense to me though."

Sam was certain that he had heard or read that phrase at one time, but he could not place where or when and thought maybe it had something to do with when the Roman soldiers, thinking Jesus was dead on the cross, pierced his side, and supposedly blood and water gushed from his wound. Again, he knew he had heard it somewhere, but the details of recall were dim.

While watching the stream flow, it occurred to him that liquid had not passed his lips in quite some time, and upon such a revelation, his thirst had become great. He got on his knees, leaned over the embankment, and drank deeply. To say the water was refreshing would be like saying the sun was hot. He felt as though a resurgence of strength, purity, and life itself emancipated his every pore, including spirit, mind, and heart. *I will never thirst again*, Sam thought with full sincerity while wiping his chin dry. As he considered that what he felt was ludicrous, he laughed just as deeply as he had drunk.

"What on earth is going on in my head?"

As he exited the room, he was sure has made himself a multimillionaire; he considered checking each room while passing down the hall for more unhidden treasure, but what he really wanted to see more than anything was what lay up on top of the spiraling staircase, if anything.

CHAPTER

27

Doctor Daniel (Dan) Baker went about his usual routine he ritualistically performed every waking workday morning, checking on the welfare of his patients. For some, there was no hope, and they would surely die before too long. Others survived their brushes with death and would soon be transferred from ICU and inevitably discharged, free to try to recapture a degree of life once known. Some, like Samuel Reed, were trapped somewhere in between, like that of a transient limbo. He took a turn for the worse the other day, his body going into a frontal-lobe seizure. He bit his tongue pretty hard, spraying down the graveyard-shift nurses with a mouthful of blood. He survived the seizure with no severe side effects detected, but he sure gave family and friends more than a bit of a scare. Four months was a long time for anyone to survive so deep a coma, completely unresponsive to painful stimuli and having a respirator breathe for him, but the doctor had witnessed some emerge from much longer a time, so Sam was not without hope.

Dr. Dan Patton was delighted to see more people were praying for him now—more Afro-Americans who were likely members of the church that Mr. John Carlton attended and had inspired to come and pray for a man they more than likely didn't even know. Yet they showed up every Wednesday morning, laid hands on the comatose man, and prayed their hearts out. On this current Wednesday, Mr. Carlton again saw Dr. Baker watching the prayers being said, which John was beginning to notice was becoming commonplace.

"Hey, Doctor," John Carlton called. "Why don't you come join us?"

Dan Baker was caught off guard. "Who, me?" He looked behind himself as if he really could be talking to anyone else. "No, really, that's all right. I have got to finish my rounds, and I—"

"You are his doctor, right?" an attractive young lady asked.

"Well…yes, I am."

"Then can we pray for you?"

"No, no, really it is not necessary."

The group of eight either didn't care for the doctor's answer or did not hear; as hands were removed from Sam, they rose to their feet and encompassed Dr. Dan, blocking any means of escape.

"No really, this is great for you and your church, but it's not met for me."

"Let them pray, Doctor," a man said from the door.

Dan turned to see who sold him out and found to his surprise Marvin and Maggie, the man's parents who only a few months ago showed zero faith in the act of prayer, had just arrived.

"Let us all pray for you, Doctor," Maggie said in collaboration with her husband.

Hands were laid upon him wherever space allowed.

"Okay, but really, I got to—"

"Dear Jesus, our Lord," the thunderous voice of Mr. Carlton spoke, "we thank you so much that you have entrusted the care of my friend, your son, Samuel into the skillful hands of Dr. Dan Baker. We ask in Jesus's name that you use him, Lord, by any means possible to bring him from his coma so that he might be returned to his family and life. We pray that even now, Lord, in his condition that you are speaking to him, that you are speaking life to him, and that even now he will open his heart to you. Lord, we cannot communicate with him, but you can.

"And we thank you, Lord, that you have welcomed his parents, Marvin and Maggie Reed, into your kingdom and have written their names into your Lamb's book of life. And in the name of the precious blood of your son, Jesus Christ, we say amen."

Dan Baker said amen in cohesion with the praying pack.

"Yes, thank you very much, but now I really have got to go," he said while departing Sam's room.

Some said, "God loves you, Dan" and, "Jesus loves you, Doctor." Each church member waited their turn and hugged him before the doc made his escape. This made Dan somewhat uncomfortable, but at the same time he could see it was important for them to express love and give thanks, so he received.

"Yes, yes, I'm sure he does. I believe that now. You are all good people."

Dan Baker retreated to the comfort of his office a bit baffled. Something happened that he could not explain. It was hard to explain something you didn't exactly understand yourself. But something did happen, of that much he was certain. Whenever the man Mr. Carlton said the name Jesus Christ, it was like a wave of glorious love embraced his very soul. It was as if each person who had laid hands acted as a channel for that love to flow. He could not explain it. It was as if each person had a direct connection with the source of all love. *God is love*, Dr. Baker thought but not quite sure as to why as he wiped perspiration from his eyeglasses.

A chorus of singing spread an angelic type of radiance through the hospital walls. *They're singing now. Their friend might be lying there dying, and they're singing gospel.* This touched him. He removed his glasses a second time, but this time to wipe his eyes of the tears beginning to gather.

A gentle knock tapped upon his door. He pulled himself together. "Yes, come in."

It was Maggie Reed, the man's mother. "Dr. Baker?" Maggie shuffled into his office, taking notice of licenses, plaques, and degrees displayed proudly upon the walls.

"Yes, how can I help you?"

"Hello, Doctor. First, I wanted to thank you once again. I know you're doing your best for my son..." Now Maggie noticed something else. The white of the doctor's eyes were red. Had he been crying?

"Yes, ma'am, we're doing all we can. But really you should be thanking the family that found your son's body. Because of them, Sam has a fighting chance."

"Me and Marvin are very grateful to that family, but even more so to God, whom we now believe used that child...Josh... to find him."

"Yes, maybe God had something to do with it."

"That's the other thing I wanted to talk to you about. I realize that you're probably not a Christian. That's okay, as of three days ago my husband and I weren't either."

This was something Dr. Baker was very interested in hearing. *Why the sudden transformation?*

"I guess our problem with Christianity, all religions for that matter, always seemed to have ulterior motives when it came to helping their fellow man. Some would even come off as know-it-all snobs. We could never understand why anyone in their right mind could say that their way of thinking is right and everyone else is wrong. But something happened to us three days ago when talking with the large black man. I believe his name is John—and his pastor Jerry. We were very delighted for their determination, along with their little church, in praying for our son. We didn't know about their beliefs and whatnot, but we at least wanted to thank them for their concern, and just like you they asked to pray for us... Well, I know that Marvin thought it was an odd thing to ask. I must admit that I did too. I mean, why waste your prayers on us when the only one who really needed them was Samuel? But they seemed like good people, so we said, yes."

Maggie paused, swallowed hard, but she couldn't stop her eyes from watering and her voice from quivering as she tried desperately to finish without a breakdown.

"I have to tell you that I don't really recall what it was that was said by Jerry, but I do remember that he asked God to give us strength, and then he asked him to touch us. Now, I don't know if it was a kinetic energy type of thing because we were all holding hands, but I felt something. I looked at Marvin, and I could tell he felt it too. I didn't know it then, but I now know it was the Holy Spirit letting us know that he loves us and has everything in control," she said as she couldn't help but sob tears of a peculiar nature.

Doctor Baker put an arm around her to console.

Maggie looked up at Dr. Baker and asked, "Doctor, did you feel anything when we prayed for you? You see, I have to ask because my hands felt like they were on fire."

"I'm sorry. I didn't feel anything…spiritual, if that's what you're asking. I only felt the warmth of your hands—and the warmth of your hearts, I might add."

"Oh, no need to apologize. I have a lot to learn as far as my new faith goes, but according to what I just read in the book of John last night, mind you, the Holy Spirit can be as unpredictable as the wind. What that tells me is that, everybody being different, God works with everyone in different ways," Maggie said while pacing his office after managing to get herself together.

"I think that God has many plans and that maybe the fact that we're even having this conversation is part of it," she said with a delightful sincerity in her eyes.

"I believe that one day you will open your heart to the Holy Spirit and one day you will feel his love. You know how I know that?"

Dr. Baker shook his head.

"Because we prayed for you, and I'm going to keep praying for you." Maggie Reed departed his office with a simple faith and quiet confidence.

Why did I do that? I looked that poor lady right in the eye and lied. Why did I lie? The doctor pondered from somewhere deep. As far as he could grasp, it was because he was not ready to share. What he felt was amazing, and until he could understand it, he would bury it in the inner file where everything personal was kept.

"Was it God? Could it have really been God? Maybe so."

CHAPTER

28

How many floors does this place contain? Drudging his way upward one step at a time, he was astonished by the immaculate craftsmanship of each ascending floor of long halls and many closed doors. Each hall ended with an immaculate balcony with an unobstructed view of the mountain's vegetation and creek exiting the mansion. The sun, beginning to rise, bounced light through the cascading balconies and countless windows, reminding Sam he had not slept. He did not care. He was not tired.

An elevator would have saved much time, but although he had not explored the bottom floor thoroughly enough to know for sure, he felt pretty certain there was no more a proper set up for a television than there would be for something as convenient as an elevator. No matter, he was very much preferring the view of the indoors and outdoors the stairs provided.

Upon nearing the second floor, Sam's ear picked up on the soothing flow of music only an acrylic grafton saxophone could create. Musically, there was nothing Sam enjoyed more than smooth jazz, going back to Jay Beckenstein and Mindi Abair, to more modern-day stylings of Greg Vail. After a rough day at work nothing could calm his nerves quite like it. When the night's agenda was to wine and dine a particular lady of interest, nothing set the mood more perfectly.

He attempted to learn to play, but it didn't last long. Sure, maybe he could have grown to be a halfway decent musician if he had the patience to buckle down and learn the instrument, but having found the talent didn't flow through him to the measure he preferred, he dropped that endeavor, perfectly content in being a full-time listener.

Somehow, someway those sweet sounds were eminent in an open door on the second floor. The music flowed from the beautiful golden saxophone that sat on display with no one there to play. He had never heard anyone play so touching a tune and didn't think anyone could, not even the greatest of jazz players he admired so—not because the skill involved was beyond capabilities but because it was because the music had purpose, not to entertain but to exalt someone or something so beautiful that it could only come from one that has seen such beauty face-to-face.

Sam cried. He had never felt so deeply touched except for one time as a young man of about twelve. It was something he willingly received and a darker source quickly snatched, robbing him of fruit's harvest up until the here and now. He could no more hear the words that touched his heart at that age than he could hear any more notes played without a complete breakdown.

He exited the music room, wiping tears away, and continued up the stairs' spiraling hike. He passed floor after floor, intent on reaching the very top, and concluded in his heart that he would stop if only another door had been left ajar. *If there are any more doors open it could only be because there is something on the inside I am supposed to see. I don't know how I know it, but I know it.*

Alas, there were no more open doors, only floor after floor, twelve of them, of long halls ending in balconies. The thought did cross his mind that maybe each floor represented a different stage of my life and each door something that said something about his particular passions.

Sam gave all credit to the spirits he encountered along the wide path. Who else could know so much about me? *The first thing they knew was I really like the fence that barricades this place; they know I'm very fond of Southern-style colonial home architecture; they knew I love large, expensive jewelry. Who doesn't? They know of my love for jazz. If they know that much, who is to say they don't know everything?* Another thought tantalized his senses. *Maybe this place is mine. It seems as if someone had me in mind when they made it, didn't they?*

The realist in Sam finally spoke up. "What's the catch? Mamma didn't raise no dummy." Gazing up at the glorious crystal chandelier sparkling in multifaceted beams of color, he said, "Think I'd sell my soul for a place like this."

The chandelier did not have a light bulb or a socket where one would go, yet light danced upon and from it in shades of yellow, blue, and red. *Fascinating,* Sam thought, eyeing the idiosyncrasies of its brilliance, asking himself the all-too-taxed-out question of the day, "How is this possible? It's not possible. Absolutely nothing I have seen in this mansion is possible. This is all like a fairy tale one would hear about of an afterlife. That would mean I would have to be dead. Is that what this is? Am I dead?"

He didn't want to believe that, but he must concur that when he weighed all the strange experiences and encounters he had suffered from before and after entering the mansion, the only way the pieces could possibly fit would be if he were dead.

"How can this be? I don't feel dead… When would I have died?"

Immediately upon such ponderings, his memory of jumping the chasm, losing his balance, and crashing headfirst into a boulder answered his question.

"That's when I died." He patted down his body starting with his head. Searching for what? He did not know. He allowed his backpack of priceless jewels to fall from his shoulders and tumble down the stairs, making quite a racket, but Sam was undeterred.

A sickly, ashen-type shock paled his skin and deadened the light in his eyes.

"Jewels mean nothing now. I'm dead. Something is on the twelfth floor waiting for me."

This wasn't a question in his mind; this was a statement—a statement of fact. He trembled in trepidation of what could possibly be awaiting his presence. In a shocked, trance-like state, he reached the brim of the top. Slowly he took the last remaining steps, and what he saw he never would have guessed, although maybe he should have.

"The spirits don't lie," Sam mumbled.

Where the floor ended was not a balcony but two gates side by side. One was high in height and wide in width, dazzled with many sparkling jewels, primarily pearls. The second reached no such heights and was pushed by the wide gate against the evanescing wall, its path through very narrow. Like most things in this palace, Sam could not put a figure on its cost; truth be told, he didn't care to try.

"Eternity awaits me on the other side of one of these gates. Which one?"

Shamir had told him of this and had cautioned him to not take the wide gate; he remembered it well. He had said that many took the wide gate and only a few the narrow. It sure was easy enough to see why. From a natural point of view, it would seem that only a fool would chose the narrow over the extravagance and majesty of the wide. The narrow gate was constructed of wood and looked like something any typical carpenter could put together.

"Shoot, I think I could do this myself in my backyard, if I had one." He pushed on it, testing its stability. It would not fall over, but it creaked sounds of very old, dampened lumber.

It would appear as if there should be no arguing about it. Sure enough the wide was the way to go. The only thing that caused hesitation was the warning of the angel Shamir. Yes, angel. He never felt right in referring to him as a spirit. He was more than that. *Whatever is left of me when I go through one of these gates is spirit.* Remembering him in his glorified angelic form before he streaked the night sky, he knew whatever his origin, he was not man and never had been. Being one not begotten of earth, he was far greater. He was eternal.

As wrong as it felt in his flesh, he felt in his spirit that he had to heed the words of the angel or be proven a fool. With great reluctance, he went to reach for the handle of the narrow gate when a crashing thud shook the foundation the mansion rested on.

"Samuel!" a voice thundered. Quickly, he removed his hand, turned back to the stairs the way he had come, and to his terror thumped the park ranger he had his encounter with at the fork in the road what felt like a millennium ago. He moved with such rage that flames of fire sat upon him. Each ascending crash of his foot somehow quickened his pace and shook the chandelier to swing to and fro. Sam's backpack full of ill-gotten gain and every jewel in the home jingled upon vibration, something like a warning. The closer the ranger came, the greater the flames intensified so that by the time he was within reach of Sam, he was completely engulfed, no fragment of cloth or feature of face to be seen.

Sam squatted down with his back against the gate he had been on the verge of opening and covered his face with his right arm, trembled, and peeked up at the man on fire. He wanted to say, "Please don't hurt me," but all manner of speech was stripped from his throat when Sam witnessed this man, this park ranger, whatever he was, transform before his unbelieving eyes from fire to pure light. This was the most beautiful creature he had ever seen, and he almost wanted to cry. A radiance of alchemy curved the outline of his figure, seeming to gather at two adjacent areas upon his back. Although he could see that they weren't, he could totally understand why some might mistake this particular radiance as two wings. It had that form.

Sam maneuvered to his knees and laid out his arms at the angel's feet in worship. The angel relished and absorbed such prais, delighted in the reverence of man. His chest inhaled deeply, thrusting forth his pecs in cut, muscular masculinity, his height at or very near seven feet.

Engulfed in the penetrating force of his persona, Sam feared to look up or to even open his eyes for that matter. It was a fear that told him he was not worthy to look upon such beauty, lest he be punished as a result. The being's light that he wore as a garment did not bring peace or joy that Sam had experienced at Christmas light displays over the years, but rather the tarnished, stained lesions of sin scarred upon his soul he tried so hard to hide. He felt like he had only just exited a shower with only a towel to hide his shame, and this being by his mere presence had yanked it free, leaving nothing hidden but the paralyzing guilt that felt efficient enough to damn his soul.

He wanted mercy. He sought any hint of grace from his accuser. His eyes, each as a flame, were fierce with hatred. And it wasn't his sins, although merited, that birthed such despised fury. It seemed appropriate to be hated for the selfish life he lived, but it ran deeper than that, and although he could not surmise as to why, he felt hated for merely existing. He wanted to scream. He wanted to curl up in a fetal position, suck his thumb, and cry for his mommy and might have done just that.

"Arise, Samuel," the being commanded.

Sam found himself on his feeble legs, retaining balance with no memory of standing.

"Samuel, you will be very wise not to open that gate." He spoke without use of speech, yet it came through louder than mouth could carry sound. His means of communication was eloquent and powerful, a far cry from the one known as a park ranger; he remembered thinking of him as slow and borderline dumb. If he had not seen the being transform from human to the angel right before his very eyes, there would be no way he would believe it was the same person.

"This..." he said, pointing at the decorated gate, "is your fate. Hear now, heed the call of your soul." Looking upon the narrow gate, he continued. "Do not forfeit your place in eternity by deciding to explore foolish things or by putting to test the unknown. Remember when you were young and your mother was cooking dinner for you and your father. You saw the flames that were broiling your food. You saw as they flickered and seemed to dance about, and it looked to you that the fire was there for your entertainment, your amusement. The flame was there inviting you to touch, and although your mother had warned you on a number of occasions, you put your finger in the fire anyway."

There was no way Sam could have possibly remembered that. That happened just a few days before his third birthday. By the time Sam was four, he had forgotten all about the incident but never forgot the lesson. Now thirty-five, the being Avah talking him through it, he remembered it all in great detail.

When his mother turned her back for just a second, he put his finger in the friendly dancing flame. He knew that that was a "no-no," but right or wrong, he could not stop. Turned out the flame was not friendly; little Sammy soon found that it was rather cruel.

His wailing screams alerted his mother to his first transgression. He remembered the pain, he remembered his tears, and he remembered the comfort he felt in his mother's arms. He felt a twinge of guilt because he had been told never to do that, yet his mother loved him anyway. His Mother seemed to feel the pain along with him, even though she was not the one who had been burned. Though his mother was upset, it wasn't directed at what Sam did, but rather it was aimed at the pain her little baby Sammy was experiencing. The reason took a backseat to the results.

He remembered his father who had been watching TV in the other room. "For crying out loud! What is he crying about now?"

"He put his finger in the fire, Marvin, but he's okay... mostly scared."

"Good. It's good to get those things out of the way. I bet he'll never do that again."

"Yes, I remember," Sam said in a whisper. "Who are you?"

"I am your every pleasure, your heart's desire. I am Avah, quencher of fleshly appetite."

"You're not God then?"

"There are many gods. Samuel. I am yours."

Sam understood now. *Does this mean hell lay behind the narrow door?* No, Sam couldn't believe such a place existed. The angel was saying the smaller gate represented the inviting, dancing flame. But the thing was, there was nothing about the narrow way that looked particularly inviting. It was the wide gate that dazzled the senses. He was not prepared to argue that point, not with a being that seemed to know all.

The angel then rested his arm around Sam's shoulders. Sam could smell the burn of flame, but the fire did not char; he felt no pain. Though Sam felt no love in this gesture, he did feel acceptance.

"Samuel, I have prepared a place for you where you will rule dry places by my side for all eternity. Don't throw that away. You and me will crush the head of the lamb that has already been slain, who even now seeks you for his own."

With these words, the being's chest rose with intensity, and his hands gripped tightly into fists. Able to see his ferocity and malevolence through the eyes of Sam and feel the numbing fear pulsating in every nerve, Avah felt exalted, pride even.

"You are mine, my son. Don't let anyone tell you anything to the contrary."

Avah was wise enough to know that fear can serve a productive purpose. Howbeit, in this case it may create a reaction contrary to his bidding.

Avah rested a gentle touch upon Sam's shoulder and spoke in a gentle, sweet tone with his free arm extended, waving him to the wide gate.

"Go now. Enter your calling."

CHAPTER

29

Along with this feeling of acceptance and a promise to rule, whatever that meant, Sam felt the most logical decision, of course, would be to go somewhere wanted, where a purpose might be served. He always thought of himself as a good man at heart and as reward would pay no dues but rather have dues paid to him. The only thing he knew about the other side of the narrow gate was that Shamir resided there, and according to Carl and Leo, he would serve in drudgery the one who created. The angels had special VIP status, while the human element ran to and fro the outskirts of heaven on errands for the heavenly hosts. *Hmm, rule or serve, it sounds too easy, doesn't it?* he asked himself. In such cases, he always asked the all-too-familiar question, what's the catch? Shamir had warned him, had he not, that the fallen lie.

Guess I'll soon find out who the true liar is because no way am I going to defy this being's wishes. It wouldn't be prudent, he thought as he saw that he was beginning to show frustration at Sam's hesitance.

"Maybe you should open it for me. Looks kind of heavy."

"I cannot, only you have the authority. Strength hath no say. Only will. Touch it. It will open."

Sam reached out for a simple touch when one single drop of blood fell before him. The ceiling of the mansion in a blink of an eye was no more. Where it had been an exotic sort of flowing delight was now a demented, dirty brown sky. The sky then bent. All at once the elemental foundation of physics fled, allowing the impossible to be possible, the sky warping itself horizontally into a large image of a cross casting shadow a mile long.

Altogether the mansion vanished along with the very mountain itself; only the gates remained and the earth on which they stood. One drop of blood was followed by fifty, then tripled, and then there were countless drops. A downpour of blood fell from the cross above all around, but not one drop touched him or the furious being beside.

Avah succumbed to a frightful rage, storming side to side and cursing God in a language unknown, but Sam knew it nonetheless. Tightening his fists as if he were ready to do battle, he shouted at the cross, "You cannot have him! He belongs to me!"

"Sir…Avah I mean, I think we're okay. The blood's not touching us," Sam pleaded, trying desperately to calm the being.

Avah pointed a long immediate finger at Sam and threatened, "Samuel, do not get the blood on you."

"I don't think I could even if I tried," Sam said as he moved about, displaying to Avah that no matter where he moved in this downpour, the rain avoided him as if it had been preprogrammed to do so. This only infuriated him all the more.

"Did you hear me! Do not even *try* to get wet. It will damn you!" Avah cried, getting right up in his face. Sam watched the flames of his eyes flicker wrath. Sam cringed at the sulfuric stench of his breath. He trembled something fierce, unable to ascertain a method of self-defense; he prayed in his thoughts in an act of desperation the simplest of all prayers: *Jesus, help.*

Shamir appeared from nowhere and, using both hands, pushed Avah with a mighty force, shoving him hard onto solid ground. He tumbled into a backward somersault and sprung to his feet with sword held in hand. Shamir held a sword of his own, and it was double-edged and its blade blazing fire. Perhaps Avah felt mismatched, as he hurled accusations rather than physical assault.

"He never called on you. You have no right to be here."

"You know I would not if he had not."

Again Sam fell on his face in his best worshipping pose in reverence of Shamir, but unlike Avah, Shamir would have none of this, immediately lifting Sam to his feet.

"Do not worship me. I am merely a servant like you."

Why would he call me a servant? I serve only myself.

"Samuel, why? Why did you call on his master?"

"I didn't. He just showed up."

"You see, Shamir, even now he lies. He can't be yours. He is mine."

"He called on the Most High in an act of resistance. It is written, 'resist the devil and he will flee from you.'"

The sword of Avah glowed crimson every time he hailed an accusation.

"Because he, in an act of ignorance, might have called on your master does not mean I have been resisted. Ask him yourself. Sam, do you wish that I leave and your promise of eternal dominion die and your judgment begin?"

Sam didn't know what he wanted anymore, and he looked upon Shamir for a rebuttal. Shamir's double-edged sword in battle radiated a flaming intensity in offence.

"'You belong to your father the devil, and you want to carry out his desires. He was a murderer from the beginning, not holding to the truth, for there is no truth in him. When he lies, he speaks his native language, for he is a liar and the father of lies.'"

Avah snarled while Shamir continued. "Samuel, God did not send his Son into this world to condemn the world, but to save the world through him."

Avah clutched his sword tighter. "Saved? Are you hearing this, Samuel? Saved, he says. What of your uncle Freddy Nosfer? Was he not a good man? Did he not have a family that loved and cherished him? Did he deserve to die? Why, I ask you? Why wasn't he saved and his wife and children spared the heartbreaking emptiness of his loss? A God of love? I think not. I ask you, who is the real liar?"

That's something I've always wondered about.

Shamir knew his thoughts. "Samuel, I know you trust that there is good in the world."

"The only good in this world came at the humiliation of your master on a tree."

"Hold your tongue, demon!" Shamir commanded.

"Of course there is. I see a lot of good in the world, and I also see a whole lot of bad." Sam thought to hear Avah's response, but he had sat himself down with mouth mute, looking like a stubborn, unruly child who did not get his way as blood continued to fall about the three of them, still not one drop making contact.

"If there is good, as you say there is, then just as the source of the tides of the sea is the moon, so is the source of all that is good our Father who art in heaven. Just as you say there is also a whole lot of bad, there is a source for this as well."

"Satan?"

"No. In his free will, he made his decision to rebel, and likewise so has all of mankind. Satan can only act as tempter, but in the end you are held accountable for your own choices, good or bad. Because God is sovereign, there are consequences. Whether or not you will see it in your lifetime is of no affect. No bad deed goes without recompense and no good without its reward. All of man is affected by the collective sin of the human race, the good and bad, guilty and innocent. 'For there is no one righteous, not even one.'"

"I know I did not live up to God's standards, but overall, as a whole, I don't think I was all that bad."

"Had Jesus been a man of sin he might have agreed with you. But he was without sin, and just as he is perfect, he calls us to be."

"Impossible! Nobody's perfect. I guess that means everyone is going to hell."

"Do you not see that this is why Jesus had to come? Born in sin, you can never be found worthy of heaven. Weighed in the balances, you would be found wanting. He took upon his body your sins and crucified them to a cross so your spirit, as a filthy rag, is wiped clean by his blood and is made perfect. Not by merit but grace."

What's the catch? "Okay, I think I'm following, but what does this have to do with my uncle Freddie?"

"Why your uncle perished was the result of a fallen world that chose self over fellowship. In his free will, the man that killed him not only broke the laws of the land but the laws of God and will suffer the consequences on both fronts. Lest he open the door of his heart soon, for his time is short. It was not God's will for Freddy to die so young. He loved him very much, just as he does you."

"Why is it raining blood?" Sam asked, changing the subject rather abruptly.

"This is for your sake. It is written, 'Unless I wash you, you have no part with me.' And because I stand clean of this blood... your sin remains," Shamir finished. "You will understand all of this very soon."

"I don't think my death can be blamed on a fallen world, more like a clumsy, falling man."

"Samuel, you must learn to forgive the man that killed your uncle."

"Fat chance. That's never going to happen. I saw that jerk in the courtroom when he was sentenced. He didn't look the least bit remorseful."

"As the Father has forgiven you, so too you must forgive."

"I think we're going to have to agree to disagree on that one."

"So be it."

"So be it? I just told you straight to your face I'm not going to do something, and with all the power and strength you have, you're not going to strike me down or force your hand on this?"

"This is something I cannot do. That is to interfere with your God-given right to choose. Just as the man that killed your uncle chose to drink and drive that night, he exercised the freedom allotted him. If you insist on hearing only what your itching ears want to hear, so be it. There is nothing more I can do."

With that, Shamir streaked across the sky, vanishing as he had once before.

Something like a spiritual gag fell from Avah's lips as he ranted. "You did well, Samuel, and you were right. He was wrong. You can never forgive the man who robbed you of your uncle and caused your family such grief, nor should you be expected to. What an atrocious request."

"He is right though, isn't he?"

"Do not tell me you believed him. All he wants is his very own servant, and that would be you, Samuel. Don't act a fool!"

"No, he is not a liar. You're the liar, demon. God is light, and in him there is no darkness."

He turned his back on Avah and walked toward the narrow gate.

"Samuel, what about your place in eternity by my side? I promise you glory, riches, anything you wish, even women. Oh, how I know you like that. I have supplied for you every woman you ever desired and will continue to do so in the hereafter!"

In spite of his greatest weakness dangled before him, Samuel paid him no mind. Avah knew then there was no stopping him and reverted to his last trick.

In the blink of an eye, Avah changed his form into his true image of about four feet tall, his face unsymmetrical with bumps and festering boils all about his bony, scaly, lizardlike skin, eyes no longer a flame but like two beady rubies just like the eyes of the six spirits he saw on the trail, the wide path. Avah leapt like a salamander and squatted before Sam. Sam had no fear and being six three in height was only going to step over him, when Avah said, "What about your beloved parents?"

"What about them, demon?"

"They know not of your savior. Will you leave them to burn in hell while you enjoy paradise?"

"Burn in hell, you say, so what happened to ruling by your side?"

Avah cackled something wicked, making the hair on the back of Sam's neck stand on end.

"So I lied," Avah said matter-of-factly.

"They are good people. I'll see them in heaven."

"Did you not hear a word the angel said? There is none right-eous. No, not one. Has not your father taught you to stay far away from those who teach the Word?"

Stay away my boy, stay away. Sam heard the gruff voice of his father as clear as if he stood beside him.

"Come with me, Samuel. So what if you don't go to Shamir's heaven? At the least you will partake in the kind of comfort only shared among family."

Although he hated it immensely, Avah was right. His folks looked upon those who taught the Bible as money-grubbing charlatans. No way would they ever open their hearts to anything said in the Bible.

"You must let me go back. I have to warn them."

Avah cackled while exclaiming with glee, "You're dead, you're dead, you're dead!"

If hell were really as bad a place as folklore said it was, with the fire and the demons and the hopelessness involved, he could not, he would not, turn his back on his parents that did nothing but love and care for his every need growing up, and even today if he were to ask. *If they are to pay the penalty of eternal damnation, then so will their loving son right by their sides. It is the least I can do.*

Samuel Reed entered through the wide gate.

CHAPTER

30

The gate slammed shut immediately upon his entrance, with a deafening thud. The first thing he noticed was that it wasn't raining there. *I guess I missed my chance to be washed of my sin*, Sam thought. He looked back at the reverse side of the gate he had admired from the front and expected to see the same glistening pearls and saw nothing like that. Instead the gate was void. Pure black. The door displayed an utter lack of color. You couldn't even call it black; it was void of this too. If it were black, in an odd way, that would lighten it up some. It was void. The epitome of nothingness. He found it disturbing to look upon, so he turned from it as if there were an inherit danger in gazing at it for too long.

Again, the laws of physics being of none effect, a spinning circle morphing into a tunnel began to form, manifesting deep, long, and utterly mysterious.

Sam had seen this before.

"I saw this right after I hit my head on Mount Kinley—right after my...death." *I rebuked it then, but this time I don't think I have a choice.* A tug that seemed to be centered in the middle of his chest lifted him about five inches off his feet and then began to slowly pull him into the mouth of the tunnel. Gravity seeming to have lost its edge, he felt like he was somewhere lost in outer space being sucked into a black hole. He wondered if there was some sort of connection between black holes and alternative dimensions. Maybe they acted as portals connecting heaven with earth, life with death, dimension with dimension, and maybe that tunnel connected the physical to the spiritual.

Soon upon entrance, Sam shot through the tunnel at what felt like the speed of light. Images of every waking moment of his life appeared before him. Everything he had ever done and thought and experienced, he was reliving once again—all his pains, regrets, missed opportunities, and all the lessons life taught. Everybody he had ever known, loved, hated, wronged, every time he had been wronged, every triumph, joy, laughter, and thought he had ever had, every hated moment, lost love, every instance he wished he could go back and change, every act of kindness and every gut-wrenching sin. He saw the true motives of his heart and how often it conflicted with the lies of intent he continually fed on.

Spiritual warfare valiantly raged on in the recesses of his life that he had willfully chose not to see, but the veil was then removed, and he saw very well Shamir, guardian, in full armor deflecting the assault of the enemy; Avah, lust, whom acted as primary agent; and the one whom Sam listened to most. Avah ruled his life, Sam giving him free reign. Try as he so often did, Shamir could not guard one who clipped the wings of wisdom. Shamir did cease, on command from the Father, every opportunity allotted to speak the love of God through those chosen before the foundation of the world was set, to him who very seldom would hear.

There were many incidents of peace and happiness he wished he could go back to and set up permanent residence and would do just that if not for the laws of time; oh, how it moved.

Of all his regrets, too many to be counted, there was one in particular that, although did nothing to change his course, would have set his place in eternity among the saints, angels, and the three that make up one God; if only he had received instead of the nagging uncertainty of a ghastly horror that awaited.

~

He was twelve years old, coming of age, with hormones beginning to rage and the opposite sex no longer an object of adolescent angst. Throwing worms at girls to watch them scream
and squirm no longer held the same appeal. Neither did it for
his fellow seventh-grade peers. His two best buds at that time
were Jimmy Keys and Melvin Baker, and it was becoming commonplace on every Saturday night to be dropped off at the local
theater, the UA6, to catch a flick as reward for chores accomplished. The movies were fun enough but were never the main
objective. That, of course, would be to hit on the older high school
girls. At least that's what they told themselves. No actual hitting
ever actually took place, just a whole lot of drooling. Although
Jimmy, to Sam and Melvin's admiration, did at one time build up
enough nerve to say hi to a cute blonde freshman, but that's as
far as it ever went.

CHAPTER

31

Jimmy noticed him first, some strange dude who looked like he had no business being there. His clothes were rather raggedy and somewhat torn. He wore faded blue jeans and sandals hanging by one strap each to support his dirty feet and a shaggy, navy blue, grease stained T-shirt.

His hair was long, just past his shoulders. He held a book in his hand and walked around trying desperately to talk to every sect of people hanging around loitering. Nobody would give this guy the time of day. They shunned him like he was some kind of salesman, or bum even.

Right off, he disqualified him as a bum by the simple fact that bums survived by taking, not giving. His mannerisms proved him to be a man with a thirst to share something, but what? Sam concluded that he had to be selling something, something his livelihood rested on, but the only thing he held was an old, beat-up book. Certainly not the kind of product demand envisions in the world of supply. Why would someone try to sell something that looked so worn and very used? Being the preteen solver of great mysteries that he falsely believed himself to be, he allowed his creative mind to create a scenario to explain the man's manner to his satisfaction.

He was a poor man out trying to get his life back together after wasting the first part of it away on alcohol and drugs.

Somehow, he managed to get himself a job selling books but was having difficulty getting the hang of it. After much travail, the books finally started to sell, unloading all product in his possession, minus the one book. The man did not get paid for each book sold but rather by each box. One to go. Soon he'd be back on his feet ready to conquer the world, providing he didn't relapse.

He probably got a bit frustrated while trying to sell that last book and let out his rage upon it, which would explain its sorry state. When he came to his senses, he decided to give selling it one last chance, which would explain the here and now. And if he couldn't sell that book, it was back to the drugs, probably heroine.

Where on earth does he get off thinking he can sell that? This guy's not playing with a full deck.

The overall lack of interest in this book by the predominantly teen crowd did not detour the man, and he was making his way toward Sam and his buddies.

"He's a religious nut," Jimmy Keys remarked as if he had experience and was well aware of the sort of man he was.

"A religious nut?" Melvin Baker asked, unsure what Jimmy was implying.

"Yeah…you know, people that go around preaching about Jesus to everyone."

Just like that, Sam's theory was dashed. Jesus was the furthest away from his expectations. Melvin was wearing a baffled look of uncertainty about his face, so Jimmy continued.

"You know, that Jesus died for your sins and everything…you know all that religious bologna."

These words sounded very familiar to Sam and not because he remembered hearing them that day when he was twelve. He recalled hearing very similar words spoken out of the mouth of his own father.

Observing himself, so young and innocent, he didn't notice it then, but hurling through a tunnel reliving the life of Samuel Reed, he saw that Jimmy did a quick look around. It was obvious to Sam now that he was looking for a place to go to and avoid the stranger altogether. Maybe the man picked up on it because he advanced rather quickly, not giving Jimmy a chance to leave.

Melvin didn't know what to do. He saw the nervousness of Jimmy and stood there frozen like a deer caught in headlights. Jimmy was able to murmur before the man arrived, "Watch, he's going to talk to us about Jesus."

"Hi, fellas," the man said, sounding very kind and chipper.

"Hey" and "Hi" were the two words mumbled out of Sam's and Melvin's mouths.

"Not interested," Jimmy said, lifting his hand in a rude gesture into the man's face

"How do you know you're not interested, son, when you don't know what it is I have to offer?"

"You're selling that book, aren't you?" Sam asked, not totally convinced he was going to preach to them. In Sam's eyes, he just didn't fit the profile of a religious man.

That question from Sam turned on a light in the man's face, and his eyes brightened with anticipation of his answer.

"No, this book is not for sale...but the words inside it are free."

Focusing in on Melvin, the man said, "This book contains the words of life, son."

"Words of life? Wha...wha...what do you mean?" Melvin asked in his nervous, stuttering method.

With this, Jimmy rolled his eyes and said, "Melvin, don't get him started."

"Let me tell you...Melvin, is it?"

"Yeah, that's my name. That's right. I'm Melvin. Some people call me Mel."

The truth was nobody called him Mel that Sam was aware of. It was a name he would rather be called, and maybe this stranger holding a Bible would oblige Melvin in this manner.

"Sure thing, Mel, my name is Louis, and you can call me Lou, if you like," the man said while shaking Melvin's hand.

"Okay," Melvin said, looking a little foolish to his friends, so he straightened himself out and put his stern, I-mean-business face back on. But it was too late for that according to what Jimmy was thinking. This man had befriended Melvin in just about a minute's time, and now they would never be rid of him.

Louis then turned to shake Jimmy's hand. It was obvious to Sam that Jimmy did not want to shake his hand, but the man had him cornered, and Jimmy felt he had no choice. Common courtesy insisted he at least do that much. Then he shook Sam's hand. Uncertainty was the best way to describe Sam's demeanor. He didn't know what to make of the man, not yet, but he was sure he would eventually figure him out. Sam was a good judge of character; it went along with being an observant person.

Louis told his whole life story, it seemed to Sam. He told of how he got caught up in drugs in the late sixties and how close he came to suicide when his wife left him with their only son. He then spoke of Jesus and how he turned his life around and quoted scriptures from the book of John. When he spoke of Jesus, there was life in his eyes, love in his voice, and passion in his message.

Sam tried hard to find a flaw in this man, but he could not. He wanted to point out that this man was no better than anybody else. So he had no right to be preaching to anybody, but Jimmy beat him to it.

"What makes you so special that you would have this connection with God, that you talk to him and he listens?"

"I'm glad you asked me that, Jimmy. I am no more special than you are. As a matter of fact, by worldly standards, if that is the marker by which you judge, I am the scum of the earth, unworthy to stain the sole of your shoes."

Jimmy nodded his head, pleased to hear Louis say what they all felt.

"But you know what, Jimmy, God loves me just as much as he does you."

"I find that hard to believe."

"It's called grace, my friends. Do you know that word? Do you know what it means?"

No one answered.

"I submit to you that it is the most beautiful word ever spoken."

Louis spoke to them on the fall of Adam and Eve, the Ten Commandments, the penalty of God's law transgressed, and how every one of them by committing the simplest of sins was worthy of eternal separation from God. Then he spoke on God giving the world what they did not deserve, through the death of his Son: the forgiveness of sins.

"Yes, *grace* is a beautiful word," Louis finished.

Sam found his words cut to his heart. The atmosphere between he and his friends became soothing and yet piercing at the same time. It was like a hovering thick, gentle cloud encompassed them. Sam felt it strongly and wondered if his friends did too. He took a quick look at Louis. He seemed to feel it himself and welcomed it with a delightful smile upon his face, as though he was in the presence of an old friend.

"Do you feel that, guys? That is the presence of the Holy Spirit. His word says, 'For where two or three are gathered together in my name, there I am with them.'"

"I feel him," Melvin said.

Jimmy was not finding comfort in this man's words. As a matter of fact, he looked intensely uncomfortable. He could not sit still; he swayed back and forth as if he were wrestling with a demon. Perhaps he was. Suddenly, he walked off and didn't even take the time to say where he was going or good-bye or anything. This kind of worried Sam because how were they going to explain the absence of Jimmy when Sam's mother came to pick them up?

But Sam could worry about that later. Right then, the man quoting from his old, beat-up Bible had his interest and heart gently in his hand.

"'For God so loved the world he gave his only begotten Son, that whosoever believes in him will not perish but have everlasting life.'"

A twisting knot of guilt convicted Sam's heart. *Why would Jesus do this for me? I am not a good person. I have such dirty, wrong thoughts.*

Louis continued quoting from his Bible, "'I have not come to call the righteous but sinners to repentance.'"

A billow of hope began to rise. *That's me. Jesus is calling me. Jesus died for me, but what can I do about it?*

"'No one can see the kingdom of God unless he is born again.'"

That's it; that's what I've have to do. I've got to get born again.

Finally the man Louis gave the answer. Louis, feeling the Spirit of the living God leading him, flipped to the book of Romans.

"'If you confess with your mouth, "Jesus is Lord," and believe in your heart that God raised him from the dead, you will be saved.'"

"'Behold I stand at the door and knock. If anyone hears my voice and opens the door, I will come into him and have fellowship with him, and he with me.'"

The scriptures he was quoting had a way of piercing through all of Sam's defensive walls and comforting his heart with truth—absolute, soothing truth.

"Jesus died for you, Mel." He Turned to Sam. "And Jesus died for you, Sam, and Jesus died for Jimmy too. I wish he knew that."

When Louis told Melvin that Jesus died for him, Melvin could hold back no longer; the flood gates of salt water opened, and Melvin was soaking his hands in his own tears. Sam didn't know what it was, but he felt on the verge of tears himself.

He couldn't tell if it was the fact that his friend was so deeply touched that it rubbed off on him, or if it was the fact that an all-powerful God who knew no wrong would take it upon himself to take on flesh, come to this earth, suffer the ultimate punishment, and ultimately die all on behalf of Samuel Reed. Sam knew he was no prize. God might want a refund when it came to Sam. This was the way he saw it because this love of God's was simply unimaginable and impossible to grasp and so deeply touching. Not in a passive tense, like the effect people could have when viewing an all-inspiring or dreadfully sad movie that it brings you to the brink of tears. This touched him in a place no man or movie could reach. It didn't touch his heart; rather, his heart was pierced.

Sam wanted to cry, but he would not allow it. Sam saw tears as a display of weakness and would not let them loose as badly as he wanted to. Maybe Jimmy would see him.

Louis then led Melvin in a prayer where he invited Jesus into his heart. "Melvin, repeat after me. Heavenly Father, I stand before you a sinner. Jesus died to save sinners. Jesus died to save me. I open the door to my heart, and I invite you in to be Lord of my life. Thank you for forgiving me of my sins. Thank you for making me a new creation. I will follow you now from this day forward. Father God, in the name of your Son, Jesus Christ, I give my life to you. Amen."

Louis looked into Melvin's tear-stained eyes and said, "Welcome to God's family."

With that statement, Melvin's eyes flooded up once again, and Louis hugged him, and they laughed and smiled.

"Melvin, a river of living water flows through you now."

"Living water?"

"Yes, it is the Holy Spirit."

Louis's fingers turned the pages of his Bible as though one familiar. He read out loud from the book of John: "'Now on the last day, the great day of the feast, Jesus stood and cried out, saying, "If anyone thirsts, let him come to me and drink. He that believes in me, as the scripture has said, 'Out of his belly will flow rivers of living water.' But this he spoke concerning the spirit, whom those believing in him were about to receive; for the Holy Spirit was not yet given, because Jesus was not yet glorified.

"Glory be to God! His Spirit has been glorified in your heart tonight."

Words could not explain the inexplicable joy radiating the face of Melvin, so much so that he wanted it for himself. Louis turned his piercing eyes of love on Sam.

I knew I had heard this before, Sam thought, remembering what was written on the embankment on the first floor's backroom.

"What about you, Sam?"

Sam knew what he was talking about but acted as if he didn't.

"About me…what do you mean?"

"Do you want to open your heart and give your life to Christ like Mel did?"

Sam wanted to; he wanted to with all of his heart. But there was the one who was very present even in situations like this. He knew what to whisper in Sam's ears; he knew Sam very well.

This is good for Melvin, but it's not good for you. Melvin is helpless and weak; he needed a savior, but not you… You're stronger than that; you're smarter. Jimmy was right about this guy. He is a religious nut; besides, think of what a fool you will look to others; think of what a fool you'll look if Jimmy came back and found you holding hands with that religious nut he warned you about, with your head bowed, eyes closed, and talking to God. What a pathetic sight that would make. And not to mention how his words touched you earlier. You know if you open your heart to Jesus, you would not be able to hold yourself back from crying… Oh, what a pathetic sight that would make.

"Don't shut him out, Sam. Life is too unpredictable and uncertain. You might never have another opportunity."

With this, Louis reached out his hands for Sam to hold in the same way he did for Melvin. Sam did not immediately clutch them the same way Melvin did. He stood there and stared at his hands, unsure of what to do. Melvin gave a look to Sam that said, "What are you waiting for? Do it."

Millions of thoughts coursed through his mind all in a single moment. Sam has always been a rational person. And when he weighed his options, he knew the wise thing to do from a spiritual standpoint would be to embrace God. It could only be him whose presence ascended here. God knew him and loved him anyway, more than he could possibly grasp. This war taking place in his thoughts found a victor. Jesus. Jesus was the answer. He made up his mind; he would receive Christ. He clutched very tightly the hands of Louis.

A smile spread across his face greater than he had ever known. The moment he opened his heart, there was a tickle in his spirit, a tickle of great joy based in the center of his being. God was touching him, and Jesus was entering him. This joy seemed to be confirmation that he was doing the right thing. It was a comfort that clarified there was not a better thing in the whole world that could be done.

Great emotion began to swell and smolder within. He knew it would be impossible to hold back his emotions before this prayer he was about to say was complete. This did not matter anymore. He made up his mind. He was going to be born again. Amen.

Louis began, "Sam, repeat after me. Father, I stand before—"

"Samuel! Samuel Reed, you get your butt over here right now. You get away from that strange man."

Sam almost didn't hear his mother. As usual, Mom arrived right on time (the worst possible time) to pick him and his friends up. But his mother was not alone. Sitting in the passenger seat was Jimmy Keys. Jimmy had a look on his face Sam became familiar with; it was a look that said, "You stupid fool."

Sam released his grip with Louis and, leaving the prayer unfinished, ran off to meet his mother, with Melvin trailing behind.

Seeing it now and reliving it all at once, Sam saw that that was the moment. That was the most important decision of his life, and Jimmy Keys and his mother were right on time to detour it.

Sam shouted out in despair and frustration. It was an incoherent holler, but it said it all. It was the ultimate release of total contempt of the selfish, unrepentant life he chose to live. There would never be another opportunity like that. He was ready then. In later episodes of his life, the walls had already been built, and he would not let anyone in, not again.

The one whom he was about to receive and embrace with all his heart somehow became the enemy, an enemy he made a habit of shutting out. In looking back on that incident with Louis and Melvin, he would from then on see that incident in the same way Jimmy Keys did, when he saw that look in his eyes that said, "You damn fool."

From then on, Sam would always see himself as a damn fool whenever he was going to open his heart to anything, whether it be a girl or philosophy, religion, or whatever. He was determined not to be made a fool, or at least not to look like one. With great ferocity, he lived his life dedicated to this endeavor. What gave Sam the most regret was that, although he did have other opportunities, he never opened his heart to Christ again.

CHAPTER

32

S ome of the perceived innocent paths of life can end in dev-astation to the psyche, stunting one's natural growth and diverting the lapse to adulthood. If dealt with on a professional or spiritual level, there can be no hanging vines of regression: an abusive, course-setting moment in life conquered. Or maybe not.

~

What a pitiful, horrible day it had already been by the time Sam had thrown all of the fifty pounds of poor little Chrystal into his bedroom wall. Experiencing it a second time did nothing in alle-viating its impact on victim or perpetrator alike. He had hoped maybe this event did not go down as he remembered, that maybe the whole incident was blown way out of proportion by the little girl and his folks. Sadly, it was much worse than he had thought. Her little head ricocheting off the solid wall, Sam shuddered in his spirit, closing his eyes, unwilling to see. He felt a measure of relief as he considered it could have been much worse. She might have been knocked unconscious. Do those who go unconscious without the ability to catch their breath ever wake up? Sam shuddered again. Yet, during this time Sam always looked upon himself as the victim. After all, it was him who was forced into taking anger management classes where he was looped together with child abusers and wife beaters; it was he who spent what should have been some of the best years of his teenage life under a microscope, having his every move analyzed and questioned by his overexaggerating, nosy parents.

This was no way for a teenager to live. Crystal was just a child, and children had ways of taking brutal-looking falls, maybe shedding a few tears, and bouncing back on their feet to play again as if nothing happened. She had the air knocked out of her; sure, it must have been a little scary, but no such trauma could rob a child of the desire to play. You had to admire their elastic-like resiliency.

That was not the case. That fleeting moment, fear of death being the primal ingredient, in a soufflé of lost love and panic-stricken paralyses that continually blanketed any hope of correlation with the object of her affection, leaving her nights bitterly unsung and alone.

She could not understand why it was that she so severely shied away from men upon the slightest inclination that the man currently dating was showing any sign of irritability or frustration, maybe or maybe not because of something she said or did. It was only normal, from time to time, to have disagreements. Nobody, not even in the greatest of relationships or the longest lasting, was not going to have some friction from time to time. That's just the way it was, and Crystal knew it, howbeit, was unable to apply such basic knowledge to her condition.

Crystal was a very pretty woman. Not model material as far as *Cosmopolitan* goes, but she had a childlike face with a glimmer in her eye that concealed a mystery that was a challenge for men to unravel. She enjoyed embracing her feminine qualities and did not lack in men who developed a healthy interest in her. She wanted that, desiring an intimacy that would last the entirety of their lives—marriage, kids, all of it—and why not? As it was, her longest relationship was a mere nine months with an electrician by the name of Alex Stangen. The only reason it lasted as long as it did was because he had a deep reservoir of understanding and patience.

Even he couldn't handle it anymore when for the fifth time in one month she curled herself up into a ball in the corner of the room, head between her knees, gasping for air, hyperventilating, and all along crying, "Don't hurt me. Don't hurt me! Don't hurt me!"

"Calm down, relax, and breathe," Alex would coach.

Alex never intended on hurting her; it was the furthest thing from his mind. There was a tone of anger in his voice when she forgot to leave him his wake-up call one morning, causing him to be late for work. His alarm clock broke down on him, so she offered the wakeup call that never came. Not a big deal; nothing worth splitting over. But because of her constant refusal to get psychiatric help, Alex, like all of her boyfriends before him, could not envision a future with someone so frail.

"A school counselor can never see a psychiatrist. It would ruin my reputation, and if word got out, I could lose my license," Crystal would repeat every time. "I will deal with this myself."

Alex hoped one day she would, but as far as he and his patience went, the well had run dry.

Sam was amazed at the results of one little incident that had occurred some twenty years ago. He had gotten over it and hadn't thought about it much, but now he not only saw but felt the screaming pain that hibernated deep in the heart of his cousin Crystal. Possibly the hardest thing about it was she did not recognize the source of the problem, thus running the risk of never conquering it and possibly being alone all of her life.

Sam wanted to reach out his arms to hug her, to comfort her. He wanted to tell her how sorry he was and to help her on her way to overcome. But he couldn't, could he? What was done was done. Sam was more than sorry for that and felt that his sorrow should be enough to merit forgiveness; after all, there were those who had done things much worse than that without the least bit of sorrow. But since when had God ever graded on a curve?

CHAPTER

33

Sam's dastardly tricks as a perpetrator at times caused grief, pain, and sorrow. Some of which were obvious to the lads while others went completely unknown.

This would be the category Ms. Clenter fell under. It was almost too hard to handle being responsible for Ms. Clenter missing her opportunity to see her father one last time before he passed.

He had been fighting prostate cancer for many years. After much chemotherapy and various other last-ditch efforts to save his life, the doctor finally had to throw in the towel and tell his family that it was time to say their good-byes.

Ms. Clenter had planned on finishing up with sixth period math and rushing out to see her father, maybe for one last time. She knew she didn't have much time; she didn't realize how little his time was. She came to retrieve her car, as she usually would, only to find her tires were shredded flat. Her heart sunk into her stomach, twisting into knots and giving birth to panic.

Something within her knew that this was beyond just a pain in the neck. Something inside her knew she had to see her father that day or never again. She had a spare but not four of them. She did her best. It took an hour and a half, but after many failed attempts to get a hold of a ride over the phone, she finally found a fellow teacher who was kind enough to offer one. The whole ride to the hospital all she could think and repeat to herself under her breath was, "Please don't die, Daddy. Please don't die, Daddy. I'm coming. Your baby's coming."

Her father was a good man. He took care of his five children to the best of his ability, being a widower and all. Lorraine Clenter's mom had passed in a horrible car accident on the way home from work twenty-eight years before when Lorraine was only six, leaving distant memories of tea parties and Mommy playing dolls with her on her sixth birthday.

She admired her daddy so much and loved him so dearly; she just wanted to say it one last time. Could it ever be said enough? She could not even begin to count all the times her father had come to her rescue. Being young and somewhat wild, she always thought of him as being overprotective, and maybe he was to an extent, but she would always be more than grateful for it in the long run.

Daddy had a way of weeding out all the bad seeds that wanted to date his baby daughter. He watched her like a hawk. He knew the nature of boys, especially of hormone-driven adolescent boys. He made sure he came off as intimidating, even a bit menacing when meeting them, anything to invoke fear, so that possibly if they were to decide they wanted to hurt his little girl in any way whatsoever, they would think of Lorraine's dad and think the better of it. Lorraine spent the majority of her teenage years hating him for it, but now that adulthood had given her 20/20 hindsight, she only wants to thank him one last time. One more hug. That's it. That was all she asked.

It was too late. He had passed an hour before. She arrived at the hospital to find family members grieving. Some looked at her as if saying, "Why weren't you here? You should have been here."

She loved her father very much and would never forgive herself for not being there for him when his time came. Upon arriving home that night, she locked all the doors, shut all window shades and blinds, took the phone off the hook, buried her face in a pillow, and wept bitterly, alone. She was alone at that time, but not this time, not in this dimension. Here, Sam was present. He was there and felt all her pain in every intricate, heart-breaking detail.

CHAPTER

34

Sometimes in our lives we can mix for ourselves a drink so bitter that it can cause the toughest of inner flesh to bleed. Some drinks are beyond being regurgitated and so easily disposed of. Some leave one with more scar tissue to be covered and deceptively hidden, even from one's self.

~

The day that ended with Crystal Nosfer started with Billy Warnic, and it was he Sam was vicariously living through now. He remembered the fear and reverence the student body bestowed upon him because of his size and quiet nature. He never earned that respect outside of the football field, but it followed him there. He never was a physical threat to anyone unless it was expected of him. He didn't want to knock out that poor freshman but felt obligated. It was what large, menacing boys were supposed to do when offended, right?

When Billy fell victim to a supposed homosexual pass, Sam could now see there was zero honesty with every swing of his bike that he thrashed into others. He was putting on a show, giving the people what they wanted. His heart was flooded in joy at the prospect of a new friend. In high school, Sam tried to stay as far away from him as possible because the rumors said Billy had a temper. True or not, he did not care to find out for himself. It was completely irrelevant to his life. It hurt him deeply that he could not go back and befriend Billy and do away with the final outcome of his sadistic scheming. Not only did he destroy Billy's dreams, but he dragged in another picture of innocence with him: Chris Fesonmer.

A picture might say a thousand words, but it never told the whole story. The truth was he always knew that, but sometimes he would choose not to.

When Billy went home that day, his heart was doing somersaults, and he could hardly contain himself. He could not care less that it was rumored that Chris was gay. Billy had been taught and knew within his heart that God created woman for man and man for woman. That went without saying in Billy's head. He put all things in there simplest terms. When it came to homosexuality, if it was right or wrong, one only needed to look at how the sexes were designed. It was easy enough for Billy to see humans were designed for reproduction. That simple truth was more than evident. Billy would make his heterosexuality clear to him and then be his friend. Billy knew where Chris lived; when he was a child, he got paid two bucks a week for mowing his lawn. Chris probably didn't even remember that.

He hated to write. His most difficult subject and the one dreaded most in school was basic English. But he forced himself to sit down at the kitchen table and write a little note for his new friend:

> Chris, I got your message on my bike seat. I am not gay, but thank you for saying nice things. I won't let people be mean to you anymore. We should hang out.
>
> Billy Warnic

If one of his parents should happen to answer the door, he could give the note to him or her and have he or she pass it on to Chris. He would definitely be sure to inform them that it was a private letter for Chris's eyes only. He figured if Chris were around maybe they would see a movie, go out and get a coke, go play miniature golf, or something like that—simple things friends liked to do.

He stood across the street hidden behind a large dumpster so he would not be seen and watched as a little girl pedaled her old, beat-up tricycle. His parents were not home. His house looked dead with no life in it at all. He was beginning to become certain no one was home when he saw the blinds of the front window flutter slightly. He considered that Chris was home and the little girl on the tricycle caught his attention.

Billy's heart began to race, and his hands became clammy with nervous perspiration. He had never asked a girl out before and was beginning to feel that such anxiety could not feel much different than making a new friend.

Chris was home. No turning back—he must go through with it. He stood upon Chris's porch when he almost succumbed to a panic attack of sorts that turned him around as if to leave. At the last second, Billy put his fear in check and decided to leave his note under the welcome mat with two frogs on two lily pads. "Have a nice day"; the frogs smiled.

"I hope so," Billy whispered.

Of what transpired next he had no memory, only that of an excruciating pain that followed the sound of a door opening and a pressing blackness to follow.

The nightmares that followed Billy's near-death experience were vivid and without mercy. A giant door would slightly creak and then fly open as if on command. Giant blue dots then danced upon the exposed tissue of his brain, swallowing white matter like Pacman, a ghost, leaving scar tissue in its wake. He always awoke from the deepest of sleep (always seemed to be ten minutes before or after 2:00 a.m.) in a sticky, hot sweat at the cry of his own voice.

Sam felt what Billy felt when someone would notice Billy's unnatural walk or noticed a slight slur of speech. Since his accident, it took everything he had to put a sentence together. He had gotten to a point where he could carry on entire conversations, which was remarkable by his doctor's standards. But he had to think about it all the time. He had to really contemplate which word he would say next in order to get his brain started on pronouncing and annunciating. Sometimes he would slip and forget or his brain would just grow plain tired of the thinking process, and an obvious clumsy slur of words would spew from his mouth. He could see it in their eyes; people noticed, although they liked to pretend they did not.

One of the means Sam used in comforting himself when it came to the damage he and the Perpetrators inflicted on Billy was the tremendous progress he was reported to have made. *Billy is pretty much normal now, isn't he?* Now he knew better. He saw now all of the effort it took on a daily basis to appear normal. If he could get through twenty-four hours without a slur or stumble, it was a good day.

Of all of this, nothing hurt Billy more than to watch football on TV and dream about what could have been. It was his muse, his passion. One of the only things he was good at, a natural at. Sam robbed him of that too.

And so the salt continued to burn and pulsate in Sam's gaping, oozing wounds—the pain great, the sorrow deep, and the future hopeless.

CHAPTER

35

The most foul and destructive of drinks are often the ones we crave the most, for they are the ones most intoxicating. Some drinks are mixed so sour it can seek the toughest, most callused of scar tissue and rip it anew—a fresh wound left oozing for all infection to huddle and abound all the more dreadful than before.

~

Just as quickly as Warnic's story finished, a grueling tale, Chris Fesonmer's saga of illicit repute, began.

Juvenile Hall was never intended for a boy such as Chris Fesonmer. He stood out as one to be taunted, teased, mocked, beaten, and even raped. It seemed that all his life he spent trying to dismiss a variety of vicious rumors spread about him and his sexuality, to no avail. After only his fifth day of incarceration, he was violently yanked from his bunk, by someone his senior, and taken by force.

People have various ways in which to deal with traumatic experiences in life. All sorts of clever methods are often utilized with the goal to move on, overcome, and be the better for it. Some never overcome. Chris fell under the latter.

He lacked the upper body strength and street smarts to defend himself. Chris's wits and creativity lay in the field of clothing design. If you needed something sewed or hemmed or just overall advice when it came to clothing, Chris would be glad to help you out. Those were things that sparked his interest, not fist fighting. He designed his entire closet of clothes and liked to wear awkward-designed fashion with bright, loud colors, and so often polka dots played a big part. To say he didn't fit the norm one would come to expect from a regular heterosexual boy would be an understatement. Girls would flock to him for advice on tips in clothing, and although often surrounded by an entourage of females, there was not one he could call his girlfriend.

At one point, Chris's father asked if he would like to sign up for Karate classes (perhaps he knew his boy was kind of on the feminine side; perhaps he knew his boy was vulnerable, lacking basic self-defense instincts; perhaps this worried him). But Chris showed no interest in the Asian arts of self-defense, and his father wasn't the type to force anything on him.

He could not fight them off. When one had his way with Chris, the news spread so that other teenage sodomites felt free to do likewise. When Chris could no longer put up a fight, he would bury his face in his arms and cry until it was over.

This went on for a dreadful three months. Things all changed when Ryan Carver arrived to serve his time and shared Chris's space. Ryan was in for murder. He'd killed his stepfather after he tired of being beaten and sexually molested. Chris felt very uneasy in his presence but never thought he had a reason to fear Ryan; after all, Chris was harmless and had no intent on molesting anyone, let alone Ryan Carver. Ryan was built like a young bodybuilder, and Chris felt very lucky to be befriended by him, the rapists leaving him well enough alone in his presence.

After a couple of weeks of relative quiet, Ryan began to show signs that he was no different from the others in his sick cravings. What he desired, he would not take by force. Chris's first reaction was to throw his arms across his face to protect himself from a beating that never came. Ryan did not want to hurt Chris but to nurture, build trust, and then eventually have Chris give it up of his own free will through constant clever manipulations. His natural God-given morality screamed, "No, this is wrong!" But another voice he could not shake did make sense, "What harm could it serve if I were to give to him what he wants than to try and fight him off over something he could take by force anyway?"

It seemed that all his teenage life he had been labeled a queer, and he fought it tooth and nail. But in this situation, he could fight it no longer. He began to ponder that maybe his high school knew Chris better than he knew himself.

"Maybe I am gay. Maybe I have always been gay. Maybe I only thought I liked girls."

By the time Chris's sentence was served, nearly eighteen, he left Juvenile Hall a dedicated homosexual.

～

Sam wasn't one of those guys who would continually rape him, and he wasn't even one who would mock or verbally slander, but he did introduce Billy to Chris. While Billy Warnic's affliction rested heavily on his shoulders, Chris Fesonmer's sins stained red on his hands.

CHAPTER

36

How dedicated Parker Emerson was in trying to share the gospel of Jesus Christ with Samuel. Sam shouted out into a dimension where he could not be heard.

"Listen to him, you fool!" Sam never did listen, not even once. Whenever hearing the name of Jesus, he would shut down faster than a virgin on prom night. For some reason, Parker liked him and would tolerate Sam's candor even when he'd sometimes become physically threatening. Sam did not understand Parker's need to share, he did not understand the light in his eyes, he did not understand joy in trial, and he definitely could not fathom how it was he was responsible for the death of his old friend.

There were times (as with all of us) when Parker went through rough, trying seasons in life, and when things got really bad Parker would tend to think of Sam. How would Sam—Joe cool—react in this situation?

The answer was drinking. He would hit a bar or liquor store and feebly try to drown his problems away in alcoholic bliss. It never worked. Parker was not a drinker as much as he would like to have been at times. In the long run, he would usually return to what he knew best, and that was attending church services. God was his only faithful refuge. Getting involved in the things of God, seeking God in times of trial and hardships was his only true comfort.

It took a good five years post Marcy before he finally found that special someone. He found her and married her, and she bore him two little girls.

"Wow, Parker is a husband and daddy." Sam almost couldn't believe his eyes, but he was proud of Parker and the life he created for himself. If anyone deserved it, it was him.

It turned out Parker's wife was one Sam had sold a car to. That occurred four years before. She was an Asian woman by the name of Bonnie. She was of American decent with beautiful, long jet-black hair reaching down to the small of her back. Sam had no idea her husband was Parker any more than she knew Sam was an old lost friend to her husband. If Sam had known that, he would have set her up with a sweet ride instead of that old lemon he sold her. That was what Sam told himself, but come to think of it, even knowing Bonnie was Parker's wife was not a guarantee that he would not have turned his tricks. Maybe it would have been on a smaller scale, but the tricks would have been turned; that was a given. It was almost as if he couldn't help it; it was second nature to him, anything to earn that extra buck and to outsell Jill Esterhouse.

It wasn't Sam's fault entirely. The car was running well at the time he sold it to her. If it had been taken to a mechanic to be inspected thoroughly, maybe the accident would have never happened. But the fact was Sam knew there were better cars in her price range he could have showed her. Sure the car needed some fixing up; most used cars did. That was not the car salesman's duty. When the car was officially purchased, it was the sole responsibility of the owner to take care of it. How could Sam be responsible for the death of Parker?

He owned three high-price cars that ran well. Bonnie wanted a fourth she could run errands in, something simple like a Ford Escort. Parker died two years ago, leaving behind his widow and two little girls, Cadney, five, and Kristin, two. The Escort was being used by Parker one spring day to pick up a gallon of milk to float dry fruit loops with at the general grocery store when on the way home doing sixty on the freeway the car died without warning. This caused a domino effect of unsuspecting vehicles to collide one on top of another. Parker was crushed on the bottom and died instantly.

Considering all he had to do was show Bonnie a better, more reliable car to avert Parker's death, Sam wept bitterly. It did dawn on him that now, Parker being dead, he might get to see him again, apologize profusely, and make things right, becoming friends in the afterlife. His spirit reminded him that Parker was where he was supposed to be and he was going where he was supposed to be, and they were two very different places.

CHAPTER

37

The veil that Sam had been wearing the entirety of his life, causing acute blindness to spiritual things, had now been removed. Witnessing angelic warfare in all of its hostilities, furious, benevolent warriors of God stood firm against the onslaught of malevolent creatures of hate. That old serpent the devil in battle with the use of his minion demons were enticing, luring, and beckoning Sam into enjoying all matter of delights of flesh, creating disaster, hardships, vexations, and tribulations mixed with such a feeling of empty abandonment, leaving him holding a load too heavy to carry alone. He was a lonely man.

Like a drug addict forever chasing the wind, finding a faulty sense of security in the life style chosen, his appetite for pleasure was never satisfied, seeking what couldn't be found in sin. Oh, how crafty the devil, and how easy it was for him to entice mankind. Howbeit, the dark was very much aware of how zealous and long-suffering God was in pursuing Sam. Therefore, they fought harder.

Such a variety of ways and methods God used to intervene and save Sam much pain and heartbreak. God was willing that none should perish but that all should come to the knowledge of Jesus Christ, his main desire being for him to be welcomed into his kingdom, a homecoming not yet realized. Sam would not have it. The church of Samuel Reed had spoken. And so it shall be.

The pages turned, and his heart was exposed. He could not count the many women he had sinned with and wronged in so many different ways. Funny thing was, he had always looked at himself as the one who had been wronged by women. But now he could see he was the one at fault more often than not. How many women did he coerce into trusting him, loving him, and opening up to him? Not only did he deceive a countless amount of women, but he also deceived himself. He deceived himself into believing the lies he dished out on an ordinary basis.

He saw it now as a defense mechanism. If he were to believe the lies he told, then it's not really lying, is it? You're not really lying if you believe it yourself, right? And if he's not intentionally lying how can it be wrong? The depths of self-deceit knew no bounds.

～

He saw Kate Suswan, otherwise known as Barbie. She was just a normal private investigator out doing her job. Someone Sam had burned had gotten a hold of her from the phone book and put her on the case.

Sam could barely remember Liz Hartley. It was because his autopilot of deception was put on cruise control. His manipulative ways were second nature. He never had to think of it. Just do it; just react. Sam reeled in Liz hook, line, and sinker and overcharged her for a 1999 Mercury Cougar.

Liz had family in the car dealership business, and they were looking out for her. They were on to Sam's tricks immediately (they probably used them on others themselves). Liz was not one to be taken advantage of, and Kate Suswan was not one to allow people to be taken advantage of. She loved her job, and to nail someone as crafty as Sam made her job more than worthwhile. It

worked out perfectly; she nabbed Sam easily, on tape and everything. It was almost too easy.

He abruptly left his job as a result, not wanting to give Mr.
Carlton a chance to fire him, and here it was the end of life as he
knew it. He jumped the chasm. Sam cringed watching his head
bash a boulder, and that was all she wrote…wasn't it?

He was unconscious; that was easy enough to see. His chest
inhaled and exhaled in a steady rhythm. "I'm still alive…or I was
still alive. What happened?" He didn't rise to his feet and move
on like he thought he remembered. He lay there bleeding, with
no one around to help.

CHAPTER

38

Josh Flenty recognized the hostile aggravation beginning to fester in his father's heart. He was becoming short tempered, snapping at the slightest provocation, and his voice was beginning to take on a "go ahead, piss me off, *I dare you*" attitude.

What a shame. Our little camping trip to the mountains was going so well, Josh thought. No point in sticking around and being the object of wrath unleashed. Josh would leave just in time with bucket in hand, rocks, sticks, and sand rattling the bottom. A little home for his soon-to-be bug collection. No time like the present to get started. He hated to leave his mother alone with his father in such a state, but there was just no point in the both of them having mysterious bruises to explain to peers. Josh, being only ten, dreamed of the day when he would be older and stronger and hero to his battered mother. Sam was reminded of Marcus Stiney and how a very similar situation landed him in prison. If Josh's father was not careful, he could very well end up deceased. You don't mess with a boy's mother.

He traveled far, toward the sound of rushing waters, picking up whatever bug he could find on the way. His main goal was to get out of range of how far sound could carry the voice of his yelling dad and crying mom. Maneuvering his way around a Stonehenge-like gathering of large boulders next to the chasm, he almost tripped right over the unconscious, bleeding man. He stood frozen for time unknown before dropping his bucket, bugs running free, and high-tailing it back the way he came.

"Da's a man…he beeding… I think he's dead." Josh's words came out tangled.

"What you trying to say, boy?" his father asked as if looking for a reason to smack him.

"There's a man… I was looking for bugs. He's laying down, and theirs blood coming from his head."

Josh's father took two angry steps closer. Josh knew what was coming and was already flinching as his father gave him the expected backhanded smack across the face, splitting his lower lip. Josh stood up to this rather well, and his mother noticed the difference. There was something very urgent Josh was trying to say. Her face was already stained with tears, having to do with whatever it was Josh walked in on. She threw her body in front of Josh.

"Bob, something happened to him. What are you trying to say, honey…slow down."

Bob Flenty also noticed there was something different about Josh, so he relented, paying closer attention to what Josh was trying to say.

"I was looking for bugs for my collection. I saw a man laying on the ground in his own blood. I think he might be dead."

Josh's mom's eyes became wide with fright. She knew Josh could not be lying; she had never seen him shake like this before. Bob firmly grabbed hold of his boy's arm.

"Boy, you better not be lying. You know what's going to happen to you if you are."

Josh nodded his head. "Yes, sir."

He did know what would happen to him. He had been locked in the closet more times than he cared to remember, and so had his mother. Unless the injured man got up and walked away,

Josh did not think he would have to worry about that, at least not today.

"Take me to him, boy. Martha, you stay here."

"He might need a first aid kit. Maybe you should bring...." Martha trailed off; what she said Josh could not decipher. Not that it would have mattered. Josh was in his father's control.

Josh hurried as fast as his ten-year-old body would allow, but his legs lagged at times, always followed by a crude kick in the rear by his very impatient father.

"Hurry it, boy. Don't be holding me up."

For one terrifying moment, Josh could not find his way back to the bleeding man. There was no question of the dire consequences soon to pay.

"Where's this body at, boy? You better not be ..." It was then Josh noticed familiar territory. The chasm presented itself upon the turning of a corner.

"It's this way," Josh said with great relief.

"Well, I'll be damned."

The fact that he was still breathing was the first thing Josh noticed; the second was that the blood was beginning to coagulate. Bob checked for a pulse and found a faint trace of life.

"He's alive. Hey, buddy...you okay? Hey, buddy," Bob said poking, Sam's damaged, unresponsive body with one finger.

"We need to get some help for this dude and quick."

"Is he gonna die, Daddy?"

"Now, how the hell am I supposed to know that, Josh? I'll tell you this, if we don't get him some help, he's gonna die."

Josh gazed the contours of his father's face and light of his eyes for any sign, no matter how miniscule, that this man might live. He did not read this, but what he did read was hard to interpret in this predicament. Greed. Suddenly Bob ripped off Sam's backpack like it was gold he had strapped on his back and emptied it in a mad frenzy.

"Daddy, no!"

"Shut your mouth, boy. Daddy is only looking out for his family."

Josh did not understand this, but he knew when it was time to keep quiet. Daddy didn't seem to find much to his liking in the man's backpack except a flashlight he kept for himself.

Now I know why I couldn't find my flashlight on the second night, Sam remembered.

Daddy then, to Josh's horror, flipped the injured man over and began digging in his pockets. Josh had to bite his tongue from crying out.

And now I know why I was facing upward when I came to. But how can this be? I died there. I never came to.

Bob pulled out Sam's wallet, but to his dismay there was no money to take. No paper money anyways. He helped himself to Sam's credit cards. He left Sam's driver's license in place and proceeded to put Sam's wallet back where he took it from now that he retrieved something of value.

"Boy, you best keep your mouth shut about this or you'll get what's coming to ya. Do you hear me?"

"Ye…yes, Daddy."

"Now I'm going to get this dude some help. I can't depend on you to come with me. You can't keep up. This man is dying, and you would only serve to slow me down. So you got to stay put."

"But, Daddy…"

"What have I told you about 'buts'? You do as I say. If this man dies, it will be your fault. Do you want that, boy? Do you want to be responsible for that dude's death?"

"No, Daddy."

"You stay right here like a big boy and keep an eye on him. You'll be fine. I'll be back."

Josh could only hope Daddy was telling the truth. He had been lied to before on a number of occasions by his father. Like when Bob had told him he'd be right there, at 2:30 p.m. sharp to pick him up from school. Daddy never arrived but instead got himself nice and toasted at Jimmy's, the local pub. Mrs. Howard had been home a few hours since school let out. As she was on her way to indulge in her nightly workout at Abb's gym, she just so happened to catch Josh Flenty sitting alone, doodling in the sand. He was awaiting a drunken father who was in the midst of slapping the fannies of young waitresses.

She was able give Josh a ride home and give his mother an earful at her workplace for trusting Josh to the care of an alcoholic.

Josh's mind began to imagine unthinkable terror as he gazed upon this dying man. What if the man suddenly reached out his hands toward Josh and said, "Help me"? What would Josh do besides wet himself? What could he do? He was just a boy. What if the man's eyes suddenly opened and stared at Josh in an insane, demonic gaze. What if the man tried to grab him? Josh was well out of the man's reach, but these thoughts caused him to back away even further. But the man remained motionless as fresh blood continued to stain the ground he lay upon.

After waiting what might have been an hour, but what felt like ten, he wanted so badly to go back to his campsite and embrace the comfort of his mother, but he thought it was possible that Dad got Mom on his way to get help. She might not be there any longer. He decided to stay put as uncomfortably terrifying as it might be.

He thought he was imagining it at first, but this was all too real. The man began to make gurgling sounds from somewhere deep in his throat, and his eyes began to flutter.

"Please don't wake up, mister," Josh spoke quietly, fear restricting volume. In spite of his request, the man's eyes opened and stared at Josh with brief clarity, and his lips mouthed something before his eyes closed for good.

That was too scary to actually have happened, but it did. Josh was paralyzed in fear and did not move for how long? He could not say, as he had every right to be as scared as one would expect from a child in such a situation. A man at death's door was staring him down. What freaked him out even more was the implication that the man attempted to say his name, Josh, before the lights flickered out. *How does he know my name? It's not possible.* That was something that would haunt his dreams for years to come.

When he was finally able to exhale and slow his pulse, he noticed a damp sensation soaking his inner thighs. He wasn't sure what it was until the all too unpleasant stench of urine hit his nose. He had heard that under extreme levels of fear sometimes people would have an accident. Josh could never understand that. How could fear suddenly give a person the bladder of a senior citizen? Now he knew all too well the power of fear and that it could do this.

Sam felt really bad for Josh. He never intended to frighten such a fragile child, conscious or unconscious. But more than that, he felt bad for Josh having an abusive jerk for a father.

Josh's father did return with a handful of paramedics. It took three and a half hours for help to arrive to this remote location. He did have a little endurance for situations like this; being locked in a dark closet from time to time did help Josh develop some coping skills. Sam watched as his body was being airlifted in a helicopter en route to the nearest hospital. He had never flown before and found it rather ironic that it would come about en route to his deathbed.

CHAPTER

39

Sam observed nurses, orderlies, and the head doctor in emergency mode checking vitals, EKG, and administrating I.V. Critical Sam would not respond to any stimuli but rather indulged in a coma-induced fantasy where rednecks chopped trees, a frightened little boy named Josh requested he not wake up, cherry trees and firewood appeared from nowhere, and a mansion not of this earth, with untold mysteries behind every door, were the new reality.

He had many visitors, and aside from Mom and Dad, Mr. Carlton was a constant. Even though Sam resigned himself to an eternity in hell, he felt comfort in Mr. Carlton praying for him. It was a kind of inner peace he could not understand, so it would be pointless to try to make sense of.

Sometimes Mr. Carlton was alone, sometimes with church members. One lonesome morning he was in tears crying out, "Dear God, have mercy on his soul." It broke Sam's heart to see Mr. Carlton in such a mess. Tears stained a trail down both sides of his chubby cheeks. Even when Carlton was alone he was never really alone. Sam recognized the man who gave him strength. He'd seen him holding Mr. John Carlton up once before, but he couldn't make out who he was. His eyes were open now, and that could only be the Son of the living God. His faithful servant was in much pain and travail. Jesus would always be there in such a time to hold him up, whether Mr. Carlton knew it or not.

"Please, God, bring him out of this, but, Lord, if it be your will to take him, then I pray you receive him into your kingdom."

Sam's spirit wept along with Mr. Carlton. He wept more on behalf of him and his sorrow than he was for himself.

"Please, God, receive me into your kingdom!" Sam shouted.

Mr. Carlton continued, "God, forgive me for not bringing him to church. I should have tried harder."

"It's not your fault!" Sam screamed into a dimension where no cross contact was permitted.

He saw women he had hurt and women who had hurt him crying profusely. Sam wondered why it was that death, or being near death, had ways of making saints of us all. A previous girl friend, Tanya, whose last words were, "I'll see you in hell," was unable to control her emotions as she embraced with Sam's mother and a downpour of tears fell.

Sam's father, Marvin Reed, shouted at Sam in his coma out of desperation. "Samuel, wake up! Sam…Sammy, please…this is your father. Come back to us!" Sam recognized this scene. He caught a tiny fragment of it back when he inhaled that mist left behind by those black, demonic figures that circled and fled. At the time, he thought it was all a powerful hallucination. It was real. All too painfully real. No symbolism involved whatsoever.

Time being of no consequence in Sam's new existence, he could not tell if it had been days or months that had transpired, but he was happy to see his folks were spending more time talking with Mr. Carlton's church. Like a dream, both of them bowed their heads and closed their eyes while all church members laid hands on them.

"What's this? Are they praying? Could my atheist parents possibly be praying?"

CHAPTER

40

Like a flash of lightning, the flick of a switch, or the blink of an eye, Sam found himself somewhere dank, drab, dry, and awful. In an instant, he went from witnessing his parents about to open up to something so wonderful he was sure to cry huge walloping tears of joy on their behalf to looking upon solid bars of rust, like that of a prison cell, breathing in an entirely new atmosphere where air was toxic and thin. He wasn't really breathing, per se, but gasping for tiny gulps of putrefied air.

Directly across, he saw more cells all the same 8-x-10-feet dimensions as his own, stacked one on top of another, reaching a skyscraper distance in height. Each cell had one above, one below, and one crammed on every side like a library of books stacked horizontal. The number of cells was beyond calculable, each with one single human occupant. There was a black, pressing darkness that could be felt enclosing, like one in a vise. He wanted to shake it off as he would an uninvited Charlie horse, but the black remained, pressing heavier still.

In the middle of this great circle of cells permeating from solid ground blazed a great fire emanating torrid heat. This fire gave just enough light for the cells to be seen and situation evaluated.

A poisonous and noxious smell absorbed into every pore, a toxic mix of sulfur and carnage, and physically would have killed any living soul no matter how well the shape of his cardiovascular system. Sam soon found there was no death in what could only have been hell. *This is forever, this is forever, this is forever*, replayed over and over in his desperate thoughts.

Echoing off the stoic walls and taunting bars of bleeding rust were the most terrifying, screeching screams of bitter physical pain and everlasting emotional hopelessness. The screams were deafening, sounding to Sam like a million vehicles all at once slamming on breaks, skidding down an endless road of perdition. These sounds never faded or dulled but remained at optimum level, each soul failing in facilitating their inflictor's wrath. In the cell directly across from him, he saw that even though the occupant was alone, he was not alone. Two creatures of enormous girth tormented the man. Sam knew without being told these creatures were an offshoot of the one they served, their father, Satan, which would make them demons. One stood at thirteen feet tall; the other was a skimpy nine feet. He could not make out their features from his distance, but he could imagine the rage in their eyes as one bashed the man's head into the cell floor while the other feasted on the man's left arm. To the amusement of his captors, the man screamed, cried, and begged for pity. They only laughed and egged him on in his worthless pleas.

The flames reached to the highest cell and beyond. Sam began to decipher that not all screams came from cells, but a great majority of these cries came from the flames themselves. That's when he began to see within the fire shapes and forms of human beings thrashing about. *Oh my God, there are people in there.* Thousands or millions, he could not say, feeling every bit the skin-eating-burn fire desires.

They crawled and pushed with every bit of weakening strength toward the embankment away from the center of earth where ground boiled, but this endeavor too was hopeless, for demons circled the pit's embankment, pushing anyone successful enough to reach right back in where they began.

Sam knew without knowing how everyone's sin as if written on their person, everything exposed and nothing hidden. Everyone there had in one way or another exalted self over the one and only supreme God and made a mockery of the sacrifice of his precious Son through their denials, rejections, and idolatries.

There were people there who were very good, caring people by man's standards, and if these were the standards by which justification were rooted, the path to righteousness would be wide indeed. But man's righteousness had the filthy stain of sin, and in itself there was no good thing. Jesus, having bridged the gap to God that sin left in its wake, made salvation as easy as one confession that Jesus is Lord and that God raised him from the dead. That made the avoidance of this living hell a reality—and an eternity where no mind could conceive the glory God had in store for those who love him, a promise.

A woman, a devout Muslim the majority of her life, who took great delight in mocking and belittling the divinity of Christ and those who worshipped him and the price paid for her on the cross, in her cell found herself nailed to a cross, gasping for air. She elevated her body against the large nail, shredding the flesh of her feet every time she pushed up to inhale that tiny gulp of rancid air that permeated the great cauldron. Her back was raw with splinters, and her wrists bared the weight of her 160-pound frame. Always feeling on the brink of death but never quite getting there, she was reaping what she sowed, an unpardonable truth that lived on in eternity.

Another man had sexually molested and murdered five innocent children sometime in the early part of the nineteenth century. He continually had his genitals mutilated and throat slit by the claws of his tormentors, and he begged for death over and over, but his violations never ceased and never would. He felt all of the pain, sadness, and fear of death his victims did in all of its detriment. These children were with Jesus now in complete, perfect peace and happiness, while this man, forever chained to the flame, sought insanity as a means of escape, but it was not forthwith to come.

Five different incubus of the most violent sort fulfilled their sickest desires through means of malignant intrusion, bringing back on the pedophile the rape he dished out on precious children.

A geyser of lava shot up in his space, disintegrating his eyes in his head and tongue in his mouth even while he yet cried. All of this continually played out before the hellacious process started over again, forever and ever.

As far as Sam could make out, there were an unlimited amount of empty cells yet to be filled. About every five seconds a new soul was dropped into eternity's bowels to begin their sentence. Some fell into cells of black and others the heart of fire.

Sam's tongue stuck to the roof of his mouth, his body grown completely void of hydration. He longed for one single drop of water to cool his scorching tongue, but he now dwelled in the belly of dry places, where the gift of water had no place.

Had not Avah promised him that he would rule this place? Had not Shamir warned him the kingdom of darkness lied? Shamir spoke truth and always had, acting as guardian of Samuel Reed the entirety of his life. *If only I had listened*, Sam's thoughts condemned. Among the last of the lies Sam bought into was that he'd be reunited with his unbelieving parents, but he knew now that if his parents did end up there, it would only add to his penalty to see them in the agony of that place.

Just as Sam thought on this, like a close up on a camera lens, in the raging flames he saw his uncle Freddy Nosfer screaming in agony. Although Sam disagreed with his atheism, he always thought of him as a good man and missed him immensely after he'd lost his life at the hands of a drunk driver. Seeing him there hurt him deeply, but no longer did he see God as unjust. Everyone there, including himself, knew they belonged there. No one attempted to argue his or her way out. All had been revealed. There was absolutely no longer any doubt about it in his heart, mind, or soul—if this place did not exist, God would not, he could not, be just.

Uncle Freddy cried out to Sam, and somehow among all of the screams Sam heard him loud and clear.

"Sammy, don't come to this place!"

"Sammy, there is no way out!"

"Sammy, there is still time!"

"Sammy, there is no death!"

He shouted four times as Sam watched in horror his face melting and twisting in ways God did not intend.

Sam had stood in speechless, utter shock and trembled, only a tearful weep making any sound.

After seeing his beloved uncle in such a state, Sam began to scream from the deepest recesses of his diaphragm, joining the unholy chorus of the damned.

Sam felt it, the very second he was no longer alone. Something was there in the dark with him. He could hear the raspy breathing but could not see. It was moving slowly closer, as if sizing him up. Then he was finally able to make out two eyes of yellow, towering from about thirteen feet above.

Sam cried. He knew what was coming; he had seen such demons unleash furious hate on others in their cells, in such painful ways that his fear was beyond scale. As he trembled, the demon giggled. Sam was finally able to see this creature as he stood in the light of hell fire.

His body was reptilian in the same manner as Avah's, but Avah was miniscule in comparison to this great beast. He grinned something evil with his giant, protruding jaw and massive, chiseled teeth. His body was disgusting, with gashes, scales, and pulsating boils. He had claws that were very much the same in texture as the rest of his body and extended a foot long, his razor-sharp nails caked underneath with torn human flesh. He had something like a nose, breathing in brimstone-like air. Sam wished to hide from what he saw in his eyes. *Dear God, why does he hate me so?*

This is forever, this is forever, this is forever, his dreadful thoughts constantly tormented psychologically. Sam was backed into the blistering bars as the beast stretched out his festering neck, sniffing and inhaling the fear Sam permeated, like a snake readying to strike.

"You're mine," the beast taunted in a deep, guttural growl.

He closed his eyes in defense to the strong whiff of the beast's pungent breath. It smelled like he had been feasting on rotting flesh for time without end. Sam stood on the edge of losing it completely, as the beast lightly dragged his claws up and down his back.

"Jesus, please," Sam muttered under his breath. The demon flinched. It was oh so brief, and he covered it well, but Sam saw it. More than that, he felt it.

The demon became furious and shouted out great blasphemies in a language unknown and then, sticking a finger in his face, shouted, "He is dead!"

Sam could see how badly the demon wanted to hurt him, but as if a force field were separating them, he did not, as if he could not.

A pleasant and timely memory surfaced in Sam's mind. It was his first encounter with Shamir, his guardian, when he had said, "When in trouble, plead the blood of Jesus, for there is power in his name and life in his blood."

"The blood of Jesus," Sam muttered with a minute twinge of faith.

This time the beast took a full step backward, and his body began to show signs of trembling. This could be a sign of fear or of rage. Sam thought it was both.

"You denied him. The age of grace has ceased for you! He cannot help you now. That is why you are here." The beast's chest rose in fury. Sam's miniscule measure of faith was completely crushed at the demons accusation.

Many instances of Sam doing just that flooded his memories as he dropped his head, downcast. The demon roared a bellowing laugh, knowing he had bested Sam, allowing his own sins to find him out.

"You are a glutton in your lust for women. This is a deadly sin, Samuel. Have you not heard? Not only this, but you have broken every one of the Ten Commandments." In reading Sam's face, the demon saw tremendous guilt with a bit of confusion, so he took liberty and delight in pointing out how he had broken all of God's law, taking him step by step through the Ten Commandments.

1. You have served yourself as your own god. *Thou shall have no other gods before me.*

2. You idolize success in your life. This is your engraved image. *Thou shall not make for yourself any graven image.*

3. You have taken the Lord's name in vain 2,688 times. *Thou shall not take the Lord's name in vain.*

4. Never have you kept the Sabbath holy, never once placing your foot inside a church. *Thou shall keep the Sabbath holy.*

5. Although you love your parents, you have not always shown them honor. *Honor thy father and mother.*

6. You hate your coworker, Jill Esterhouse, for outselling you at your place of work. Did not Jesus call this murder? *Thou shall not kill.*

7. You commit adultery in your heart with every woman that strikes your fancy. *Thou shall not commit adultery.*

8. You watch television every day with cable you have not paid for. You are a thief. *Thou shall not steal.*

9. And as I have already mentioned, you've lied to your parents as a child, you lie to your boss as an adult, and you lie to all the women you promised to love. Your lies know no bounds. *Thou shall not lie.*

10. And alas, you covet every woman you want but cannot have. *Thou shall not covet.*

"Samuel, that is every commandment transgressed. Yet, you have the gall to call on the Christ when he is the one who has condemned. He cannot help you now!"

With every accusation hailed, the demon bathed in pride while creeping his way back into Sam's space. What could Sam do? Everything the demon had said was true. God's law had been defiled time and time again. *Guilty, guilty, guilty.*

Excruciating pain brought Sam to his knees as the demon thrust his claw into the virgin back of Sam and twisted and turned. He cried in agony.

"You think you know pain. I will show you pain." The demon grinned. "We have only just begun," he said as he gnawed upon Sam's left shoulder.

He couldn't tell if it were a result of delirium or if a meaning was involved, but he saw a vision of a lost sheep. It was the same lost sheep he saw in his dream on the first night camping up Mount Kinley. Ironic that the meaning of that dream would become clear in such a horrific state of being.

I was the sheep on my way to hell, and Jesus was the good shepherd trying to show me the right way. He thought on how the sheep had bit him (Jesus) when he was only trying to save him/her. Even so, the shepherd loved the sheep and would not relent. Alas, the sheep of its own freewill chose damnation.

Sam thought about one day when he was twelve years old, with the street witness, Louis. *I was so close to confessing Christ as my savior just like Melvin did. I was going to do it; it was in my heart.* A distant memory of Parker Emerson appeared in Sam's mind of him countering Sam's statement about God knowing that he was a good man at heart. Parker said God knew that the heart was deceitful above all things. Sam rationalized in his thoughts, *If God knows the bad in the heart, then it makes sense that he would also know the good. He has to know that in my heart I already said the sinner's prayer (isn't that what it's called?) along with Melvin. In my heart of hearts, I know I did.*

He continued to keep his eyes closed tightly, afraid to see what the demon was concocting, when suddenly, in his mind's eye, like the crawl on the bottom of a TV screen, Scripture appeared. It was one of the exact same scriptures Louis had quoted on that fateful night:

> My sheep listen to my voice; I know them, and they follow me. I give them eternal life, and they shall never perish; no one can snatch them out of my hand. My father, who has given them to me, is greater than all; no one can snatch them out of my father's hand.
>
> John 10:27-29 (NIV)

A cautious joy began to develop in his heart as he juggled the pain of his shredded back and shoulder with a new developing revelation. *If this is true, I can never perish. God is holding me in his hand, and he will never let me go.* His rational side asked a logical question: *If this is so, what am I doing here?* He had no answer. Sam replayed the very recent memory of the flinch of the demon when he had first said the name of Jesus. *Not only that, but did the demon not tremble upon the second time I said that name? Shamir said there is power in his name. I believe there is.*

"Now, Samuel, you will suffer for your sins."

"I am forgiven of my sins."

"By what authority?" the beast asked in a coarse, snipping fashion.

"Jesus forgave me when I was twelve."

Oh, how he laughed at Sam's insolence.

"Tell me then, Samuel, why are you here?"

"I am not sure, but I know I am forgiven."

With every reply, the demon's wrath grew to the point that Sam almost couldn't tell what was said, his growl becoming deeper and muffled. This made no difference; Sam understood him in his spirit.

"There is no place for you in God's heaven, for you would defile it through and through."

It sounded logical and true, but Sam stood steadfast.

"I am forgiven!"

"Stop saying that!" The beast wanted to annihilate him, he could feel it, but again, it was as though Sam was protected. "God can never forgive you. You are filth and out of his reach. You are mine!"

"No one can snatch me out of his hand!"

"You are a dreamer. Give it up. You are mine!"

There is power in his name. There is power in his name. This is no longer something he was dabbling with; he now believed it with all of his heart.

The creature reached out his giant arms with claws in position to slaughter as Samuel Reed exclaimed with full faith and authority, "In the name of Jesus Christ, Satan, I command you, leave me!"

Sam felt the wind of claws pass by and over as the demon became no more.

CHAPTER

41

Dr. Baker was thankful to have such an experienced staff working beneath him the night Samuel Reed in room 2A stopped breathing. "Code Blue 2A" echoed down the hospital's halls as a crash cart was called for. He had been technically dead for seven minutes and forty-two seconds before a pulse was found. Just like that he was thrust from the great beyond back into his coma.

The doctor wanted just as much as his praying friends and family to see a happy ending to this saga that had tarried on for close to five months. He thought it odd for Sam to have such a setback, considering that he had been responding to minor stimuli, which usually was an indication that the patient might be on the crux of emerging.

He thought the prayers of Blessed Hope on every Wednesday had been working. He hoped, most sincerely, that they were. When informing Mr. Carlton of Sam's cardiac arrest, he simply responded, "Looks like we're going to have to pray harder."

Dan continued to be amazed at such faith. Amazed but not without understanding. He got it now. It had all started with this small but dedicated church that radiated love like a rose, a pleasant smell, in full bloom.

He wanted what they had, for he had a taste of it every time they had prayed. It had become a frequent occurrence that someone would request to lay hands and pray for him. He tried to resist that at first, always pretending his presence was needed elsewhere. After a while, he began to enjoy their prayers and even looked forward to it. He began to recognize the presence of the Holy Spirit and had difficulty explaining to himself why he should resist love incarnate.

"How do I…um…become a…um…Christian? Is there a certain amount of money I need to give to your church, because I could run to the bank real quick…" Dr. Dan asked Pastor Jerry Renolds.

The pastor smiled big and rested an arm around the doctor's shoulders and chuckled. "Forgive me. I'm not laughing at you. I'm laughing because God is good. Oh, he is so good. What you have asked is the sweetest question that can be uttered. Like honey to my ears. Praise Jesus."

"You have something I don't have, and I want it. I think I need it, and I know it is good because I can feel it. I feel it every time you pray, and it is very real."

"Hallelujah! A seed was planted, and now spring has arrived in your heart. In answer to your question, no. No money is required, my friend. It is a free gift."

"But I am such a bad person. I sin all of the time. I'm sure I have to do or give something." Dr. Dan Baker removed his glasses, unable to hold back tears of guilt.

"No, Doctor, the only thing you have to give is your heart. Jesus did the rest on the cross. Your debt of sin has been paid in full.

"Listen, Doctor…"

"Call me Dan."

"Dan, repeat after me. Father, please forgive me my sins, for I have broken your laws and have been separated from you. Help me to turn away from my sinful life. I believe that your Son, Jesus

Christ, died for my sins, was resurrected from the dead, is alive, and hears my prayer. I invite Jesus to become the Lord of my life, to rule and reign in my heart from this day forward. Please send your Holy Spirit to help me understand your Word and to do your will all the days of my life. In Jesus's name I pray. Amen."

Dan felt like a heavy, burdensome weight had been lifted from his shoulders. A sense of freedom and joy tickled his heart. He didn't know whether to laugh or cry, so he did both.

Jerry walked Dan into room 2A where the church had been praying for Samuel and announced, "Hey, everyone, guess who just received Christ as Savior?"

The room broke out in uproarious shouts of praise and applause, so much so that nurses had to drop what they were doing to check in on the commotion.

Dan walked directly to Maggie Reed and said, "You were right about me. Thank you for your prayers. Thanks be to all of you."

Everyone took a turn in hugging and welcoming him to the family of God. Mr. Carlton declared, "God truly does work in mysterious ways."

"How do you mean?"

"If it wasn't for the unfortunate condition of Sam, you'd still be lost in your sins."

The joy that had been doing cartwheels in Dan's heart suddenly took a backseat to the condition of his patient.

"I wish there was more I could do."

"Ya know, Doc, there is."

"No, you don't understand. I've done all I can do. I've taken him as far as medicine will allow. In light of his recent cardiac arrest, there is no telling if Sam will pick up where he left off in his progress or sink back deep into that comatose nether world. I hate to say it, but as long as he went without oxygen, there is just no telling if he will ever be the same, even if he does come back."

Marvin Reed embraced his wife upon hearing this. "No, Doc, you don't understand. You're a believer now."

Pastor Jerry flipped the pages of the Bible until he found what he was looking for. "You see, Dan, right here in Mark, 'and these signs shall follow those that believe; in my name they shall cast out devils, they shall speak with new tongues, they shall take up serpents, and if they drink any deadly thing it shall not hurt them, they shall lay hands on the sick and they shall recover.'"

Dan did not understand what all of that met, but immediately he understood what Jerry was getting at when he read that last sentence, "They shall lay hands on the sick, and they will recover."

"Does that mean what it says?"

"It sure does. God has been in the business of healing the sick a lot longer than modern medicine, that's for sure," Mr. Carlton said, followed by many amens.

"Is this why I always see you guys laying hands on him?"

"You got it. You have to be a doer of the Word, not just a hearer," a lady exclaimed, coming from somewhere in the back.

A childlike excitement and an innocent growth in faith took Dr. Baker captive.

"I'd like to try."

"Sure thing, Dr. Dan. Just lay your hands on his head and pray from your heart."

CHAPTER

42

A radiant, all encompassing wave of living light shone down. Physically penetrating, like the finger of God, his cell became consumed, unable to retain the alchemy of such a force; it sucked away to nothing, leaving Sam naked and abandoned in this great expanse.

All of the underworld rattled on edge in fear that judgment had come early. Not only did those made in the image of God who missed the whole purpose of life while living suffer visions of all of hell cast into the lake of fire, but their tormentors did as well, as they all screamed in fear of what the glorious light might mean.

The second the light fell upon Sam he felt a gentle presence awaken his sleeping spirit, baptizing him with fire. He was lifted from his feet and drawn upward, toward the heart of the light, the heart of all existence.

He could see that his physical form looked horrid, like roadkill; although he had not been engulfed in flames, it was painfully apparent that he did not escape penetrating, skin melting heat. His mutilated body not only showed the stripes from the claws of the beast and bite marks on his shoulder, but welts and charring also.

As Sam was lifted from his feet, drawn into the light, he could see all light was coming from a giant circular-shaped opening. He felt so small and insignificant, like a speck of dust or hovering lint drawn into the sun. Back over his shoulder he could see the black of hell he was leaving behind and heard a faint echo of screams exiting his ears. Upon drawing closer, he could see the opening as a tunnel. Looking along the length of it, he could see what could only be the source of all light and pondered if that was the end of the universe or if it was merely a beginning. He watched in utter amazement as a wave of radiance leapt off the source and touched him. All the terror that had strangled his soul departed in an instant as he exuded warmth and comfort, bathed in living light.

Rays of substantial brilliant light flowed from the central core of all existence. *God is light*, Sam realized as he felt his spirit naked and all the filth of every sin exposed. Where he was going he was not worthy of. Feeling heart-wrenching guilt, he began to pull back and resist, when a wave of unconditional liquid love shot through him like the warm embrace of a mother to her newborn child.

Sam wept. "Lord, you can't love me. I have walked away from you. I have mocked you and cursed you and have lived my life indulging sin. You can't love me," Sam cried. Yet more rays of love and forgiveness caressed him tighter still.

He noticed his body was no longer the temporal wounded flesh-and-blood capsule he inhabited for thirty-five years but a transparent spirit emanating the very light that rested on him in waves.

Once having passed through the opening and the day's second tunnel, he moved at what had to be the speed of light. He transferred into the atmosphere of earth, about seven stories above ground, looking down upon magnificent waters and the land that separated them. *How great the hand of God*, Sam marveled. He thought upon Shamir, and in doing so, Shamir appeared in full angelic armor by his side.

All around the atmosphere, from the air itself, Sam saw movement but without being able to make out what it was his eyes spied. It was like millions of bugs scampering about, beneath a tightly fitted blue sheet, morphing air.

"Look, I will show you what you are looking at around you," Shamir said as he motioned with his hand from one side to the other. Sam's eyes were then opened to a multitude uncounted, legions of demons about serving their fathers purpose upon the earth.

"What is this?" Sam asked.

"This is the celestial realm of darkness that Satan and his demons inhabit. Demons come to the earth from this realm and cause all forms of destruction and wickedness on the race of men."

"How is it he has such power?"

"He is the prince of the power of the air and only has the power that man allows. From the beginning, his kingdom has been at work in deviating the plans of God and man through lying knowledge and foolhardy deceit. The fruits of which are destruction, death, and damnation."

"How can any man stand against this?"

Shamir waved his arm again from side to side, and Sam's eyes were this time opened to millions of beams of light shooting up from all over the earth into the third heaven.

"Do you see these beams of light, Samuel?"

"What does it mean?"

"These are the prayers of the saints to the Father."

Again Shamir waved his arms, and this time Sam saw great multitudes of angels responding to the prayers of the saints wherever required. The kingdom of darkness did its best in intercepting the prayers of the saints as they raged on in warfare against the servants of God. The angels had the advantage with their double-edged swords blazing fire, dressed in full armor; the only hope of the minions of Satan was to attack in numbers, for they wore no armor of defense and on offense only the sword of tongue.

In spite of such numbers, one prayer said in faith could send thousands a flight in retreat. Wherever on earth that prayer was void, demons gathered like flies and had their way in the affairs of man. Wherever prayer lacked, the kingdom of darkness ruled, but wherever prayers were said, the angels of God punished the dark with flames of holy fire. Sam was awakened to the importance in praying for the Father's will to be done on earth as it was in heaven. It was the one thing that kept God's Holy Spirit alive and well on planet earth. *God help us if it is ever removed.*

Sam knew without knowing how that this war would rage on until God saw it fit to send his Son a second time—this time not as servant but conquering king.

CHAPTER

43

To seize a moment while current is a fine art, one that is difficult and hard to master. First the moment must be recognized as significant, held on to, milked, cherished, and sucked dry of all its sweet, dripping nectar. Otherwise such a moment might slip through fingers, never manifesting its impact to be fully savored and shared by those aware.

~

Samuel and Shamir streaked across blue sky, leaving behind the boundaries of earth, and treaded where stars and planets spun, proud to view everything in all of creation perfectly set in its proper place in motion, like an architect admiring his design.

Sam gazed upon earth, overwhelmed by the beautiful blue ball that hung on nothing, circling the greater yellow ball of fire. Trillions of stars scattered all about the universe, every single one crafted by the hand of God, all for the purpose of facilitating life on our tiny blue planet. Try as he might, he could not comprehend all that his eyes beheld. Not just the magnificence of creation itself but the love behind it all, all so man could live comfortably in contentment with the Son of the living God on earth. All of this he has freely given us.

"It is all so beautiful."

"Samuel, now that you have seen the beauty of all of creation, it is the Father's desire for you to see more."

"What do you mean?"

"Close your eyes, Samuel."

Sam closed his eyes as bidden. Shamir rested his hand over his eyes for what felt like two seconds before Shamir said, "Now, Samuel, open your eyes and see."

Sam's feet were set upon gold in its purest form. "Is this heaven?" he asked as he found himself looking upon great mountains, giant vociferous trees, green grass, birds flying, and an incalculable amount of people enjoying the delights of an Eden-styled version of earth.

All of the various wild beasts of creation were friend to man and to each other. There, the lion truly did lie down with the lamb. Sam witnessed that it was God's good pleasure to reunite people with their long-lost pets of yesteryear. He never did own a dog, cat, or even so much as a miniscule hamster as a young lad, his parents never allowing flea-ridden varmints into the home. A large calico cat took the liberty to rub up against his leg, an exact replica of a cat he wanted and begged is farther for as a child but never got.

The topography here was very much like the earth he left behind, but it was new, unblemished, and undefiled by the filth of man. Everywhere he looked his senses were dazzled like a child witnessing the spark of fireworks for the very first time. The soothing, all-encompassing light that lifted him from the depths of smoldering earth ruled this place. *Everything is alive*, Sam realized. The trees, the grass, the hills, mountains, and even water itself permeated as living beings. This he could not explain in mortal words, but a glorious love exuded from all creation and testified of God's majesty to Sam's spirit, and he rejoiced from somewhere deep within.

People were reunited with their loved ones and to those who had spoken truth, showing the way to salvation. Sam's heart was glad to see such joy in the afterlives of so many, but deep inside there was a measure of sorrow, for he had come from a long line of agnostics and atheists. There would be none to greet him.

He looked upon the new body given him; no longer was he a capsule of flesh or a transparent spirit in transition but a spirit full of the light of heaven. He took on the form of man, with all distinguishing features and the very essence that was Samuel Reed. Upon his head sat a golden crown of salvation set with varied priceless gems, of which he felt unworthy of but was glad to have. He wore a dazzling white garment of humility, for truly he had been humbled. He was unable to shake the pestering perceived truth that he did not deserve to be there.

"You do deserve to be here."

The sound of this voice certainly did not match the tone he had become used to when spoken to by Shamir; he turned to face him, and nothing could have prepared him for the joyous surprise of seeing his old friend Parker Emerson.

"Parker!" Sam embraced Parker in a mutual hug for what felt like time without end. Although his joy was beyond scale in seeing his friend, Sam broke down in tears having remembered being responsible in a roundabout way for his physical death, stripping him of a life with wife and kids.

"I am so sorry, Parker. I am so sorry." Sam wept upon Parker's shoulder.

Parker held him at length, smiled, and said, "Sam, I forgive you."

"How can you? I've—"

"Sam, as Jesus has forgiven me, so do I forgive." He understood this. Because he had loved us first, we love him. Because he had forgiven us our sins, we can forgive. The both of them laughed from the joy in their hearts. Shamir had departed upon Parker's appearance, respecting God's plan for Parker to act as Sam's guide from then on.

Everyone there wore only the garment of humility, but Parker wore three garments. The first was the same white garment of humility that Sam wore, and on top of that was a long shiny garment known as the robe of righteousness. The final was a luxurious gift Jesus himself placed upon his shoulders: a sleeveless coat that came down to his knees and was set with all kinds of diamonds, rubies, and jewels known as the garment of praise. He was adorned like a king, the emeralds tantalizing Sam's eyes, and of course the same crown of salvation was set comfortably upon his head.

"This is where we all come after experiencing physical death. Those who acquire no treasure with the gifts God has given remain here, and those who have been faithful to plant seed and meet the needs of their fellow man are rewarded fully in the holy city."

Upon the mention of the holy city, Sam saw it in the distance in all of its radiant glory, fully aware that where he was, although awesome in beauty, was merely the outskirts of a glorious city where saints danced.

"Is God in the holy city?"

"Yes, Samuel. He awaits your coming."

"I would like to go there."

Immediately upon his request, they moved at the speed of thought and stood in front of one of twelve awesome gates impacted by great walls of jasper, and what sat upon the walls were rubies, sapphires, and brilliant pearls. The walls and gates shrouded the city like a fortress. They were massive in height, width, and depth. They faced the eastern gate, which stood at 1,200 miles wide and 216 feet thick. Aside from the pearl radiance of its splendor, written on top was a name that caught Sam's eye: Isaskar. Parker explained that that was the name of one of the twelve tribes of Israel, and above every gate (three on each side of four squares) was written such a name.

Sam saw a luring light as he looked upon the gate. As he was drawn, he walked through closed gates that weren't really closed at all (the laws of matter of no effect); with Parker, he stood inside at the beginning of a long hallway where on each side in rows were archways a third of a circle to what looked like offices, where records were kept.

He wished to explore this further when the most beautiful sounds of music caressed his ears. This far exceeded anything he had ever heard on earth, even from the most gifted of saxophonists. Oh, how he longed to join them, to be one in song, harmony, and spirit.

At the end of the hall of records, before entrance into the holy place, stood an angel. He stood seven feet in height, as did Shamir, and like Shamir his body was as smooth as the flesh of a newborn baby yet powerful. Sam could tell straight off that this angel was not a warrior, for he was not equipped with sword and shield or any armor one would need for battle against the demons that swarmed like flies where prayer was stifled. Evidently it was his job to greet and welcome.

He stood before a podium (or at least what would be considered a podium on earth) with a large glowing book. Parker and Sam walked down the hallway passing many archways that contained all of the records of man and stood before the angel.

The angel looked upon Sam, smiled, and said, "Samuel Reed." He opened the book to the date of his birth and then to the date of his spiritual rebirth, his passage from death to life recorded down to the very moment. That helped in allowing Sam to feel that yes, he did belong.

"Welcome, Samuel Reed, to your inheritance among your fellow saints. Father God is waiting for you."

Samuel Reed entered into the holy city of God and was greeted by multitudes of angels and saints. Sam took notice that the saints in the holy city wore the same three garments Parker did. It felt like a homecoming, a long time coming.

He saw large groups of angels in fellowship with saints, arms raised, singing from the deepest recesses of their spirits. Sam heard instruments but saw none. He then realized that the sound of instruments was a result of a spiritual phenomenon, not of a physical nature, brought forth by the collective praise of angels and saints in one accord. Sam began to sing, not from his throat but from his spirit, a beautiful tribute to the Lamb of God.

"Worthy is the Lamb…" he sang through tears of joy. He soon caught on that not everybody was singing the same song. They all sang a song close to them that spoke to their hearts individually. This was not like on earth where attempting to mix multiple songs at once would result in chaotic noise; here every song accentuated perfectly with one another no matter how versatile.

Every sect of people from all over the earth was represented. No one spoke their native tongue, but a spiritual language not of earth, understood by all.

The beauty of the angels mystified Sam. They had brilliant white hair, whiter than snow, and eyes that were fashioned like pearls. The difference between the saints and the angels was subtle. Their color was of pure, brilliant white, from their hair down to their feet, but the saints wore golden crowns of salvation while the angels did not. Sam was surprised to see that not all of the angels had wings as folklore depicted. Only the Seraphim that circled and attended at the throne of the living God wore wings like an appendage and glided with the equal ease of a bird.

Sam would have been completely content to stay there among fellow saints and angels exalting the Lamb, but Parker reminded him that there was so much more to see.

The next thing he knew, he was standing before great rows of trees that stood about fifty yards from a great river, each one bearing different fruit. Some of the fruit he recognized; some he did not. Multitudes of people stood around the trees indulging in the fruits of God. Immediately, upon one fruit being picked, another would appear in its place. Sam picked a large fruit that looked somewhat like a pear and did taste. It was among the most delicious of fruits he had ever partaken. Very similar to the cherries he had indulged on Mt. Kinley. Juice ran down his hand, down his arm, and off his elbow. He thought his garment would be stained or his arm would be sticky from the juice of citrus, but there was none of this.

"This is the tree of life. Those who partook of its fruit while living may have as they desire in God's city," Parker said.

"The cherry tree. It was the cherry tree that I ate from on Mount Kinley that represented the tree of life in heaven. God spoke to me through symbolism during that time, but I did not recognize it."

"It was important for you to be spoken to in that manner, in order to prepare you for the things that you are seeing now."

Tremendous joy tickled his spirit as he let loose and ran past the fruit-baring trees toward multiple knolls of flowers, like a child chasing butterflies. It was then that he realized that he and the others moved without the use of feet but hovered at any speed desired. The choice was theirs to move at thought or at any lesser sightseeing pace.

For a second time, the sound of music caressed his ears, but he could not see from whence it came.

"You're wondering where the music is coming from?" Parker asked on cue.

"Yes."

"Look at the flowers."

Sam dropped to his knees and looked intently at the beautiful flowers that decorated the land. Sure enough, that was where the music emanated. He studied the pedals as they vibrated in a gentle rhythm, annihilating the realm of ethereal possibility.

"How can this be?" Sam giggled with fascination.

"All of creation shouts out, even the very rocks," Parker said matter-of-factly. Sam had only just begun to absorb such wonder when Parker exclaimed, "Let us now see the River of Life."

Instantly Sam and Parker stood waste deep in the river among multitudes of others who greeted and loved upon them. The water was smooth, accelerating, and cut like crystal, this being the same waters he fished in on Mt. Kinley. He was able to see clear the river bed with its precious stones and the idiosyncrasies of the bedazzling gold on which the bed was set.

There was a great harmony of joy and laughter, the kind of laughter that could only come from spirits with no worry or angst of any sort, only the surreal, exhilaration of being in the hand of an all loving God for all eternity.

There were many groups of people that would move into deep water until their heads were completely covered and yet breathed freely. They did this not for fun (although it might have been), but it seemed to serve a greater purpose.

Parker, being aware of the questions dancing around in his head, said, "Sam, although God has forgiven, forgotten, and has separated our sins from him as far as the east is from the west, we still have our guilty recollections. When we bathe in the River of Life, our sins are erased from memory so that we may see ourselves the way God sees us: without sin, washed clean by the precious blood of the Lamb." Parker went on. "The river itself is a tangible manifestation of the Holy Spirit."

Sam was speechless.

"Come. Now I will show you the mansions God has prepared for those who love him."

Miles and miles of mansions surrounded the city capable of housing such a multitude no man could count. Some were magnificent, while others were miniscule in comparison. Even the miniscule far exceeded what the hands of man can construct on earth.

In an instant, they stood upon the porch of Sam's mansion.

"I've been here before. It is so beautiful… The River of Life flows right through it."

"Yes, it starts at the throne of God and then winds through all the mansions of the saints. When it gets to the bottom, it comes up in fountains, falls down bases, and is gathered together and flows out into the river. It then flows in twelve circles through the Holy Place, out of the eastern gate down to earth, falling upon those who worship in the Spirit. God allowed you to see this from an earthly perspective. He prepares all mansions with those delights that are accustomed to the individual. The very large table that resides inside will soon be filled, with you on one side, Jesus at the head, and all of your friends, family, loved ones, including all of those you have yet to meet, will feast in fellowship at your table, as will you at theirs."

"I was told that it is still under construction."

"And so it is."

"But how is that possible? If God awards us for the good we've done on earth in heaven, should not my mansion be complete?"

"These things will be revealed to you very soon...but come with me now for there is another preparation the Lord wants you to see."

Sam found himself looking upon a massive structure, a humongous table that stretched for miles upon miles, capable of sitting comfortably millions upon millions of souls. The table, as well as every chair, was crafted in finest of what might have been redwood, while crystal plates and golden goblets were set upon the table in preparation for a great feast.

"What is this?"

"God has prepared his table for his bride. When his church is ready, we will all sit and eat at his table."

"Is his church the bride?"

"Yes, and the groom has made all the preparations to receive her when she is ready."

Sam had seen so much, so many wonderful blessings, treats, and delicacies."

It was almost too much for his spiritual eyes to absorb. He could not begin to contemplate all that was left to see and experience, knowing full well the majesty of heaven he had witnessed thus far was merely like a gem reflecting the sun. But there was one thing he wanted more than anything, and he wanted it now, and that was to look upon the face of Jesus Christ and God his Father.

"I think I would like to see Jesus now."

"And so you shall."

CHAPTER

44

All strength fleeing his body, like a human stripped of a skeleton, he fell upon his face and worshipped at the throne of the living God. Parker left Sam to this endeavor alone in respect to God's command. Sam now understood the scripture, "...out of your bellies (your inner most being) shall flow rivers of living water." He could not—nor did he want to—contain the gusher of praise, adoration, glory, and honor to Jesus. He shouted hallelujah to the one who died for his sins, the reason for him being there, the Lamb of God. The glory of Jesus filled his soul like a dam flooding parched land and could not be contained as he sang, "Holy, holy, holy!"

There were three glorious, radiating lights of person, each occupying tremendous thrones above and beyond scale. He saw them as one that exuded three manifestations. They occupied an oval-shaped dome of sapphire jewels like a sea of glass, where saints worshipped underneath a rainbow of brilliant colors around the thrown. They worshiped and danced as multitudes of Seraphim that stood at forty feet sang hallelujah.

Crystal set about the parameter reflected the colors of the rainbow. Sam saw colors never seen before that were overwhelming—so radical and beyond comprehension that a vocabulary to describe was nonexistent. Just like so many things it reached beyond the boundaries of imagination. There were as many colors as there were saints; he marveled at his Lord's diversity. The colors moved in sync with the sounds of music. Sam at first could not tell where the music came from. It was not from saints and not from flowers but from the portion of the River of Life that ran through the throne room of God. Lightly the river flowed over jewels that lined up a path for the water to travel, creating sounds reflecting the epitome of beauty.

He who sat on the right side stood, and when he stood, three became one. The light was great, and had he been in human form, he would have been consumed to nothing; in his spirit, he felt gentle warmth fall upon him like a mighty waterfall. As his Savior approached, the spirit of Samuel Reed shook in joyful trepidation.

He tried to make out a figure, an aura, or an outline of the face of God but could not, unaware that no man could look upon the face of God and live. He pondered that all of heaven received its light from this source and knew that with one spoken word all constellations, universes, and life itself, perfectly crafted before the foundations of the earth, were set and received all energy from this source. He suffered no fear, but trembled in awe and reverence.

He wrapped his arms around his bare feet and kissed them.

Around his ankles were dazzling white robes. These were not garments of cloth but garments of light. Light was emanating immensely bright, deflecting his ability to make out the features of his face, but Sam would have guessed that he stood at about six feet two in a radiant white robe with a purple sash across his chest where it was written "King of Kings, Lord of Lords," and there was a solid gold belt across his waist.

His arms were outstretched as if to welcome Sam's embrace. "Rise, my child," the Lord thundered in perfect annunciation.

Sam's knees knocked together, his body trembling like that of one with Parkinson's. He stood, and they embraced. Sam buried his face in his chest and wept in joy and gratitude over the grace allotted him. Never by anyone, not even his parents who would sacrifice anything for him, had he felt such love.

Jesus rubbed his back the way a father would his son, the only words escaping Sam's lips being, "Thank you, thank you, thank you, thank you, thank you…" He could not forget his stay in hell and was finding it very difficult to express gratitude in any other way then to simply say thank you.

Jesus then took on the form of the man he was two thousand years before. This was done for the sole purpose of easing Sam's uncontrolled trembling. His skin was an olive complexion, his cheeks swollen and disproportioned, and chunks of his beard vacant, ripped away. His hands and feet still bore the wounds that nailed him to the cross. Sam could only assume his back remained shredded with the stripes of his flogging, for he wore the same garments as the saints he saved. Very much the way artists throughout history depict his image, his brown hair reached to his shoulders, and his brown eyes that saw all things showed kindness, gentle and wonderful.

Of all the questions circling his thoughts, first he asked, "Why, Lord, why do you still show your wounds?"

"So that you may know that always your sins are forgiven and your body made whole. My death, your sins; my body your healing."

Quickly, Sam jumped to his next question. "Why, Lord, why did you allow me to spend that time in hell?" This he asked not accusing but with honest uncertainty.

"Great it is the multitude who do not believe hell exists. Many are among my own people. You must tell them, Sam, for your time in hell was necessary in order for you to serve my purpose on earth."

"My Lord, I do not understand."

"It is not your time, Samuel. You must go back."

"Go back!" The very thought of going back to a world of such turmoil and strife broke his heart. "Please, Lord, do not send me back. I want to remain with you. I have no wife and no kids. There is nothing for me there."

"My son, Samuel, I will not leave you alone, for I will be with you always." Jesus waved his arm side to side and said, "Look, Sam, and see all the souls who will be lost to hell if you do not share with them your experience."

Behold, Sam saw great multitudes of people.

"But I do not know them."

"But I do. Many will not listen, but these I have set aside will hear."

"But, Lord, I want to reside with you as I am now."

"Because I love you so very much, I want you to be with me as well. But as it is, you cannot, for there is a barrier."

The Lord then took Sam to the earth-like surroundings of where he first began when brought to heaven by Shamir, howbeit, this time invisible. "My son, this is your lot in heaven, for you have done nothing in my name with the life I've given you, thus far."

"How can this be? Parker showed me my mansion."

"Whether you reside in it or not depends on what you do on earth. My reward is with me, and I will give to every man according to what he has done. I want everyone I have chosen to occupy their mansion in my holy city, but you will reap what you sow, and I can only give to everyone according to what they have sowed."

Sam looked upon multitudes who resided eternally in what might be called the suburbs of the holy city. All who remained there wore a garment of humility just like him, but those who went on to the holy city received the garment of praise and garment of worship, as did Parker. He then watched multitudes being led by their angel beyond the great barrier and into the holy city to receive their many rewards, the greatest of these to be in the presence of God and look upon his face. As Jesus longed to have fellowship with his saints, Sam longed to continually partake of the delicious fruits of the tree of life and to swim in the River of Life/the Holy Spirit, to sing with the angels of God, to have Jesus Christ sit at his table, and also to partake in the unlimited, unknown, forever-changing treats of heaven. But more than this he desired to serve God's purpose.

"Lord, I wish to do your will."

Jesus smiled wonderfully before he said, "First, I will show you a great need." Jesus took Sam back to the holy city and onto a field of beautiful green grass that looked as though God had sprinkled crushed diamonds upon his lawn, where multitudes of many thousands of children played under various trees.

"Who are these children, Lord?"

Jesus pointed at one group and said, "These precious children have died in wars, accidents, and disease." He then pointed at another group of children and said, "These precious children were sent back to me through murder and abortion."

Sam heard the Lord's voice beginning to change as one who was emotionally in great pain.

In his eyes, tears were beginning to well up as he said, "The third group of children you see playing were sent back to me in secret by my people. They did not trust that I would provide for their family, for my family. In so doing, they have committed murder under the guise allowed by man-made law.

Jesus found it hard to continue, but he pressed on, "I had a plan given to me by my Father for every child."

The pain in the voice of his Savior brought Sam to tears. "My Lord, will these children ever grow, or will they remain children forever?"

"They will grow to full adulthood as they learn."

"Learn?"

In an instant, they were transported to a dome known as the Temple of Instruction where many went to grow in wisdom through the delights of learning the character of God. The children rejected by their parents watched the crucifixion of Christ. That was somewhat like watching a recorded video of a serious incident from the history books, but it was a play on dimensions, as they were actually there in real time witnessing his brutal death from the vantage point of the crowd as they heard the words, "He saved others. Why doesn't he save himself?"

Soon after the words of Christ, "Father, forgive them, for they know not what they do," the children cried, for they feared for the Son of God as they could see with spiritual eyes the kingdom of darkness celebrating their hour. But it was the Son pleading to his Father for forgiveness for those who did not deserve that caused all of the children to likewise forgive and love their mothers and fathers unconditionally. Sam found it difficult to understand how these children could show such love and mercy, having been snuffed out before life began. Jesus quoted his Word, saying, "Their angels always do behold the face of my father."

Having witnessed the forgiveness of the children for their parents, Sam felt the sword of hate and unforgiveness buried deep in his heart for the drunk driver that killed his uncle Freddy vacate. As a replacement, a genuine love and hope the man would one day open his heart to Christ, before it was too late, filled his spirit.

～

Sam wanted to stay among the children so that he could witness the resurrection of Jesus Christ and the celebration of all of heaven, but Jesus informed him that it was not yet his time to witness this and that he would see it soon enough, when the time was right.

"Sam, you must tell my children everything that you have seen. Some will mock and some will spit. Turn the other cheek, my son, for great is your reward in heaven," Jesus said in love and with a measure of urgency.

"Behold, I come quickly."

"How much time is left before your return, Lord?"

Putting his thumb and forefinger together, he answered, "There is none. Only the grace allowed for the saints to spread the gospel to all the people of the world."

Sam thought on modern technology and how he once spoke to a man in Italy and a woman in Ethiopia at once on the Internet. He knew that technology was already there; time was short indeed.

"Lord, how do I return?"

Jesus hugged him as he said, "Close your eyes, my son." Sam did. "Now allow liquid to drain from your left eye. Now open your eyes and see."

45

"Dear Jesus, Holy Spirit, heavenly Father..." Dr. Baker started, being so new to his faith he was not exactly sure how to address his Savior.

"Your Word, your Bible is a beautiful book... I have just read a passage that says that if I laid my hands on one who is sick he will recover. I think this particular passage first said that I must believe. My Lord, my God, me and my present company do believe, so by the authority given to me through your Son, Jesus Christ, I command you, Samuel Reed, be made whole. Come back to us!"

A scream from the back of the room was the first inclination that something had happened. Ninety-nine percent of the church opened their eyes from their agreement in prayer with Dr. Baker, and all heads turned to the startled lady. She held her mouth in resistance to any further outbursts, but her eyes were wide in a welcomed shock. Again all heads turned in the direction her stunned eyes looked. Sam's eyes were open.

The church in room 2A bellowed out with thunderous praise. Dr. Baker simply switched gears to doctor mode, checking Sam's vital signs and pupils. Everything appeared to be in proper functioning condition. Overcome by faith, throwing caution to the wind, he removed Sam's respirator, and sure enough Sam breathed on his own. The church sat him up in his bed as Mrs. Reed wrestled her way through the crowd and smothered her son with kisses.

"I knew you would come back. I knew it! I knew it! I knew it! We all knew it. Thank you, Jesus!" she screamed, and the church shouted exaltations to the Almighty.

Sam moved his head all about until he spied Mr. Carlton. Someone noticed Sam's lips moving and realized he was trying to speak.

"Shh, quiet, everyone! I think he's trying to speak."

"He may be hoarse. He has not spoken in five months," Dr. Baker warned the crowd through tears of joy.

Pastor Jerry put his ear to Sam's mouth, and although difficult (Sam only able to speak at a whisper), he was able to decipher what sounded like, "Mr. Carlton."

Pastor Jerry stood up and shouted, "Mr. Carlton! He wants to speak to John Carlton!" In all of the excitement, Jerry did not realize that Mr. Carlton was standing right beside him.

Mr. Carlton leaned down, putting his ear up to Sam's mouth, and said, "Yes, Sam, I am here. We have all been praying for you. Are you okay?"

It was then that Mr. Carlton heard some of the sweetest words, like honey to his ears, he had ever heard.

"Mr. Carlton…I want to be baptized."

Endnotes

1 John 12:8

Matthew 7:13-18

2nd Corithians 4:4

Romans 1:20

John 8:44

John 3:17

Romans 3:10

John 13:8

Matthew 18:20

Luke 5:32

John 3:3

Romans 10:9

Revelation 3:20